ABOUT THE AUTHOR

Originally from Northern Ireland, Jacqueline Harrett has lived in Cardiff with her husband for over thirty years. Her two grown-up children also live in the capital city.

A multi-genre author, Jacqui has published non-fiction; *Exciting Writing,* (Sage), *Tell me Another…* (UKLA); children's stories; and short stories in anthologies. She has co-authored a novel with Janet Laugharne, *What Lies Between Them,* (Dixi, 2022) as well as flash fiction and blog at www.jlharland.co.uk.

With Grave Consequences is the third novel in her DI Mandy Wilde series.

Published in Great Britain in 2023
By Diamond Crime

ISBN 978-1-915649-32-4

Diamond Crime is an imprint of Diamond Books Ltd.

DIAMOND
BOOKS

Thanks to…

Steve, Phil and Jeff whose patience, hard work and good humour is much appreciated. Also, to the Diamond Crime team of authors. Members of the Criminal Fairies: Linda, Gwyneth, Duncan and Jan for reading a very rough first draft and giving me constructive criticism.

Writers Enjoying Words for constant encouragement and interesting conversations.

The Welsh crime collective Crime Cymru who are an amazing group of friendly and supportive writers. I am delighted to be a member.

For all the lovely readers who left reviews for *The Nesting Place* and *The Whispering Trees*; a special thank you. Reviews are like gold for writers, more important than readers realise. I hope you enjoy Mandy's latest adventure in *With Grave Consequences.*

Cover photo: Radek Kilijanek

Book cover design:
jacksonbone.co.uk

Also by Jacqueline Harrett:
Books One and Two of the DI Mandy Wilde Novels
The Nesting Place
The Whispering Trees

Published by

DIAMOND
CRIME

For information about Diamond Crime authors
and their books, visit:
www.diamondcrime.com

For Margaret.
Thank you for always making me laugh,
even on the dullest days.

With Grave Consequences

A D.I. Mandy Wilde Novel

JACQUELINE HARRETT

CHAPTER ONE

DAY ONE

It was December and cold as hell. At just after nine o'clock Grace Mathias entered Cathays Cemetery. Three hours later she was dead. In Cardiff Central Police Station DI Mandy Wilde was frowning at her computer screen, an empty soup bowl at her elbow when DS Josh Jones burst into the room.

"Boss, we've got a body. Cathays Cemetery."

"No shit, Sherlock. We can see why you're a detective.

DC Olivia Wyglendacz sniggered. Josh coloured.

"We'd better move our arses then. Pronto."

Pulling her coat on and grabbing hat and gloves, Mandy pounded out of the office, Josh trying to keep up. The fitness routine they'd established in October had gone to the dogs with the cold snap. No-one wanted to be out running in freezing weather when the pavements were like skating rinks. Mandy suspected Josh was relieved. Maybe he'd join the rugby team again – if Lisa, his wife, let him.

Outside the cold air hit them like a slap with a wet fish. Their breath hung in the air. Overhead a weak sun struggled through heavy clouds and a low mist crept across the grass of Cathays Park. Even the traffic noise seemed more subdued, as if the mist blanketed the sounds.

A couple of police vans were parked outside the cemetery entrance and the main gate was closed. Mandy spotted the pathologist's car. Good, Rishi was there already. It meant everything was in place and they shouldn't have to hang around for too long in these near freezing temperatures. A uniformed officer stood at the side gate, preventing anyone from entering. Mandy waved her warrant card at him and asked directions.

"To the right of the chapel, Ma'am. Follow the path and you'll see the team."

It was a bleak place, the trail leading them through the Victorian section of the graveyard onto a track, dead leaves making it muddy underfoot. Mandy was grateful for her boots and glad to see Josh had worn something less designer and more practical for the job in hand. A pair of jackdaws cackled as if giving them a warning before flying to the uppermost branches. Skeleton trees, maple and sycamore, reached for the sky, witches' fingers, gnarled and knotted. It was easy to locate the SOCO team. The low murmur of voices and figures moving around contrasted with the loneliness around them.

What they found was not what Mandy had expected. Somehow, she'd imagined an elderly person had keeled over and died. What lay in front of them was the body of a young girl. Fifteen or sixteen at most she reckoned. She was on her side rolled up, half-undressed, her discarded clothing lying close by, and she appeared to be trying to hide. Who had done this?

These were the worst ones to deal with. They'd seen enough dead bodies but the young ones, lives cut short, were the hardest. A blackbird fluttered past and landed on a nearby branch.

They stayed on the path and waited. Josh had a quiet word with one of the officers standing close by. The SOCOs were busy and Rishi would speak to them when he was ready. He was focussed on the body, so hadn't seen them approach. A squirrel bounced past and shot up a tree. There were fewer of them about in the cold weather. Vermin. In the distance the drone of traffic reminded them of the proximity of the city and the roads around.

As if suddenly aware of their presence, Rishi raised his head. Booted and suited, they made their way from the path closer to the little copse of trees. It was uneven underfoot and Mandy's feet snagged on brambles and bits of branches. The leaves had turned a dirty brown, almost black, and there was a dank smell. It was a difficult spot to reach. Everything was so overrun with grass and weeds. How, and why, had this young girl ended up here. The area surrounding the body provided a little shelter. Pine trees, evergreens giving a sort of canopy and their distinctive sharp smell. One tree trunk looked as if it was almost growing along the ground before turning heavenwards. A dismal setting, yet also quiet and peaceful. The body looked out of place in these sacred surroundings. Even the birds were silent in this little patch. Silent and watching.

"She's young." Mandy was reminded of Tabitha, her niece, in the unlined face.

"Teens, I think," said Rishi. "I'll know more after I get her to the lab."

"Any ID?"

Rishi nodded. Something positive. "We have her personal effects. It seems this is the body of Grace Mathias. She also had tablets in her bag for a Mrs Eleri Mathias. Her mother perhaps. There's an address too, on the label."

"Thoughts?"

Rishi took a deep breath. "Not until I can get a look inside her. The tablets for her mother were collected this morning and two are missing. Plus, an open packet of paracetamol. But …" His voice tailed off and Mandy knew why.

"You're thinking?" The question remained unspoken, but Rishi knew what she was implying.

"I cannot establish anything until after the post-mortem." His speech was, as always, formal, precise.

"Do you think she was attacked? I mean the clothing has been removed. Any signs of a struggle? Marks on the body?"

"Her fingernails have mud under them. It looks as though she was scrabbling under the tree."

"Trying to hide something? Or get away from an attack?"

"It is too early to say."

"When can you do the PM? Today?"

"Late afternoon. Say five? It will mean I have a valid excuse to miss the weekly dinner with my mother-in-law."

"Every cloud." Anyone who would rather cut up a dead body than have dinner with an in-law needed some sympathy. Rishi's ongoing feud with his mother-in-law was a standard part of their conversations. "I'm sure Mrs Crocodile will be devastated."

Turning to Josh she said, "Someone needs to break the news to her family. Give Helen a ring will you, please? We can put her in as family liaison. She's bloody good at that." She glanced at the body again and sighed. "Poor kid. Why?"

"According to the uniform," Josh nodded towards the officer he'd spoken to, "the old boy who found her is still in one of the chapels. Do you want to talk to him before we see the family?"

"Yes. Let's see what he has to say and let him get home. The sooner we speak to Grace's family the better."

A train rattled past.

"I didn't realise the railway line was so close."

"Yeah. In Victorian times they had a station there to drop off the dead. It would have been out of the city more then," said Josh.

"How the hell do you know that?"

"Probably read it somewhere." He shrugged. "I'm a mine of useless information."

"Not for a pub quiz. You'd be pure gold. Teams would be fighting over you."

They tramped over the grass on to the path again and made their way to the chapel. Mandy noticed cameras high on the walls. She pointed. "Get someone to check the CCTV. It might help us to establish when she got here and if anyone else was with her. Maybe she was meeting a boyfriend."

"In a graveyard?"

"Stranger spots have been known as clandestine meeting places. Yeah, a coffee shop would be warmer but not as discreet. There's something odd with this one. I'm sure of it. Gut instinct or whatever. I suppose we'll know more after the PM."

CHAPTER TWO

It was nearly as cold in the chapel as it was outside, the door having been left ajar. It had an unused musty smell. A high vaulted ceiling and white walls with chairs stacked against them. The creaking door alerted the occupants and two pairs of eyes watched as Mandy and Josh entered, their footsteps echoing in the space. On one chair sat an elderly man, his hands wrapped around a steaming paper cup, with a uniformed officer on another. The man appeared dazed, his eyes blinking as if in bright sunlight. He wore a blue beanie hat pulled low and an anorak in a similar colour that had seen better days with a tartan scarf wrapped around his neck.

Mandy addressed the officer first, flashing her warrant card with a nod towards the man. The officer, dark hair and sympathetic blue eyes, turned to the man.

"These are detectives who will want you to tell them what happened. I know you've already told me, but they need to hear it directly from you. Are you up to that, sir?"

Mandy noticed that the officer kept a sympathetic hand on the man's arm as he explained proceedings to him. Empathy in bundles by the look of it. No doubt not too long on the job. Mandy hoped he managed to keep that quality, like DC Helen Probert. It helped in cases like this. Too often they found themselves hardened by things they witnessed on the job, and it was sometimes difficult to remember that not everybody was a potential criminal.

"Yes." His voice rasped and he took a sip of the tea before raising watery eyes to Mandy's face.

Realising that her height, at almost six feet, was intimidating, Mandy knelt on the wooden floor of the chapel, feeling the cold penetrating her trousers and hoping she wouldn't have to spend too long down there. Her face was level now and she saw faded grey eyes and a gap between stained front teeth.

"Can you just tell me, in your own words, what happened here today, Mr...?"

"It's Jeff. Jeff Davis. Without the e. People want to always put the e in the surname."

Oh God. He was one of those. Don't say it in five words if you can say it in five hundred.

"Right Mr Davis. We'll make sure we spell it right. DS Jones has made a note. Now, what happened?"

"I come here to speak to Lily every day and to pick up litter. You'd be surprised at what people chuck over the walls. A disgrace it is. I used to come with Lily, but she passed a year or more now." He paused, staring into space.

It was going to take forever at this rate. She'd have to guide him a bit to get on with it.

"So, what time did you come to the cemetery?"

"Well, I usually come about ten but with the fog and the cold this morning my old bones were a bit stiffer than usual. I looked out and I said to myself, 'best wait until it warms up a bit, Jeff. No point in rushing. It could be icy. Don't want to fall, do you?'" He looked at Mandy, expectant.

Mandy drew in a breath and forced what she hoped was a sympathetic smile to encourage him to continue.

"I made another cuppa and sat down. I must have dozed off as it was getting towards midday when I looked at the clock. I was going to have a bite of lunch, but I could see that it was still grey outside. I figured if I didn't go out then it would be dark after lunch." Another pause as he considered his movements. "It must have been near, no, after perhaps, twelve when I got here. I don't live far away you see. Down on Robert Street. The old legs don't move as fast as they used to."

"And you found the girl soon after that?" The call had come in before one o'clock.

"I try to start in a different place each time. Sometimes near the library end. The newer graves. Today I thought I'd start with the other side. The Victorian bit is overgrown so it's not such easy walking."

"It's very uneven in places. Perhaps, in such poor weather conditions, you should stay at home sir. Safer."

He looked at her and seemed more wary now. "I could see the girl under the tree. Just lying there, she was. I thought I'd go and speak to her. See if she was alright. I've seen her here before. I don't talk to many people. Most folks these days have no time. People are always dashing here and there. Years ago, I knew all my neighbours but now it's all younger people and students."

It was going to take forever. Mandy felt her shoulders tense. Why had he even bothered to come out on such an awful day? The litter wouldn't have gone away.

Josh was gentle. "Did you touch the body or try to revive her, sir?"

"Oh no. When I got a bit closer, I could see she wasn't with us no more. Like one of those statues. All white as marble and blue lips. And," he paused, "clothes lying about. I wondered if someone had... you know. Proper shook up, I was. I rushed back up and banged on the door to the lodge but there was no-one in. Then I spotted a young lady passing the main gate. I told her to dial 999 and my legs gave way. I suppose it was the shock, see. I sat on the bench with the young lady until the ambulance and police arrived."

"Young lady?" Mandy asked the officer.

"We spoke to her, Ma'am. She didn't know anything; just thought he'd had a turn so stayed with him. He was shaking."

It didn't seem that they were going to gain much from further interrogation of Mr Davis, so Mandy turned to the officer. "Get someone to take him home and see that he's alright. And speak to Social Services. Maybe get some help for him. They must have a befriending service or know of charities who do that sort of thing. Salvation Army perhaps. Ring his doctor as well?"

The officer nodded. "I'd already made a note, Ma'am. I'll pop in and check on him after my shift. Thank you. If I say DI Wilde asked for some assistance for Mr Davis, it will have more clout."

CHAPTER THREE

The house where Eleri Mathias lived was down near Waterloo Gardens, terraced, red brick with a small front garden. Josh rang the bell, but they could hear no sound from inside. The front door was half wood and half obscure glass and Mandy stuck her face against it to see if there was any movement. She thought she saw a shadow down the hallway so tapped on the glass. They were rewarded with the door opening seconds later. A tall, dishevelled man stared at them.

"Mr Mathias? I'm Detective Inspector Wilde and this is Sergeant Josh Jones." They showed their warrant cards.

"My name is Stefan Nowak. What is this about?" His face, strained and with grey stubble matching his grey eyes, had a mystified expression.

"We believe that a Mrs Eleri Mathias lives here."

"Yes. Eleri is my wife. She kept her previous name when we married. I did not mind. Nowak is not easy to say or spell for some people." What could have passed for a smile flickered briefly.

"We need to speak to your wife. Perhaps we could come in? It's about Grace."

"Grace? She's out. She was going to do some shopping. She should be home soon." He stopped. "Has something happened?"

"I think it's best if we come in, sir."

He nodded and stepped to one side to open the door wider. He pressed one finger to his lips. "My wife is sleeping. It's the medication. It helps."

The hallway had the original tiles in brown, deep red, beige and blue like Mandy's house in Brithdir Street, except these were in better condition. He led them down past the stairs and two doors to the kitchen. As they passed the second, Mandy glanced inside. A woman was asleep in what looked like a hospital bed with cot sides up. There was an odour of disinfectant and other less pleasant smells. Stefan said nothing until they entered the kitchen at the back of the house. It had been extended at some point and held a pine table and chairs as well as a door leading into what was either a utility room or bathroom. There was no view of the garden, just the side of the neighbour's wall.

"Your wife is ill?" The medication found in Grace's bag was not the general sort of painkillers doctors prescribed and, from her appearance, the woman in the bed was seriously ill.

"Not long now. Maybe weeks. Maybe less."

Oh shit. No wonder the poor bugger looked knackered. And they had come with more bad news. The worst sort. There was no point in prevaricating. Mandy waited until they were all sitting down at the pine table.

"I'm sorry to have to tell you, sir, that the body of Grace Mathias was found in Cathays cemetery a short time ago."

He said nothing for a moment, looked from one face to the other and then shook his head.

"No. No. There must be some mistake. I saw her this morning. We had breakfast. Not Grace. She… her mother…" His voice tailed off and he leaned forward, elbows on the table and cradled his head in his hands.

"The body will have to be formally identified, but Grace's bag with her student ID card and your wife's prescription medication were beside her."

Josh nodded towards the fridge freezer door where there were several photographs. One of them, a close-up of a smiling girl was Grace. No doubt then.

Stefan dropped his hands. His eyes were full of tears. "She went to collect the tablets. She said she was going for a walk. I don't understand. What happened? An accident? How do I tell her mother? She's not going to be able to …"

He seemed distraught but thinking about how they had found the body and a possible attack meant difficult questions needed to be asked.

"So, the last time you saw her was early this morning? How did she seem?"

"A little quiet. Pale. She said she had pain here," he pointed to his lower stomach, "but she wanted to go out. Get her mama's tablets. Fresh air would help she said."

"And where were you this morning? Did you go out? Follow her to see if she was alright, perhaps?" In many cases of assault a family member was responsible. Mandy wanted to check if Stefan had an alibi.

"I stay with Eleri. Very sick. She sleeps a lot but needs someone to watch."

"Did anyone call? Anyone confirm that?"

He frowned, as if unsure why she was asking the question. "Eleri."

"But if she was asleep?"

His jaw clenched as he realised why Mandy was pushing him. "I haven't left the house. A carer, agency woman, came just after Grace went out. She was here about twenty minutes. Here. Evidence." He got to his feet and picked a file from the windowsill, throwing it on to the table. It was the record of visits made by the care team, dated and signed with comments. "Someone else rang about an hour later. They are going to give me some night support now too."

"I'm sorry. I have to ask these questions. We don't know what happened to Grace but we intend to find out. I can assure you of that."

CHAPTER FOUR

Josh's phone buzzed and he glanced at the screen. "Helen's just parking." He stood and made his way back up the narrow hallway, ready to open the door.

Thank God for that. The poor man needed support and they had already got his hackles rising with the questions. Helen would be able to organise something to help and make sure everything was in order. She was also quite astute and would know if there was anything amiss in the household.

"Do you have anyone we can call to be with you, sir? Family? Friends?"

"No. There is no-one. My family is in Poland. Eleri has a sister, somewhere, but they had a big falling out many years ago. They do not speak." He was shaking a little so Mandy filled the kettle and put it on to boil. Perhaps he needed something stronger, but tea would have to suffice for now.

"Our colleague, DC Helen Probert, will stay with you for a while. She's your liaison with us. If you have questions, or if you remember anything, then Helen will be able to contact us. Would a neighbour come and stay with you for a while?" Surely there was someone who could help him.

"Mrs Long, two doors down, is a kind woman. She's always dropping off cakes or flowers since Eleri took ill. People are kind, but practical help when someone is dying is not so easy. People do not like to see sickness."

It was true. People tended to shy away from the ill and dying. It was too painful to see the crumbling of the human body and a reminder of one's own mortality. They'd get Helen to see what could be done and then shoot off to the post-mortem. She could hear Josh whispering to Helen, bringing her up to speed. They'd need to get Mr Nowak over to the mortuary soon to do the formal identification but that would be dependent on someone attending to Eleri Mathias. It was obvious she could not be left alone. The timing was dreadful. Christmas looming and from what Mandy had seen that poor man would be having a double funeral. Life was a bitch.

* * *

When the others left Helen made a mug of tea for Stefan. He declined milk, but Helen added a spoonful of sugar. There was a bottle of vodka on a shelf in the cupboard but with his wife so ill she figured he was in enough of a state without adding intoxication to the mix. A glance into the sick room assured her that Mrs Mathias was asleep. The figure in the bed was a pathetic sight, skin sallow and shrunken, one arm draped over the bedding while the other secreted underneath. Her breathing was steady, not laboured, and an assortment of tablets, a glass of water and a plant sat on a table close by. A small window looked out on to the passageway at the side of the house which led to the garden but, like the kitchen, there wasn't much of a view.

"How long has your wife been ill?" she asked.

Stefan was like a man in a trance. "A while now. Two, maybe three years. At first, they don't know. Perhaps it's this. Perhaps that. Tests. More tests. Then the diagnosis. Tumour on the brain. Nothing to be done. Too dangerous to operate."

"That must have been very difficult for all of you."

He nodded. "At first, we don't believe it. How can there not be some way, some cure." He closed his eyes, then opened them again meeting Helen's in a direct way. "We don't understand. Grace – she started to research. On the internet. Some people have this new treatment but it's expensive and only available in America."

"Not here?"

"No. We asked the doctors, but they said it was not advisable. Eleri could die during the operation. The techniques were revolutionary and results variable." He rubbed a hand over his eyes. "Eleri wanted to take the risk. But the money…"

"No NHS in the States. You could go bankrupt." said Helen.

"I wanted to sell the house. There's no mortgage. Eleri's grandmother brought the girls up and left the house to Eleri."

As Helen was about to ask more questions a faint coughing could be heard. Stefan paled, has hands trembling.

"Eleri is awake. I don't know how to tell her." He stood, a grim expression on his face as he left Helen sitting in the kitchen.

Muffled voices could be heard and then an animal sound, a low keening. Helen boiled the kettle again.

CHAPTER FIVE

"We've a possible murder on our hands," said Mandy when they got back to the station. Superintendent Ross Withers was interested. A mysterious homicide was relatively unusual in the capital city.

"I heard." Withers sniffed. "What have you got so far?"

"Not a lot, sir. She was half undressed, and it looked as though she was trying to hide. Not much chance at this time of the year. Apart from the evergreens the undergrowth is sparse. PM at five so let's hope Rishi can enlighten us."

"Family?"

"The mother is terminal, and the stepfather seems genuine. He was at home all morning. Olivia has been scouring the CCTV from the cemetery."

"Good God. They have CCTV there? What are they expecting? Zombies?" He chuckled as he went back to his office.

"How's it going?" Mandy asked. Olivia was peering at the screen. The footage wasn't very clear, and the early fog hadn't helped much.

"It's dead boring, it is." Then, realising what she'd said she clamped a hand over her mouth. "Oh, I didn't mean to make a joke." Her eyes were sparkling with mischief.

"Sorry. I mean there's nothing much happening." She paused the video.

"Well, it's not exactly a nightclub." Josh appeared, coffee in one hand and a chocolate biscuit in the other.

Olivia giggled and lifted a notepad where she'd been scribbling. "I've been able to run it through to near noon. There's not much."

They looked at the notes.

09.00. Figure of young woman enters through the main gate. Bent over. Seems to be carrying something. Makes her way to the right of the chapel and disappears from view.

10.21. Two schoolboys enter. Move to the other side of the chapel where they light cigarettes. Appear to be engaged in conversation. Stamping feet.

10.28. Boys leave and turn left out of main gate.

11.05. Woman with wreath enters. Takes the left-hand path. Seems to be hurrying. Takes a phone out. Stops for a minute before disappearing out of range.

11.17. Same woman, minus wreath, leaves.

Mandy and Josh pulled up chairs either side of Olivia and motioned for her to press play again. If Jeff Davis had the times right, he should be appearing on screen quite soon. Josh munched his biscuit despite the dirty look Mandy gave him. He sounded like a squirrel crunching acorns. Distracting. As the time on the recording passed the mid-day mark, they sat upright, eyes fixed. Just after noon, Jeff had guessed. Five minutes, seven minutes, ten minutes and then at eleven minutes past the hour they spotted him.

"Stop," said Mandy. "That must be Jeff Davis. He's shuffling along, poor bugger."

"But he's turning to the left. Grace went to the right," said Josh.

"He said he went to talk to Lily every day. Why the hell he didn't go home after visiting his wife's grave is a mystery."

"You don't think he had anything to do with it, do you? He looked pretty shaken up to me," said Josh.

"There he is again, now. Time 12.26." Olivia's voice held a hint of excitement. "He's going down to the right and he's taking something out of his pocket. Look."

They watched as the old man shuffled along, pulling something out of his pocket as he headed towards the Victorian side of the cemetery.

"Can we zoom in a bit?" asked Mandy. "There. That's it. A bag of some sort."

The picture became more pixilated as Olivia zoomed closer to the figure in question but still recognisable. It was, without a doubt, Jeff Davis.

"His rubbish collection bag. He told us he picked up the litter. He didn't have it with him when we saw him though," said Josh. "We can get uniform to look out for that in case there's anything in there."

Mandy raised an eyebrow but said nothing. The grainy screen was motionless again except for the odd bird flying past and a squirrel darting about. At 12.33 Jeff appeared again. This time he was stumbling and almost falling in his attempts to hurry. He still had hold of the bag but as they watched, he tripped, almost fell and lost his grip on it. A gust of wind lifted it into the air like a balloon and then impaled it on the uppermost branches of a tree. As he neared the chapel building, the man had a hand to his chest. They watched as he approached the lodge and thumped on the door with both fists. As there was no response he seemed to stand, confused, head bobbing from one side to the other before shuffling towards the main gate. They saw him wave his arms to attract attention and speak to a woman who held his arm and guided him to a bench before taking a phone out of her pocket.

"It's all exactly as he told us. Poor sod. And now we know where his collection bag went." Mandy glanced at Josh.

"Could someone have come in from another way? There are several entrances to the cemetery, aren't there?"

"I checked that," said Olivia. "They're short-staffed. Some bug doing the rounds, so only the main gate opened this morning. Nobody could get in without climbing over the railings, now."

"We may need to check out any cameras along Allensbank and Fairoak Roads depending on what Rishi has to tell us. Speaking of which we'd better shift our butts up there." She got to her feet. "Do a check on those roads will you, Olivia? There are a couple of businesses and flats which may have cameras. And look closer at the picture of Grace. It's not very clear if she's carrying anything apart from her bag."

Without looking to see if Josh was following, Mandy was out of the room, taking the stairs at speed as she zipped up her coat and pulled on a hat. What information would the body provide? Was Grace attacked? It certainly looked that way.

CHAPTER SIX

Visiting the mortuary at any time was grim. Mandy wiped a sliver of Vick's vapour rub under her nose and passed it to Josh. She found the forensics fascinating but the smell was something she could live without. Rishi seemed immune. The body was laid out on the table, naked, ready for the post-mortem examination.

"First thoughts, Rishi?"

"I have not had time to do more than the initial assessment. I will need to open her up, but I think it was natural causes. Hypothermia."

"What? I thought that happened to old people without enough heating or folk stuck in snowdrifts and the like. I don't understand. It looked as though she'd been attacked, her clothes ripped off. Plus, she was almost hiding under that tree." Mandy frowned. She'd assumed a murder and set things in motion. And she'd told the Super.

"Indeed. I agree, Inspector. That's what it seemed. However," Rishi pulled himself up to his full height, "I see no evidence of an attack. I think this is an example of what is known as paradoxical undressing."

"Come again?" Mandy glanced at Josh who looked as perplexed as she felt. She could see Rishi, with a slight smile of satisfaction, about to impress them with his knowledge.

"When some people, statistically about twenty-five percent, are in the final stages of hypothermia they exhibit strange behaviour. As the body cools it induces vasoconstriction, which basically slows the blood to the skin in an attempt to keep the core warm. For example, on a cold day your hands and feet may become cold to the touch, but your body will still retain heat."

"That makes sense but why remove clothing? If you feel cold, you put on more layers, not strip off."

Rishi was enjoying himself. "The body cannot maintain vasoconstriction and will become exhausted. When that happens, in severe hypothermia, the person has a sudden rush of heat from their core. They will feel very hot and remove clothing. Some also exhibit a sort of burrowing."

"Not an attack. It would explain why Grace was in the position we found her, looking as if she was trying to hide. Poor kid. How does a young girl die, in the centre of a city, with hypothermia? Wouldn't she have been aware? Shivering? Feeling cold?"

"Shivering is a sign, but she may not have been able to recognise she was in danger until it was too late." He turned to the side where Grace's clothing and effects were laid out. He picked up a paper bag with a medical sign printed on it. "This is the medication for Mrs Eleri Mathias. Opiates. Dispensed this morning. I think Grace took two of these and it made her sleepy. She was probably unaware of the danger."

"Why would she do that? You don't think...?" Too many young people suffered from undiagnosed stress and depression. It wouldn't have been the first time they'd witnessed self-harming and death by suicide.

"My theory is that she knew the medication for her mother was very strong. If she had taken more, I would suspect suicide, but two tablets would just make her drowsy. I won't know more until the toxicology report comes back. Two or three days perhaps."

"The paracetamol?"

Rishi shrugged. "In her pocket. Again–"

"You won't know until the toxicology comes back. I get it. Why take her mother's meds?"

"Perhaps she was in pain. Her underwear is blood stained and," he paused again, "from my preliminary examination it is obvious that she has given birth recently. Possibly in the last week."

"What?" Both Mandy and Josh said in unison. That put a new slant on the investigation.

"Why the hell didn't you tell us that in the first place. Bloody hell, Rishi. There was no sign of a baby. Does that mean we're looking for another body?" Mandy thought back to the visit to the house. No indication of any baby to be seen. Just that poor woman dying. They'd have to go back. And they'd need to get the sniffer dogs out in case Grace had left the baby in the cemetery. They'd assumed she was bent over her bag, but what if it was something else?

"Do you want to stay and observe?" Rishi had a scalpel poised, ready to open the body.

Josh coughed. Mandy glanced at him then the clock. "We need to start a search for the missing baby and get back to speak to Grace's parents. Find out what they know. If she had a baby in the last week, it's something she couldn't hide."

CHAPTER SEVEN

A subdued Helen opened the door to them. The surrounding houses had twinkling lights and two doors down a giant blow-up Father Christmas wobbled in the stiff breeze. Light spilled out into the pavement, and they were glad of the almost cloying warmth of the house. The frost had come hand in hand with the darkness, making the pavements glitter. Her windscreen would take ages to defrost if they stayed too long. Mandy hoped the gritters were out. It was going to be another bitter night.

Her voice was a whisper as she asked Helen, "How's things?" How was any household when they'd been given the news of a death? Shock, disbelief, numbness – grief arrived in many guises.

"He's told Mrs Mathias. We had to call the doctor to give her a sedative. It's been an uneasy couple of hours. They have a night-sitter who comes in about ten. I said I'd stay until then."

"What about your boys?"

"Tom will sort things and put them to bed. He's great with them. Loads of patience. More than I've got." She smiled at that. Mandy couldn't imagine anyone with more patience than Helen. Tom must be a saint.

"Have you seen any signs of a baby in the house? Or anything unusual? Any edginess, covering up stuff? You know what I mean? Uncomfortable about having the police in the house?"

"No. Nothing." She frowned. "A baby? What baby?"

"It appears Grace gave birth sometime in the last week. We're going to have to search her room and the house. Where's Mr Nowak?"

"Kitchen. He's still reeling."

"Let's see if he knows anything about the baby."

The door to the sick room was closed but they still tip-toed past, aware they were intruders in the space. Stefan looked drained, weary. Despite the hushed atmosphere in the house the kitchen was warm and inviting with a bench under one window heaped high with cushions as well as the pine table and chairs. He glanced at them, eyes glazed, as they entered and sat down. Helen stood behind him, leaning against a work surface, aware of the bombshell Mandy was about to drop.

"We've spoken to the pathologist." Mandy cleared her throat. "It appears Graces's death was possibly hypothermia. She had taken two of her mother's opiates and the drowsiness would have made her unaware of the danger."

Stefan's brow knotted as he struggled to understand. "Why would she do that? I don't see…"

With a quick glance in Helen's direction, Mandy continued, "There's more. Grace had given birth in the last week. Where is the baby?"

Stefan Nowak reacted as if someone had prodded him with a hot iron. He half stood, eyes wide and then collapsed again into his seat, shaking his head from side to side.

"A baby. A baby. I… not possible. Grace… no."

"What makes you think it's impossible, Mr Nowak? Did Grace have a boyfriend? Did you not know she was pregnant?"

"No. No." Stefan repeated.

"No boyfriend? No baby?"

"She had a boyfriend, but I didn't think they were … Grace had a baby? But… she was away last week. Staying with Ashley."

Josh made a note. "Who's Ashley? Where can we find her? Perhaps she knows something."

Stefan stared at Josh. "The three of them were close. Ashley, Sunil and Grace. Friends since primary school. They were all going to university together, but Grace deferred for a year because of Eleri. She wanted to spend time with her mother and to organise more fund-raising activities. We were so close to the target."

"Fundraising?"

Stefan sighed. "I tell Helen all about it."

"Do you think you could tell us too, please?"

He looked at them for a moment. "Two years ago, the doctors told Eleri there was nothing more they could do. The tumour would continue to grow, and her quality of life would go, until… They couldn't predict how long she had." He swallowed. "Grace refused to accept it and did some research. They were experimenting with a new treatment in America, but the trip and the cost of treatment was more than we could afford. We couldn't get a loan, or re-mortgage. Eleri didn't want debt and the house, as I tell Helen, was Grace's legacy. So, Grace set up a GoFundMe page and began to organise events and activities to raise money for the trip." He swallowed. "She was a powerhouse. In the first six months we raised thousands but still far short of the mark. We need about another twelve thousand. Then last week, while Grace was staying with Ashley, we had the news. It's too late to do anything now. Palliative care only. Grace was devastated when she found out."

A lead to follow but it didn't answer the question. Where was the baby?

"Where will we find Ashley?" asked Mandy.

"Bristol University. That's where Sunil and Ash went to study. If only Grace had gone with them."

If only. Too late to think that way. "May we have a look at Grace's room, please? There may be something there that would help with our inquiry?"

"Top of the stairs and first on the left." He rubbed his forehead with a hand as if he could push away all the horror of the day.

Spying the bottle of vodka on the side Mandy said to Helen. "Mr Nowak might appreciate something a bit stronger than tea."

CHAPTER EIGHT

The room was neat and tidy, bed made, and clothes hung up. Photographs of Grace with friends and her mother and stepfather plus leaflets of some of the events she'd organised were pinned to a noticeboard. A chart indicated the target amount and a monthly indication of how the money was raised. Mandy spent a moment studying it. All the determination and effort and for what? Grace was dead and Eleri dying. And a missing baby. Mandy suspected it was dead too and been concealed somewhere. Stefan said Grace was away last week. Had she given birth secretly or did her friends help? They'd go to Bristol tomorrow and find out what had happened.

They pulled on gloves and scrutinised the room. In one alcove was a small desk with a lamp and Grace's laptop. Josh was already putting the laptop into an evidence bag.

"No sign of a baby." Josh's voice was a whisper. "Do you think Rishi could be wrong?"

"You know as well as I do that Rishi is never wrong. But you're right. No inkling that there was anything to do with a baby. Not even any soft toys. It's a little too neat." As she said the words, Mandy had a vision of Tabitha's room. It was always tidy too but also lived in, with odds and ends scattered on the chest of drawers;

slippers on the floor and dressing gown draped behind the door. This was almost sterile, as though Grace was a visitor in her own home. Weird.

A pine wardrobe took up half of one wall. It held a selection of jeans, jackets and jumpers, all on hangers. At the bottom sat two pairs of trainers, one white, one black alongside ankle boots and strappy leather sandals.

"She didn't have much, did she?" Mandy sat on the edge of the bed. Something didn't fit. "Do you have sisters, Josh?"

"Yeah, two. Both younger than me. Why?"

"Would you say this was the room of a typical teenager? I know when we were in our teens Mam used to go spare with Joy and me. Mess everywhere and we were always buying new clothes."

"God, yes. My sisters are the same. Bitching over who is going to wear what. Shopping all the time. Not so bad now Samantha has moved out. I think my parents are hoping Becky will clear off too. She leaves a trail of destruction behind her."

"Exactly. This girl lived like a bloody nun. Hardly any possessions. She must have had things when she was a child. Toys. Books." Mandy shook her head. "This is too austere."

"What are you thinking?"

"I don't know. Maybe Stefan will be able to enlighten us. Let's see if the chest of drawers holds any clues. I can't get much sense of Grace. There are the photographs and the fundraising charts but little else. Have you photographed that noticeboard?"

"Yes. All these photographs seem to be recent. The last couple of years. Maybe her mother has others?"

"Do we know how long since Stefan married Mrs Mathias?"

"It'll be a matter of public record so easy to find out. Are you thinking Grace wasn't happy here? Didn't get on with the stepfather?"

"I don't have any theory yet. All I know is that a young woman is dead and her baby, dead or alive, is missing. There's no sense of despair or neglect here. Everything has a place."

"Do you think she was into Feng shui or a follower of that woman, whatshername… Marie Kondo? You know, all that minimalist stuff."

"Bloody hell, Josh. You never cease to amaze me. What do you know about Marie Kondo?"

"Lisa's always going on about clutter. Clear house, clear head and all that. Maybe Grace needed to clear all the clutter to help her concentrate on the fundraising activities. Maybe she had stuff and sold it to raise money." He shrugged his shoulders. "I know what you mean. It's all a bit too spick-and-span."

Nothing until, right at the back of the bottom drawer of the chest of drawers, they found a notebook.

"At last. Let's see what this says. I hope it's not her bloody maths homework." Mandy flicked through several pages. "It looks like some sort of diary. Dates and initials but nothing else. Let's take it with us. You never know. There could be some sort of connection to something else." She sighed. "I'm clutching at straws here."

Josh took another evidence bag out of his pocket. He was about to write when the pen slipped out of his hand. "Damn, it's rolled under the bed." He dropped to his knees. "Can't see where it's gone."

"Better get on your belly then. We need to check under there anyway." Mandy suppressed a chuckle as Josh sprawled on the carpet, arm stretched under the bed in an attempt to find the missing pen. He grunted, sat up and took his phone out of his pocket.

"Dark. Can't see. Got it." There was a pause. "There's something else under here. Right in the corner. I'll see if I can reach it." He grunted again and pulled something out. He got to his feet and handed it to Mandy.

It was a bag about the size of a small loaf, plastic, navy with purple spots and contents bulging.

"What do you think it is?" Josh asked.

Mandy prodded. "It's full of something and not toiletries. Let's see." She unfastened it, revealing the contents. "Bloody hell's bells."

CHAPTER NINE

Josh whistled. It was stuffed full of banknotes. "How much do you reckon? It's not pocket money, is it?"

"No, it damn well isn't. All fifties by the look of it. Could be as much as ten grand. What the hell? We'll need it tested for fingerprints."

"And it was hidden away. Do you think the parents knew?"

With a shake of her head Mandy said, "From what I've seen so far, the mother's been too ill to know what's been happening and the stepfather's equally as ignorant of Grace's life." She bit her lip. "This changes things. We need to know where this cash has come from and what secrets Grace Mathias has been hiding, along with the money."

"Drugs? Prostitution?" Josh said.

"Could be, but I doubt it somehow. Look at that noticeboard. She was determined to raise the funds for her mother's treatment. Is this money she raised but didn't add to the fund and why would she do that? It doesn't make sense. Let's go and talk to Stefan."

When they entered the kitchen again, Stefan was sitting in the same chair with the same blank expression on his face. Helen had made tea and a mug sat in front of him along with an untouched sandwich.

Josh showed him the bag. "Have you seen this before, Mr Nowak?"

Stefan frowned and shook his head. "No."

"We found it in Grace's room hidden under the bed. We wondered if you knew what it contained?" Mandy asked.

A shrug was the only reply.

"Grace's room is very tidy, everything in its place. It seemed odd that she should have hidden this out of sight. Are you sure you don't know anything about it? Have you seen it before?" asked Mandy.

"Why should I know about this? I don't go into her room. Grace was a very private person. I respected that." He pointed to the bag, his tone belligerent. "Why do you think I should know what is in there? It looks like something for make-up or toiletries. The sort of thing any teenager would have in their room although Grace was not like other teenagers. Her whole world became focused on her mother when we had the diagnosis. She was devastated when she found out all her efforts had not–" His voice cracked. His eyes filled with tears.

Helen raised an eyebrow.

"Would it surprise you to know it contains a large amount of cash?"

"Money? I don't understand. She was working in the supermarket sometimes. Zero hours contract as she wanted to be flexible. Little pay."

"How long have you been married to Eleri?" There seemed little point in pursuing the money so maybe they'd find out more from a different approach. Family background might provide some clue to Grace's state of mind.

"Five years. Grace was thirteen."

"And did you get on well together? Teenage girls can be challenging. My niece lives with me." Mandy hoped offering a glimpse into her private life would help make a connection.

"It was difficult, at first. She resented me, I think. An awkward adolescent. She didn't want to share her mother. It took a while. Then, when she saw how happy Eleri was, she changed. I wasn't trying to take her mamma away."

"I understand Mrs Mathias doesn't have any family. Is that right? No-one to help?"

Stefan sighed and looked at the sandwich as if he hadn't seen it before. He pushed the plate away. "That's right. Eleri has a sister, but they haven't spoken in years. Not since long before we met. Eleri's grandmother looked after the girls."

Interesting. Family secrets always intrigued Mandy. "Why did Eleri's grandmother bring her up? What happened to her parents?"

"It's a sad story. Eleri's parents went on holiday to Switzerland, and they died in a plane crash. The girls were with their grandmother, and she just took over. Eleri was five or six at the time and Sîan almost fourteen, I think. That's what Eleri told me."

"That's a big age difference. Eight years."

A shrug of the shoulders was Stefan's response.

"Where's Sîan now?"

"Eleri doesn't know. Her parents' deaths hit Sîan hard. She was a difficult teenager and left home when she was about sixteen. Only ever came back a couple of times when she wanted money by all accounts. Eleri lived with her grandmother, even after she got married and had Grace."

They were beginning to build a picture of the family background now but not much about Grace. She prodded a bit more. "And Grace's father?"

"He was not a good man, either to the grandmother or Eleri. Eleri divorced him after Grace was born and carried on living here, just the three of them. She looked after her grandmother until she died of a stroke."

A sad story indeed. That explained why there were no family members to support them. No wonder Grace and her mother had such a close bond. And Stefan was the outsider.

"How did you meet Eleri?"

"I'm a painter and decorator. I came to do some work. Eleri is a kind woman. I fall in love, big time. We got married and have happy family until…" He pulled his lips together and turned away, eyes glittering.

"Grace must have been very upset. She's had a lot to deal with in her life."

"Grace is, was, a strong person. Once she decided her mother was going to have the treatment in America, she started to raise money. The goal was over one hundred thousand pounds. Another ten thousand to reach the target." His shoulders slumped. "But it's too late. That's what we found out this week. The latest scan shows the tumour has started to grow faster. When

Grace got back from staying with Ashley, and I told her, she was devastated. It's been hard for her to see her mother so ill. We had hope. Now, nothing." He blinked.

"We'll organise for someone to sit with your wife tomorrow while you identify the body." Mandy gestured towards Helen. "DC Probert can go with you to the mortuary. It won't take long. A formality really." Her voice softened. "Will you be alright?"

Stefan met Mandy's eyes. "She wasn't my daughter, but I loved her as much as if she was my own blood."

There was no answer to that. They left Helen to deal with things while they made their way out of the house into the inhospitable winter's night.

CHAPTER TEN

"What do you think? Is he genuine? Or do you think he's mixed up in all this? Not telling us what he knows?" asked Josh.

"He seems genuine enough but ask Olivia if she's got the background checks on him sorted yet. See if there's anything there. For all the talk about happy families I'm not so sure. And I want forensics in Grace's room. See if they find anything else. Maybe I'm just a grumpy and suspicious so-and-so but I want to make sure there's nothing dodgy there. If he's had as much as a parking ticket, I want to know."

"You don't think–"

"That he's got something to do with Grace's baby? God knows. Stranger things have happened. It's late and we've got a shitload of stuff to do tomorrow so best warn Lisa that life is going to be hectic. I'll drop you off at the station."

"Where are you going?"

"Back to the Heath. The mortuary. See if Rishi's still there and if he's found anything else of note. Do me a favour, Josh. If Withering's in give him the lowdown for me, please? Just tell him where things are at the present and that I'll fill him in tomorrow."

Although he didn't seem thrilled at the prospect, Josh agreed and, as soon as she'd dropped him at Central, Mandy headed back up to the Heath hospital. Relieved to see Rishi's car still in the car park, she hurried to the mortuary.

The vibration of the fridges was the only sound she was aware of as she entered the room. She could almost taste the formaldehyde the smell was so strong. Rishi was no-where to be seen although Grace was still lying on the table. Still dead. Mandy gazed at the body. She looked more like a fifteen-year-old than a young woman of eighteen who had given birth.

"What happened to you, Grace? Where's your baby?"

She jumped when a voice said, "A very good question, Inspector."

"God, Rishi. What the hell do you think you're doing creeping up on people? You scared the shit out of me."

"My apologies. I was obeying the call of nature now I have finished here for the night. I just need to tidy up and put the body into cold storage."

"You've finished the PM?"

"Indeed. I think I know why the poor girl took the opiates." He went over to the side of the room where various bowls held substances that Mandy preferred not to think about. Using long tweezers, Rishi lifted something out of one of these bowls. "What do you see?"

"A piece of liver? Something quite bloody anyway. Are you going to explain?" Mandy was puzzled. What was Rishi on about?

"This is a small fragment of the placenta. It must have been missed at the birth. It caused excessive bleeding and extreme discomfort. I am surprised she did not go to a hospital."

"She must have been in considerable pain which is why she resorted to taking her mother's opiates," said Mandy.

"It seems that way. Of course, we need to wait for the toxicology report to confirm there was nothing else. If she had gone home, then she would have been alright. She could have slept it off." His shook his head. "I do not know why she did not go to her doctor. There are drugs to expel the placenta. A tragedy."

"A waste of a life. A young woman with everything ahead of her."

"Apart from the pregnancy there were no signs of disease, all organs in good health, no bruises or needle marks to indicate drugs. I would say she lived a clean life."

"I'll speak to her doctor in the morning and see if we can make sense of it." Mandy turned to leave then a thought struck her. "Can you do a DNA test from that sample? Could we determine paternity?"

"Of course. The sample from the placenta will have the same DNA as the baby." His voice dropped. "Have you found anything yet?"

Mandy shook her head. "No. We've got the sniffer dogs out at the cemetery but nothing yet. I've got a bad feeling about all this." She glanced at the body. "Poor girl. All I can do is find out why and what happened to her child. It doesn't look good. Would the baby have been full term?"

"It is difficult to say but from examination I think so. If not full term, then close to that. Her skin has been stretched considerably."

"She would have looked pregnant?"

"Inspector, we both know that if a woman wishes to conceal a pregnancy there are ways to do so. Not all of them are good for mother or baby but," he gestured with his hands held apart, "it happens."

CHAPTER ELEVEN

Joy was sitting on the sofa watching some TV drama when Mandy got home to Brithdir Street. Although she loved her twin there were times when she wanted some space and Joy and her belongings seemed to fill the house. Extra shoes and coats in the narrow hallway; magazines and empty mugs littering the lounge; a bathroom with wet towels and bottles of various liquids and a bedroom that looked as if the place had been burgled. All Mandy wanted to do was to sleep but there was Joy, alert and showing no signs of going to bed.

"Hey, sis. Late one."

"Yeah. I'm knackered." Mandy yawned to add weight to the statement in the hope Joy would take the hint. She'd been sleeping on the sofa bed in the lounge since Joy had arrived home in October. It was supposed to be a temporary arrangement which seemed to have stretched.

"I've seen the doctor today. Scan next week. Do you want to come with me?" asked Joy.

It was a loaded question. Did she want to go and sit in the hospital when her workload was already making her feel every minute of the day was precious? Mandy shrugged and tried to inject some enthusiasm into her voice. "Sure. If I can. Depends on work. We've a new case today. I don't know how long it's going to take."

Joy pouted, "Whatever. No pressure."

"Is Tabs alright? She's got a lot on with this drama club and end of term exams as well. I hope I'm going to be able to get to the play. That's the trouble with this job. Unpredictable." She flopped down beside her sister.

"And you can't talk about it? I saw something on the news about a body in the cemetery. Are you investigating that one?" Mandy didn't respond so Joy changed the subject. "That boy was here again with Tabs. The posh one."

"Daniel?" Mandy's heart sank. She thought Tabitha's crush on Daniel would have passed. It would end in tears. Boys like Daniel Levin married posh girls, not the illegitimate offspring of former drug users.

"They were rehearsing their parts for the play. She's a bit sweet on him, isn't she?"

"Yeah. I just hope she doesn't get hurt." Mandy yawned and stretched. "I'm going to have to shift you from my bed. I'm desperate for sleep and a full day ahead tomorrow again."

Joy stood up and stretched, making no attempt to help Mandy pull out the sofa bed. "Will you be able to pick some food up from Lidl on your way home? I've got awful cravings for peanut butter, and we've run out."

"I'm sure, even in your condition, you can manage to carry a jar of peanut butter." Mandy gritted her teeth. Her sister didn't even look pregnant and she sure as hell wasn't going to start running her errands for her. The sarcasm was wasted. Joy stretched again and went up the stairs.

Mandy sighed.

CHAPTER TWELVE

DAY TWO

Superintendent Withers was waiting for her. She hoped Josh had briefed him.

"DS Jones has given me the details in the Mathias case. Anything else I should know? What next?" he asked.

"We'll need to speak to Grace's doctor. I'll ask DC Probert to do that when the doctor calls at the house this morning. DC Wyglendacz can trawl through the social media and see if there's anything there that might help. I'm going to Bristol with DS Jones to speak to Grace's friends."

"The pathologist's report?"

"Rishi says she had a fragment of placenta retained in her womb. It would have caused heavy bleeding and extreme pain. She must have been desperate to have taken her mother's medication. We don't believe it was an act of self-destruction. She couldn't have known the effects until too late. Plus, there's the missing baby."

"Hypothermia, according to DC Jones. The cemetery is still closed, and bereavement services have been asking when they can open again. What are your intentions?"

"I asked for the sniffer dogs to do a round of the grounds. From the CCTV it didn't look as if Grace was carrying a baby. But she was bent over. I want to make sure no-one comes across the body of an infant."

Withers looked pensive. Neither of them wanted to think about that possibility. From what Stefan had said about Grace's visit to Bristol it was likely she had given birth there. Nothing was certain and it was always best to cover all eventualities.

"A missing baby? Nothing in the family home?"

"That's the way it looks, sir. No baby or indication that the family knew she was pregnant. The money is an added complication."

"Theories?" He glared at her through his specs.

"It's complicated. We don't know if the baby is dead or alive. She could have had a stillbirth or a premature baby who died. She covered up the pregnancy with her family at least. We don't know why. It's a puzzle and finding the money has muddied the waters further. Are the two things connected or not? Frankly, sir, I'm not sure what's been going on. I've a few theories rumbling around in my head but no clear picture yet."

"Well, don't let me hold you up." Mandy nodded made for the door. "What about the press? What have they been told?" asked Withers.

She stopped, turned back. "I haven't spoken to anyone, sir, although somebody has. My sister said there was a news item last night. No particulars given. Probably the old boy who found her or the woman who rang emergency services."

"I'll brief the press. Give them the bare minimum. Keep the details to ourselves for now." He glowered at her. "Well, what are you waiting for?"

* * *

The main CID office was buzzing with machines, low voices and spoons stirring in mugs. The other teams were involved in different investigations. Olivia was already logged on to her computer. She flipped a strand of purple hair out of her eyes and gave Mandy an expectant look. Eager beaver.

"Where's Josh? We need to get on the road."

"Loo, I think. Helen rang. She said she'd go straight to the house again this morning and report back later."

"Give her a ring and see if she can speak to Grace's doctor. Could be the same one as Mrs Mathias. I want to know what antenatal care Grace was given. Anything that could be relevant. She'll also need to organise a trip to the mortuary for Mr Nowak to identify the body."

"Sure, boss. What do you want me to do now?" She peered over the top of her specs.

"Get forensics out to the house. Tell them I want Grace's room searched. They need to be sensitive. There's a dying woman in the house. It's a delicate situation."

"It'll be tough for Helen, it will." said Olivia.

"She's skilled. Empathetic. As well as background on Stefan Nowak, I'd like you to go through the social media stuff and find out about Grace's relationships as well as this fundraising stuff she's been doing. Anything odd turns up, make a note. Go back a year or more." Mandy scratched her head. "Actually,

go right back to when she set up the GoFundMe page or whatever. We need to try and trace her movements, especially in the last year. She didn't get pregnant through the holy ghost so there's someone out there who knows something."

CHAPTER THIRTEEN

"Ready to go to Bristol?" Josh's voice broke Mandy's train of thought. He had dressed for the weather with a thick pea coat and new shoes.

Mandy commented on them. "Like the shoes."

"Soft-soled." He grinned. "I just hope they've got a good grip. It's still frosty but the gritter's been out. I dropped the laptop with tech in case there's anything that could help."

Mandy glanced at the clock. "Let's go. Sooner we get to Bristol the better. Let's hope Ashley or Sunil can enlighten us about what Grace did on her weekends with them. Especially last week. If she gave birth in the halls of residence someone will have heard or seen something. Screaming. Crying. Whatever."

She headed downstairs at speed, Josh following. They said nothing until they were on the way.

"You don't really think she had the baby there, do you? I mean student halls. Not very likely. And what would they do with it?" Josh was puzzled.

"Agreed. It's not likely, but it's the only damned lead we've got so far. Our best hope is to find out something about Grace's life and piece things together bit by bit. God, I hope there's no delay at Brynglas this morning."

As they made their way along the M4 towards Bristol, Mandy thought about the forthcoming interviews. The traffic was thick and slow-moving giving her time to ruminate. Both students had been informed of the death and knew the police wanted to speak to them. How had Grace's friends reacted to her death and what did they know? They'd soon find out. It was windy on the Severn Bridge, the Juke rocking a bit as they crossed and the Severn below grey and choppy. Mandy took the M5 towards the city.

"Left fork after we see the suspension bridge," said Josh as they neared Clifton. "Both students are based in West Village. We need to meet at Clifton Hill House. That's where the Student Support Centre and security are based." He had Google maps up on his phone.

The river flowed along to their right. Before long the bridge was visible hanging above them, a feat of engineering and, before barriers were erected, a place for potential suicides. Even after the barriers went up some desperate souls had managed to throw themselves into oblivion, ignoring the helpline number for the Samaritans on the bridge. Mandy stole a glance upwards. Heights she could live without.

"Parts of this building date back to the 18th century," said Josh, as Mandy pulled into a parking space at the front. They made their way through the main doors and had to wait for a student to let them in. Then through double doors to a room which must have been a canteen but where a more modern looking structure held a reception area. "How can we help you?" asked a notice. Mandy and Josh produced their warrant cards and explained their mission to the young woman behind the desk. She had long brunette hair tied into a bun but still looked like a student herself.

"We've been expecting you. I'll take you over to Ashley's room. It's in the other block."

They followed the young woman as she teetered on high heels, across a pathway and into the modern building, gaining curious glances from a couple of students on the way.

"We're very security conscious. You wouldn't be able to get into any of these buildings without a card. We like to know who is in here, at all times," said the woman. It was as if she felt she needed to tell them about the security. Perhaps her boss had given instructions or maybe it was the sort of spiel they gave to prospective students and parents on open days.

Josh smirked and Mandy wondered about his university experiences. No doubt there were ways around security. She'd have to ask him later about his student life. It was something she'd never considered before.

Long corridors and various odours accompanied their journey. The receptionist knocked on a door. "Ashley. It's your visitors." She left them as the door opened.

A young man, sandy-haired with a wispy beard, stood facing them. That was a surprise. She thought Ashley was a girl. He stood to one side to enable them to enter the cramped room before introducing himself.

"I'm Julian, Ash's peer support."

Ashley was sitting on the bed, curled into one corner, red-eyed and arms wrapped around herself.

Julian spoke to her. "Do you want me to stay with you while the police are here?"

She shook her head and gulped. "I'll be alright. I'll see Sunil, Sunny, later. His seminar finishes at ten. Thanks Jules." She attempted a half-smile.

"If you're sure. Call me if you need me." Julian patted her on the arm and left.

While Mandy sat on the edge of the bed, Josh lifted a soft toy from the chair in the corner and made himself comfortable. The room was compact but held a desk and shelving as well as a slim cupboard. A suitcase sat at the end of the bed, stopping Josh from stretching his legs too far. A diffuser dispensed a scent. It said White Linen on the label but was so indistinct it could have been toilet cleaner as far as Mandy was concerned. The sort of cloying scent that seemed to catch your tongue and throat. She wanted to open a window and let some fresh air into the room but didn't want to upset Ashley by asking. They had more important things to think about.

"We're sorry about your loss," said Mandy. "It's hard to lose a friend when you think you've your whole life ahead of you."

Ashley's eyes were brimming with tears. She sniffed and dabbed her nose with a tissue already twisted into knots. "What happened? Mam rang but she just said Grace was dead. Did… did someone kill her?"

"No. Nothing like that. We can't divulge any information at this point, I'm sorry."

Ashley was young and vulnerable. In a few years Tabitha would be at university. Mandy's heart gave a lurch. How could she let her go not knowing what dangers she might face.

"We're just trying to piece some things together and find out a bit more about Grace and her life. Are you able to help us with that? You've been friends for a long time."

"Since primary school. Me, Sunny and Grace. Our mams used to say we were stuck together with superglue. It's been strange not having her here in uni with us. That was the plan. The three musketeers together. Then Grace's mam got ill, and everything went to pot."

"Did you notice any change in Grace over the last year or so?"

Biting her lip, Ashley asked, "Like what? She was obsessed with the fundraising if that's what you mean. It sort of spoilt things a bit."

"What do you mean?"

"She didn't want to do anything unless it could raise money. She sold off loads of her clothes on eBay, all her stuff. Then there were all the sponsored things. At first it was fun, you know. We dressed up as superheroes and ran around Roath Park lake ten times. But it became obsessive, like it was every weekend."

"No down time for her?"

She shook her head. "She worked extra hard at school and weekends there was always something." She stopped. "That sounds awful, but we couldn't keep up with it. Plus, she became fussy over food. She kept thinking all the time about nutritional values. I thought she had anorexia or bulimia or something. She lost a lot of weight early in the year, said she felt sick. But then she seemed to get over it and put a bit on again. She had to borrow my trousers once as her zip broke from overstretching."

In the corner Josh was making notes. He asked, "How did she get on with her stepfather? Any discord there?"

"Not that she said. She wasn't too thrilled about him at first, bit jealous like. But he's such a quiet bloke, isn't he? I don't think they had any big rows or anything. Why?"

"Just trying to get a full picture," said Josh. "This isn't a big room. Are you happy enough here in Bristol?"

"I love it. Plus, we've got everything and so close to the centre too. There's always someone to talk too. Jules said he'd see about me talking to a counsellor. My tutors are very good too. I've told them about Grace." she swallowed. "I'm going home tomorrow. Few days early. I just want to be with my Mam."

An urge to hug the girl came over Mandy. She might be a young adult but there was a lot of the needy child in there too. Like Tabitha.

"Security is good, isn't it? Did you have to sign Grace in when she came to stay? Bit cramped too." Mandy said.

Ashley frowned. "Grace hasn't been to stay. I haven't seen her since September."

CHAPTER FOURTEEN

"Did you know Grace was pregnant?"

Ashley seemed unable to reply. Her eyes, still swimming with tears opened wider. At last, "Pregnant? No. Grace? She didn't. She couldn't." The girl sat, open-mouthed, gawping at them.

"Her boyfriend, Sunil, didn't say anything?"

"Sunny? He isn't, wasn't her boyfriend. I mean, he's her friend, but I don't think Sunil would… he's not that type." She stopped and flicked a lock of curly hair out of her eye. "You'll understand when you meet him. We've been friends forever. It wasn't that sort of relationship." She seemed very sure, so Mandy didn't pursue it.

"We need to speak to Sunil. Where can we find him?" asked Josh.

"He's got a room in this block too. Upstairs. I'll take you. He should be back from his seminar now." Ashley slid past Mandy and went to the washbasin to rinse her face. She ran a comb through her short hair, slipped on a pair of trainers and picked up her key card. Her eyes were swollen from crying, but she blew her nose, took a breath and said, 'Ready?'

There was no-one in the corridor although mumbled voices and laughter could be heard from somewhere in the building. They followed Ashley upstairs and along a corridor until she got to the end of the block. She knocked the last door.

"Sunny? It's me."

A rustling noise and then the door opened revealing a room almost identical to the one they'd just been in except it was pristine in appearance; bed made; shoes in neat rows; books arranged on shelves and even a plant growing on the windowsill. The young man who opened the door looked as drawn and shocked as Ashley. His eyes were puffy as though he hadn't slept much.

"These are the detectives. I'll see you later. My Dad said he'll come after work and pick us both up. Okay?" Ashley asked.

Sunny nodded then wrapped his arms around Ashley. "I can't believe it. It's too horrible. I didn't go to my seminar. Couldn't face it." He bent down over her, and Ashley patted his back.

"I know." She sniffed, trying not to cry again. "Be brave." Pulling away from his embrace she gave him a brief smile and turned away so he couldn't see the tears. She almost ran back down the corridor, leaving Mandy and Josh to introduce themselves.

As they entered the room Mandy spotted the shelf above the washbasin which had more toiletries than in her whole bathroom. Sunil was good looking, clean shaven, wearing a tight purple t-shirt and skinny jeans. The room smelled fresh with a sharpness like lemon or lime. Was he responsible for Grace's pregnancy? Somehow, Mandy didn't think so.

Sunil sat on the chair while Josh leaned on the desk under the window and Mandy perched on the edge of the bed.

"You know why we're here," Mandy began. "We're trying to find out a bit about Grace's life so we can work out what happened."

"Yes." His voice wobbled but he met her eyes.

"When was the last time you saw Grace?"

"September. Just before Ash and I left for uni. We wanted her to come out with us for a last wild fling, but she said she had to stay in with her mam. I met her in the afternoon, after she'd finished her shift. She had a temporary job in a shop. We just had a walk around the cemetery."

"That's a strange place to walk."

"Not really. It's quiet there and vast. Grace loved it. She used to take me around and tell me about various people who were buried there. She loved the statues too. Her favourite was one of a mother and child. Virgin Mary, I suppose. She often put flowers there."

"Why?" asked Josh.

"Dunno. She said some people had no-one left to remember them, so it was a nice thing to do."

"Were you Grace's boyfriend? Her stepfather had that impression."

"We were friends. Not in the romantic sense. Just friends. Like Ash." He coloured and looked away.

Mandy said nothing and waited for Sunil to break the silence that followed his statement.

"Grace was – how can I put it? Perceptive. Sensitive. Empathetic. She was the first one to guess that I'm gay. She didn't want me to be teased or picked on, so she pretended that we were a couple." He paused. "My parents don't know. I've only come out since I came to Bristol. I'll have to change my clothes before Ash's Dad comes to pick us up later – look like the son my parents expect to see."

Leading a double life. It wasn't a surprise to Mandy. Sunil was unlikely to be the father of Grace's baby. Ashley hadn't said as much but her reactions showed she knew too. But she had to be sure.

"Did Grace have a boyfriend?"

"Not that I know."

"Did she confide in you? Tell you secrets she might hide from her parents, for example?"

"Like what? She talked about her mam's illness and how it made her feel. She was obsessed with the fundraising. I think she'd have done almost anything to raise the cash to send Mrs Mathias to America."

"Unfortunately, it's too late for that." Sunil didn't seem surprised to know Mrs Mathias was not going to recover. What else did he know? "We wondered if Grace ever became depressed about the future, with her mam's illness and then deferring her place at uni. That must have been hard."

Sunil considered the question. "She was pragmatic. Old beyond her years my Mam says."

Now for the bombshell. "Did you know Grace was pregnant?"

The reaction was immediate. Sunil gasped. "No. Never. My god. How? Who?"

"That's what we'd like to know too. Could it be your baby?"

With his hand on his chest Sunil said, "Mine? I'm not into girls, as I told you. I loved Grace as a friend. I'm devastated she's dead." His eyes glistened. "I didn't know she was expecting. That's so," he paused, searching for the right words, "well, I don't know."

"You won't mind giving a sample of your DNA so we can eliminate you from our enquiries?" Phrased as a statement, it was more a question. She didn't believe Sunil was the father but best to be thorough.

"Of course."

Josh had come prepared with a kit and swabbed the inside of Sunil's mouth then put it into a container, labelled and dated it. Sunil appeared to be deep in thought. When Josh had finished, he turned to Mandy.

"And the baby? Did it die too?"

A good question. She wished she knew the answer.

* * *

"Thoughts?" Mandy asked Josh when they were sitting in the car before the return to Cardiff.

"He's not the father, is he? We'll send the swabs off, but I believe him. In fact, from their reactions I'd say they were both telling the truth. They didn't know about Grace's pregnancy." The seat belt clicked into position. "Leaves us with more probs though. If Grace didn't spend weekends here with her mates, where was she?"

"Where the hell did she go? I'm not sure if Ashley is telling us everything. I mean, if your best friend is being sick and you think she's got bulimia, then she's put on weight, so her zip breaks." She shook her head. "It doesn't add up. Wouldn't you ask questions? Support her. At least you might have suspicions. Let's go and talk to Ashley again when she's back in Cardiff."

"And Sunil?"

"Not sure. Maybe those two agreed on a story. Time will tell. Now, let's hope there's some news when we get back to the station."

CHAPTER FIFTEEN

Olivia was glued to her screen when they got in. She had a sheet of paper beside her covered in scrawled notes. Mandy hoped it was a good sign. They needed something.

"What's the news? Did Helen ring?"

"Yeah. It was the nurse seeing Mrs Mathias this morning. Said if you want to speak to the doctor then ring the surgery, now. No other info. She's taking Mr Nowak up to the mortuary this afternoon to identify the body. They've got a sitter for Mrs Mathias, so he can leave her for a bit. You could probably meet them there," she looked up at the clock, "if you go now, like."

"I'd like to watch his reactions when he sees Grace's body. Josh, perhaps you can make an appointment to see the doctor while I'm at the mortuary. Unless you want to come with me?"

Josh cleared his throat. "It's okay. I'll sort it. Do you want me to go and speak to her if she's available?"

"Good plan, Batman. See you in a bit."

She made it to the mortuary at the Heath hospital just as Helen and Stefan were entering. No-one spoke, just acknowledged each other. Stefan seemed in control, subdued but calm. He held his head up and his hands loose to his sides, his walk confident, steady.

"I'll just check they're ready," said Helen, as she disappeared through a door.

Stefan took a few deep breaths before he was admitted to the room where Grace was lying covered with a sheet. A mortician was in attendance and when Stefan indicated he was ready, uncovered the face. Stefan crossed himself. "My God. Grace." His shoulders slumped. He raised a hand as if to touch her and then changed his mind turning away, his hand covering his mouth.

"Would you like a few moments alone?" asked Helen, placing a hand on his arm.

He shook his head. Tears filled his eyes as they left and he almost staggered, leaning against the wall outside. It was genuine grief. Even though Grace was not his child he watched her grow up into a strong young woman. They'd need a DNA sample from him to ensure his relationship with his stepdaughter was not more than paternal. Now was not the time to do that.

* * *

Josh was at the doctor's surgery. Morning clinic was just finishing so only a handful of people sat in the waiting room on blue plastic chairs which lined the perimeter. An elderly man sat wheezing on one and a harassed mother was struggling to placate a snotty-nosed toddler, wriggling and protesting at being restricted in his pushchair. Josh was distracted by a screen on the wall which flashed whenever a patient was summoned. A wet dog odour from a young man huddled in the corner almost overwhelmed the lingering smell of disinfectant. Josh showed his warrant card to the receptionist.

"I believe Dr Gupnik is expecting me."

"I'll ring and check if she's free." It didn't take long. "Go through. Down the corridor. Third door on the right."

The doctor, a skinny woman with grey hair tied into a plait over one shoulder, was staring at a computer screen. She turned when she heard him and gave a wan smile.

Weary and with no time to waste on niceties, she said, "You wanted to talk to me about Grace Mathias. Such a lovely girl and so caring. And Mrs Mathias too. It's not good. I've just been checking my records. We haven't seen Grace at the surgery for about fifteen months. She had a throat infection then."

"Were you aware she was pregnant?"

Dr Gupnik looked surprised. "Good gracious. Certainly not. If Grace was pregnant, we should have known."

"Could she have been seeing another doctor? In another practice?"

"Not without requesting a change. We would have been informed. I've seen Mrs Mathias a few times over the past few months. Grace was often there, but I didn't suspect anything." She shook her head in disbelief. "In the early stages it wouldn't be noticeable, of course. How many weeks?"

"From the post-mortem it appears she gave birth sometime in the last week. The pathologist thinks it could have been a full-term baby."

Dr Gupnik digested the information. At last, she spoke. "And the baby?"

"Missing. We've no idea if it's alive or dead," said Josh. "This is confidential, of course. We haven't released anything to the press until we know what we're dealing with."

"I don't know what to say. Poor girl. A tragedy. I can assure you there is nothing on her medical records about a pregnancy." She glanced at the clock. "If there's anything else?"

As Josh left the surgery, he received some scathing looks from the people waiting to see the doctor. For once, the dead had precedence.

CHAPTER SIXTEEN

"Anything?" asked Mandy.

"Only that Grace's pregnancy was a secret, even to her doctor."

"So, we've a missing baby that no-one knew about, and it could be dead or alive. Bloody great. Talk to me Josh. What are you thinking?"

"If the pregnancy and birth was kept secret from the family then somebody else knows something. Who was she close to? Where did she go last week as it's likely she gave birth there?"

"If she'd given birth in university halls, I don't think it would be a secret for long, do you?"

"No way. Those walls are paper thin. You can hear everything – and I mean everything. The guy next to me had a different woman every night and it left nothing to the imagination," said Josh, grinning.

"Finding out who the father is might help. We'd better get Stefan's DNA sample sooner rather than later. He was shaken after seeing the body. Real grief. He won't be happy about being asked for his DNA. Has to be done though."

"And the missing infant?"

"I need to talk to the Super again. Until we know where Grace was when she gave birth, we don't have a search area. I suppose it will have to be a nationwide alert. Can't see it going down well with Withering."

"Especially as we have no details. A baby or a body. Good luck with it, boss. He's in his office." Josh scarpered while Mandy straightened herself, patted her hair and headed for the Superintendent's office.

Ross Withers was reading a file. He peered over his gold-rimmed specs at her and waited to hear what she had come to say.

"Grace's doctor didn't know she was pregnant. There's no sign of anything in the house and her friends know nothing. We have a missing baby and no way of knowing where she gave birth. No starting point for a search." The words came out in a rush. There was no way of sugar-coating the facts.

The Super leaned back in his chair and steepled his hands on the desk. "And she gave birth about a week ago. No babies found on doorsteps or bodies found in bins in the vicinity. You think she gave birth out of the area somewhere?"

"It seems likely. I think we need a nationwide appeal for information, sir."

"I agree. I'll get the press office on to it right away. Keep me informed." He paused and added, "This sort of thing is unsettling. My first case was a dead baby. Little mite found in the river. Haunted me for ages."

It was a rare insight into the Super's experiences. Crimes involving babies had that effect. She didn't respond. No need.

* * *

It was already dark when they got to the house. Helen opened the door to them, her face taut. It had been a difficult day. The door to the sickroom was ajar and Stefan was sitting with his wife who seemed to be sleeping. Mandy indicated to him, and he slipped out of the room.

"Inspector Wilde. Is there a problem?"

Stefan seemed to be looking through them as if they were invisible. In present circumstances the police presence was an irritation.

"We're trying to establish where Grace went to when she wasn't here. We know she didn't go to stay with friends in Bristol so who else was she close to? No relatives you told us. What about her biological father?"

"He emigrated to America a couple of years after the divorce. He didn't keep in touch with Grace. Washed her out of his life. It was his loss."

"And no-one else? Her aunt, Eleri's sister?"

Stefan pursed his lips. "Eleri told me she had no idea where Sîan went. She hasn't seen her, or her child, for years."

"Who would be able to tell us more about Grace? Where did she work? She must have contacts, colleagues, people who helped with the fundraising, social worker, medical people."

With a dazed look in his eyes, Stefan considered the question. "She never mentioned anyone by name. She was just doing temporary work in different places. If her mother needed her, she didn't work. The fundraising was the core of everything."

"We probably need to look more closely at her employment records. Speak to various people," said Josh, making a note.

"We'll need to take fingerprints and a DNA sample from you, for elimination purposes. DC Probert can do it if that feels better for you, or DS Jones has the kit with him."

They watched him as he processed the information. "Why do you need my DNA? Can I refuse?"

Mandy attempted to explain. "Having a sample will help us to establish who she has been in close contact with."

Stefan blinked and his expression changed as he became aware of the implications. "You want to see if I'm the father. You think I'm pervert? What the hell?" Anger replaced resignation.

"I'm sorry. Routine. It's necessary otherwise we wouldn't ask." Mandy waited. She knew it wasn't going to be easy.

With a look that displayed his disgust, Stefan allowed Josh to take the samples before returning to sit with his wife. Mandy hoped it didn't destroy the fragile relationship Helen was forging with the family.

* * *

A frost was setting in, the silvery sparkle just beginning to spread over the windscreen. Pretty but a nuisance. It would take time to scrape it off in the morning. They headed back to the office for a brief meeting to establish next steps. Helen joined them, about ten minutes later, just as Mandy was about to speak.

"He wanted me to leave. I'll go back in the morning when he's had some time."

Turning to the whiteboard Mandy asked, "Any forensics back from the money and the bag?"

"Nothing flagged, there isn't," said Olivia. "Grace's prints and other partials but no matches on the system."

"Whoever was involved with Grace must have met her at least nine months ago. One night stand? From what everybody says it's unlikely. Where did she go to socialise? We'll ask her friends again." She made a note.

"I suppose the school might give us some insight into her personality. She would have been in sixth form with Ashley and Sunil back at the start of the year," said Josh.

"She went to sixth form college. Stefan mentioned it when we were talking about Grace and her friends."

"Thanks, Helen. Which one?"

Adding the information to the board Mandy said, "We need to go back and trace things from there. I wonder if we missed anything else? The money was concealed but not hidden."

"There's a difference?"

"I think she put it there out of sight but if she'd wanted to hide it completely, she'd have put it somewhere less obvious. Like in the attic – or shoved the cash into her coat pockets and hung it up in the wardrobe. Strikes me under the bed was a temporary place."

Josh grunted and twisted in his seat. "We didn't check everything, did we?"

"No. The forensics team will do a thorough job. Stefan's not going to be receptive to us for a while. I hope you'll be okay Helen. You've gained his trust."

With a yawn, Josh asked. "Next steps, boss?"

"Home first. Tomorrow a visit to the school and another chat with Ashley and Sunil. It'll be a few days before the DNA results are back."

Josh's phone pinged a message. "No baby found yet. They've checked hospitals, asked doctors and midwives. What do you think happened?"

"I think the baby is alive. Somewhere. Why Grace kept the pregnancy a secret remains to be seen."

CHAPTER SEVENTEEN

DAY THREE

Neither Ashley nor Sunil had mentioned attending a sixth form college instead of continuing their education at the comprehensive school. It didn't seem a deliberate oversight. Too shocked by Grace's death perhaps. Mandy rang and asked to make an appointment to see the principal. When the purpose of the visit was explained, it was suggested the Head of Pastoral Care might be more appropriate. She should be able to give them more help as she knew the students better. It made sense. Ms Cooper was available to see them at ten-thirty, so they had time to sift through Grace's phone records first. For a while there was little noise except the tapping of keyboards and the clink of mugs.

"That's odd, now." Olivia's voice broke the concentration.

"What?"

"Grace started this funding thing about eighteen months ago, right?"

Attention was now on Olivia and what she had found.

"Well, look here." She pointed at her screen as both Mandy and Josh crouched behind her.

"She got a good start, she did. Publicity in the Echo and some local councillor pledging support. The fund totalled over three grand on the first go. You can link the fundraising events with the income on the page. See?" She pointed at the screen.

"Now, about fifteen months ago something else was added. About once a month a thousand was donated anonymously. Money into the account but no name. Regular pattern, like."

"How would we find out who donated that money? Is there any link on the page?" asked Mandy.

"No. Nothing. I suppose the bank would have details of all income. What you think? Bit dodgy, like?"

"Not necessarily," Josh interrupted. "We used to do fundraising for the rugby club. Cash in hand or buckets. That sort of stuff. The treasurer took it and deposited it in the bank."

Mandy's eyes narrowed as she thought about it. "Anyone could make a regular payment from their bank but unless they had access to the account, I don't think they could put cash in. Could explain the money we found. Well spotted, Olivia. We'll go to the bank after the college. Maybe there's a link there. Give Helen a ring and get her to ask Stefan what he knows about it, if anything. We aren't exactly flavour of the month there."

"Yeah, okay."

"Come on, Josh. Let's go and see what Ms Cooper can tell us."

As they turned to leave Superintendent Withers appeared, his complexion more florid than usual.

"Any progress on the Mathias case?"

"It's an odd one, sir. No new-borns have been left at hospitals or anywhere else. But no bodies have been found either." She took a breath. "My gut feeling is that the baby is alive, and someone is looking after it, keeping it hidden for some reason. I could be wrong–"

"–but it's a plausible explanation. And a sensitive situation. We've put out a national appeal to the good in the community. Maybe someone will come forward."

With a cynical smile, Mandy agreed.

"We're trying to build a picture of Grace's life. The best friends were unforthcoming, but we'll talk to them again. We've an appointment to see one of Grace's teachers this morning, sir. Olivia has discovered a pattern in the donations to Grace's GoFundMe page. It could have a bearing on the case."

"Good. Get on with it then." He turned on his heel and left. Mandy rolled her eyes. What the hell did he think she was trying to do?

As they left the station a gust of icy wind made Josh shiver and pull up his collar. Mandy wrapped a scarf around her neck and pulled on a beanie hat. The damp in the air would play havoc with her hair and she wanted to look less like a mad professor and more like a competent detective when they met Ms Cooper.

At the college it was difficult to find parking, so Mandy slewed the Juke into a space reserved for governors. Josh grinned at her. Whether at her lack of respect for authority or the thought of Mandy being a governor she wasn't sure. When they arrived at the front door of the college, they had to press a bell for entry.

"Sad that all this security is essential these days," said Mandy, as they waited to be admitted. "When I was in school anyone could wander in. Not that anyone with any sense would want to be surrounded by adolescents."

The door swished open at that point, so Josh had no time to respond. They showed their warrant cards. The receptionist, a thin woman with a face as pale and sour as curdled milk, indicated for them to follow. She knocked on a door and opened it to reveal a small room with tables and chairs, a whiteboard at one end and three computers to one side. Ms Cooper stood as they entered.

"Good morning. I'm Gemma Cooper, Head of Pastoral Care. I believe you wished to speak to me about Grace Mathias. Terrible tragedy. The headteacher did a special assembly in Grace's memory. I'm afraid I didn't know her personally. I just started in September."

Damn. Why didn't someone tell them before now? And Ms Cooper with her slim skirt, high heels and full make-up looked more like a model than a teacher.

"What about the other teachers? Would any of them be able to give us some information? Who taught her? Who was Head of Pastoral Care before you?"

Gemma Cooper clicked on one of the computers. "I pulled up Grace's details when I knew you were coming in. I thought there might be something on file to help. She took Art, English Literature and Drama. The art teacher has left. He's gone to live in France with his wife – lucky bloke – and it was Nia Jones who taught English and Drama. She's on maternity leave."

"When did she have her baby?" asked Josh.

"About July, I think." Another click. "Yes, she was teaching until the last minute, I was told. Wanted to get her group through their A levels. There's devotion to duty. And she was Head of Pastoral as well. Nia would be the one to talk to."

"Do you have her particulars?" Josh had pen poised.

"I'm not sure…"

"We are investigating the death of a former pupil. I'm sure we can find out by other means but that could hold up our enquiries." Mandy gave Gemma a demanding look and waited. It had the desired effect.

"Yes. Well, under the circumstances, I suppose it's not a breach of confidentiality. They have a farm out past Rumney, towards Marshfield." She clicked on the computer and rattled off the address and contact number.

"We'll give her a call. Thank you for your help, Ms Cooper."

Gemma Cooper was a little flushed, unsure if she had behaved in the correct manner in disclosing the information. Mandy beamed at her. "This must be a demanding job. Do you teach as well as dealing with the pastoral stuff?"

A sigh escaped her lips. "Yes. Some days I feel like a mouse on a treadmill."

"Don't we all?"

Outside again Josh said, "Not a great help, was it?"

"At least we've got a name of someone who knew Grace and who could have some insight into how she was thinking. She could have spoken to Nia Jones. Confided in her. We'll give her a ring and maybe she'll talk to us. Every bit of information could help."

"Bank now?" asked Josh. "Time to grab something to eat first?"

"Lisa still not feeding you?"

"There's stuff in the fridge. I forgot to take anything with me today." He looked away. "The bank's on either Wellfield or Albany Road, isn't it? I can pop into Tesco after and grab something. Won't take a minute."

"Sure. Can't have you passing out from hunger, can we? Just don't get something that's going to stink out my car like that wrap thing you had last week. It's too bloody cold to drive with the windows open."

CHAPTER EIGHTEEN

It was lunchtime and the bank had a queue outside, plus all the students from the local college had flooded Wellfield Road looking for food. It was like trying to weave through opponents on a rugby field.

"To hell with this crap," said Mandy pushing her way to the front, oblivious to the disgruntled murmurings and contentious looks. She flashed her warrant card at the startled cashier. "We need to see a manager now, please." She attempted what she hoped was a friendly smile and the startled cashier disappeared, returning in minutes with a middle-aged man. His paunch and ruddy complexion spelled out too many nights on the sofa drinking beer and watching television. He introduced himself as Colin Higgins and gestured for them to follow, as he opened a door to let them enter. They trailed him upstairs to a bland office, one of many, where he had a glass topped desk and a view of a brick wall. Soulless.

"What's it about?" No procrastination over business and that suited Mandy. She spent little time in outlining the problem.

"So, if we can find out who deposited the regular payments it could help. We can get the necessary paperwork but that would hold up our investigation." She waited, expectant, jaw set, as he deliberated. Then, deciding it wasn't worth the effort to protest, he brought up Grace's account on the screen and swivelled the monitor around so they could see.

"Grace deposited those amounts herself?" Mandy's voice was incredulous. It wasn't the information they'd hoped for and another non-answer to their questions. "These are regular cash payments of large amounts. Didn't anyone think to talk to her?" asked Mandy. "Did they not ask her about things like money laundering, for example? What if this was drugs money? No checks?"

Mr Higgins shrugged his shoulders. "There was no reason to suspect anything. Grace Mathias and her mother have held accounts here for a while. We knew it was going into a charity fund. What would you expect the bank to do, Inspector?"

Now, Mandy wasn't sure how to answer. She was pissed off, but she couldn't really blame the bank. Another hurdle in their journey to find out about the enigma that was Grace Mathias.

Once outside again, Josh dived into Tesco, elbowing his way through the students while Mandy sat in the car and pondered. A regular payment in cash. Did it coincide with Grace's alleged monthly trips to Bristol? Trips that didn't happen. Would Stefan know?

She was so lost in thought she didn't notice Josh until he opened the passenger door. He had something in his hand.

"What did you get today?"

"Roast beef on brown."

"You'd save a fortune if you made your own. Or got Lisa to do it."

"Some chance. Are we going back to the station now?"

"Yeah. Check to see if anything has happened and ring Nia Jones. If she's been on maternity leave, she probably needs a warning before the police turn up at her door."

Just as she was about to pull out of the parking space, they heard a commotion. Two young lads were belting it down the street with a plump woman in pursuit. One of the lads was gripping a large pink handbag. They were weaving through the crowd towards where Mandy had parked.

"What the hell? Josh out!"

As Josh leapt out, Mandy opened the door wide causing the one nearest her to fall over. His mate hesitated a fraction too long. Josh was in pursuit. As they neared the corner of Albany Road he tackled him, bringing the lad to his knees. A crowd had gathered to watch. Cuffing his hands behind his back, Josh walked him back to the car. Mandy was grinning from ear to ear, the other one similarly cuffed and leaning against the side of the Juke.

"I've rung and uniform are on the way." The owner of the stolen bag was standing beside Mandy. "This lady will be making charges against these two clowns. Good tackle, DS Jones."

"I know you," said the first one. "I seen you about with your daughter. She won't be so pretty if–"

"If you come near me or my niece I'll tear you–"

A siren interrupted her, but the grim expression on Mandy's face left him in no doubt about his future should he harm Tabitha. She'd have to warn her niece to be extra vigilant.

* * *

The appeal about a missing baby was not connected to Grace to spare the family any more hassle, but Tod Blakeney, one of the local reporters, was waiting for them on their return to Central.

He was stamping up and down outside, his breath making little puffs of smoke and his arms wrapped around his body. He had a nose for a story and was one of Mandy's least favourite reporters. She pretended not to see him as they headed towards the steps up to the entrance doors.

"Hey, Mandy. What's the gen on this missing baby then? Whose baby? Do you know? Any connections to recent events?" His beaver eyes watched for her reaction.

"Piss off, Tod. Go and crawl under a stone. Superintendent Withers gave the press release. You won't get anything else out of us. And it's Inspector Wilde to you."

"No connection to the dead girl? Grace Mathias. I heard a rumour."

"Well, you can stick your rumour where the sun don't shine. Where did you hear crap like that?"

Aware he had her attention, Tod grinned. "If I tell you that then you have to give me something in return."

Mandy stretched out her arm towards him and he took a step back, almost falling in his haste. Josh put a restraining hand on Mandy's arm, and she lowered it again.

"If you are withholding information you'll get the insider on it – from inside a bloody cell. Now spill. Where did this bullshit come from?"

With a grimace, knowing he wasn't going to get anywhere, he said, "I've a mate works in the hospital. A cleaner. Big ears. He sometimes drops little titbits of info for the price of a pint.

Gritting her teeth, Mandy almost spat at him. "You tell your mate to buy his own pints and to be aware of patient confidentiality. He could get into big, big trouble if he opens his mouth too wide. Now go and find a hole to bury yourself in."

Not waiting to see what Tod would do, Mandy stomped up the steps and through the doors. For once the only person there was the desk sergeant, so she was able to vent her anger as soon as the doors closed behind them.

"How does that little shit do it? You watch. He'll print something about this. No names will be mentioned but I bet there'll be something. I'd like to wring his bloody neck."

Gogo, the desk sergeant, exchanged a look with Josh. "A kick in the balls might do the trick," he said in a mock serious way before laughing. The tension melted.

"What next?" asked Josh.

"We start with what we've got. Grace's laptop and her contacts. Let's ring this teacher. Nia Jones. We can go and talk to her. See what she can tell us. And I want another word with Sunil and Ashley. There's something they aren't telling us, and I want to know what it is."

CHAPTER NINETEEN

Helen was back in the office and reported Stefan seemed a little taken aback by the forensic team's intrusion. It was difficult but she had managed to explain everything to him. Although she was as calm as ever, it was easy to spot how weary she looked.

"I don't think the poor man knows what's happening. He's aged ten years in two days. The doctor has prescribed stronger sedation for Eleri due to her distress."

The missing infant was a complication which just added to everyone's heightened emotions. Mandy rang Nia Jones. She picked up the phone on the third ring. She sounded listless and they could hear a baby crying in the background.

"Craig. I told you not to ring. He's only just gone to sleep."

"Mrs Jones? It's Detective Inspector Wilde here, Cardiff Central Police Station–"

"Oh my God. Has something happened? Is Craig alright? He hasn't had an accident or something?" A touch of panic.

"I can assure you this has nothing to do with Craig. Is that your husband? This is an entirely different matter. We're trying to find out a little more about Grace Mathias. You'll have seen the news. We'd like to come and speak to you."

"Yes. Awful. And such a lovely girl." The baby's cries had reached a crescendo and Nia Jones said, "I can't talk now.

He'll want a feed. Can you come out in about half an hour? He's usually better after that." She sounded distracted, and it was obvious they were not going to gain anything by trying to continue the conversation with the accompaniment of a screeching child.

"Of course. We've got your address."

"It's a bit hard to find but there's a blue house on the corner–"

"Don't worry. We'll use the satnav."

With a sound of relief Mandy put the phone down. "How can a small thing like a baby make so much noise? My ears are ringing."

"They can drive you to distraction," said Helen. "My two only slept when I took them out in the car. Ear-piercing screams every night just as Tom came through the door. He thought I'd put them up to it."

Mandy had a sudden vision of Joy and a new baby squashed into her house in Brithdir Street. They had talked about Joy moving out or building an attic extension. Having a baby in the house was not going to fit with Mandy's erratic routine and need for respite after work.

"The joys of parenthood. Thank God Tabitha is past the baby stage."

"Teens are worse," said Olivia. "My sister and me, well, we gave Mam hell. For a couple of years anyway."

"My sister's still giving me hell," said Mandy. "I should be the one screaming. Which reminds me. She's got a scan sometime soon, so I'll leave you to sort things out one afternoon, Josh. Good experience. Have you thought about the inspector's exam?"

Helen and Olivia paused as they waited to see what would be said next.

"Yeah. I've had a look but I'm not sure if I'm ready."

"Bullshit. Of course, you are. More responsibility. Different team."

With a shuffle of his feet and head bowed towards the floor he replied, "Not sure it's what I want. I'm quite happy with present company."

"Now I know you've got a problem. If you can put up with me then perhaps you are destined for sainthood." She grinned at him, pleased in one way. She'd have to push him out of the nest at some point for his own sake. "Right, let's go and see Nia Jones."

CHAPTER TWENTY

It took them longer than expected to find the farm. The satnav suggested they had reached their destination in the middle of a narrow road with no buildings in sight. Mandy had to do a three-point turn and retrace their steps. At last, they saw a blue house and headed towards it on what was little more than a glorified dirt track.

"What's the name of the farm again?" asked Mandy, tempted to stop at the blue house.

"Whistletop Farm. That's not it," said Josh pointing at the sign. "That's called Bluebell Cottage."

"Which is why it's painted blue. We'll carry on up here a bit and see."

The road twisted and seemed to be climbing steadily until they turned a corner and below them spotted a house and outbuildings.

"That looks like the place," said Josh. "I had a look on Google maps, satellite view, before we left the office."

"The wonders of technology. Good. Pray the screecher doesn't waken up."

As they approached the house, a solid looking stone built building, two dogs approached the car. One, a collie, appeared curious while the other, some sort of indistinguishable breed, barked in warning, baring his teeth.

"Bloody hell. A Rottweiler," said Mandy, as she parked the car and switched off the engine. She was reluctant to get out.

"Don't be daft. It's just a mongrel. He won't attack." Josh was grinning at her.

"That's okay for you to say, country boy. If it's not on a lead and it's snarling, I'd rather not take the risk."

"I'll show you." He opened the door and stepped out, waited until both dogs gathered around him. As Mandy watched, Josh held his hand out and allowed the dogs to sniff him. The barking stopped and Josh patted the mongrel on the head, talking to him all the time. Mandy took a deep breath and got out, stiffened as the dogs approached. The air was fresh, despite the proximity to the motorway. Although it seemed a long way from when they had turned off the main road, Mandy could see cars in the distance and hear a faint rumble.

"Bandit. Heinz. Come away." A woman had appeared at the door of the house, a baby on her hip, her sandy coloured hair pulled into a careless bun at the back of her head. The dogs sloped off and the woman beckoned. She looked about thirty, stick-thin and dressed in joggers and loose top.

"DI Wilde?"

They took out their identification and Nia Jones invited them into the house. The house had been renovated at some time and the dining room and kitchen were combined into one large room with a settle, a long oak table and chairs at one end. The original flagstones were half covered with a rug and a rocking baby chair sat on top. A carrycot on a stand was by the wall. The baby was wriggling in Nia's arms.

"I'm sorry. I thought he'd be asleep, but I think he could be teething."

The baby grizzled as if to confirm, pushing one chubby hand into his mouth and gawping at the newcomers.

"If you hold on to him for a minute, I'll put the kettle on. I'm gasping for a cuppa."

She pushed the infant into Mandy's arms. Mandy wasn't sure who was more surprised as the infant's eyes opened wider. He smelled of milk and baby shampoo and was heavier than she expected. Josh was trying not to smile but the ends of his mouth were twitching. The child lifted his hand and grasped Mandy's hair. She winced and tried to prise the tiny fingers away. He held on tighter. At least he wasn't screaming. Nia seemed pleased.

"He likes you. He doesn't see many people out here. Neither do I."

Mandy rocked the baby a little and his eyes drooped. Next thing she knew his hand flopped, and he was fast asleep.

"Seems you've got a magic touch," said Josh as Mandy handed the baby back to Nia. With infinite care she put him into a carrycot. He snuffled a bit but carried on sleeping.

"God, I'm exhausted. Give me a room full of teenagers any day. At least I know how to deal with them." Nia dropped into a chair and Mandy and Josh also sat down. She'd poured tea and offered milk and sugar, heaping two spoons into her own mug. She wolfed down a couple of digestive biscuits and sat back at last, eyeing the two detectives. "What do you want to know?"

"You were Head of Pastoral Care and taught Grace Mathias. We're trying to get a picture of her life over the past year and build up a profile. What can you tell us?"

Nibbling a third biscuit Nia thought for a moment. "Bright girl. Loved literature and read widely. She had a thing about Du Maurier and wanted to be able to write like her. She was bubbly, full of fun – until her mother's illness. Then she changed. Driven. She still studied hard but seemed obsessed with finding a cure."

"And raising money to do so. Did she ever speak to you about the fundraising?"

"Believe me, anyone who came in contact with Grace knew all about it. She did a school assembly on it. Sponsored events. Every weekend there was something. Local councillor got involved as well. She was hoping to take her concerns to the Senedd, but I don't think he was up for it. Gave her a lot of support though. It helped with publicity."

"When was the last time you saw Grace?"

"Results day. August. I went in to see my former pupils when they got their grades. I worked my socks off with that group and wanted to share the excitement. Rhys," she waved a hand towards the carrycot, "was still tiny and the girls made a fuss of him."

"And her friends? Any special boyfriend?"

"She hung around with Ashley and Sunil all the time. The three of them were like the Three Musketeers. All for one and one for all." Nia smiled. "Grace was a very loyal person. She'd fight for what she thought was right. And she was altruistic too. I've seen her defend Sunil against rude comments. A spitfire when needed but a sweet nature."

How much did a pastoral care teacher know about her students? Mandy wasn't sure what Nia Jones knew about Grace's private life.

"Did Grace confide in you? Tell you any secrets? About her private life, I mean. Did you know if she was in a sexual relationship, for example?"

There was silence while Nia regarded them both. The fridge freezer purred in the background and the old house seemed to creak now and again.

"What exactly is all this about? I was Grace's teacher. A support and, I hope, a friendly listening ear. Sometimes she was upset about her mum and just needed to talk. That's all. She didn't tell me if she was sleeping with anyone. You need to ask Sunil. He's the only boy I ever saw her with."

"You are aware that Sunil is gay?"

"I suspected as much, and I think that's why Grace felt the need to protect him. Teenagers can be evil towards one another. Grace had natural empathy with people and would go out of her way to help others. She had a bright future ahead of her. Such a waste."

The baby stirred in his sleep making little chirruping noises. Time for them to go. They thanked Nia and left the warmth of the house for the bitterness of the winter day. The sky looked laden and tiny flakes of snow danced in the wind. Not enough to cause a problem and despite the keen wind it didn't feel cold enough for snow. The dogs were nowhere to be seen.

"She wasn't much help, was she?" asked Josh.

"Not really. Grace Mathias is as much a mystery as ever."

As they drove past the blue house a man got out of a car. He stared at the Juke. Not much traffic along this road she guessed.

"Let's get back to civilisation," said Mandy. "I'd hate to live out here in isolation. Bloody countryside. Hate it."

CHAPTER TWENTY-ONE

"Anything new?" asked Mandy when they got back to the office.

Helen smiled. "Nothing on Stefan, I'm happy to report. I'm just going over there now. Try to smooth the waters after the forensic team have been. He was a bit tetchy with me today. It's quite understandable. At least he doesn't see it as my fault."

"Nope. All the blame is on me. Good. Don't hang about too long. There were a few snow flurries in the air out at Marshfield. Too wet to stick but you never know."

As she gathered her things together Helen said, "You don't really believe he's got anything to do with all this, do you? My feeling is he's completely out of his depth here. His wife is dying; his stepdaughter is dead; her baby, that he knew nothing about, is missing," she hesitated, "it's overwhelming for him. And the forensics team going into the house as well. It's enough for anyone to come to terms without–"

"–being? under suspicion. I know. We're all aware of it, but we have to challenge everything. If the DNA test eliminates him and then we can all breathe. I hope you can explain it to him. We should have results in a couple of days." They all had their jobs to do.

Without another word Helen left. Sometimes Mandy wondered why she preferred being a DC instead of looking for promotion. But Helen had other things to deal with apart from a career. A husband, two growing boys, ailing parents and ancient aunt. It was more than enough for one person. Mandy didn't even dare think about her own home situation. The only way she could work was to focus on one problem at a time. Today it was the missing baby.

"Anything?" she asked Olivia.

"Loads of social media stuff. Seems as though she was on every platform available but all to do with the fundraising. It's going to take a bit of time, now."

It wasn't what Mandy was hoping for. How much time? Every hour could make the difference although the missing baby would be a week old now – if it was still alive.

"Nothing from forensics?"

"Nah. Want me to chase them?" Olivia grinned.

"It's a bit too soon. I'm expecting a miracle, I suppose. I'm going to have a look at the diary we found."

"There wasn't much in it, was there?" said Josh. "It's as though she knew she needed to keep it all a secret. A separate life."

"We haven't had toxicology back yet either. I'll push for that tomorrow although I doubt there'll be anything unexpected. What have we got so far? A teenage pregnancy, hidden from everyone. A baby missing – alive or dead. No clue as to paternity. All we know is that Grace Mathias was obsessed with raising money for her mother's treatment. That last ten grand we found would have almost hit the target."

"But she returned from a few days away to discover her mother was going to die anyway. You don't think…" asked Josh, his voice tailing off, reluctant to voice what they were all thinking.

"That she took those tablets deliberately? In a state of distress? No. From what we've found out about Grace Mathias I should say that was extremely unlikely. The pregnancy is linked to the money. I'm certain of that. What was it Ashley said? Something about her selling stuff to save her mother? Obsessive fundraising."

"You think she sold the baby?" Olivia was appalled.

"Possibly something like that. Or the father insisted the child was given up at birth."

"Maybe she got pregnant and blackmailed the father for the money to pay for her mother's treatment," said Josh.

"If we rule out prostitution or drugs then there must be another way she could get hold of so much money. What if she had a relationship with a married man and he didn't want his wife to know–?"

"–then she had a hold over him. She could keep the pregnancy secret in exchange for the money." Josh was becoming animated at the new train of thought.

"It might explain why the cash was paid in instalments. Hush money. Final payment when the baby was born."

"It don't explain where the baby is," said Olivia. "What happened to it? What if the man didn't want the baby? If it was the result of an affair, is he going to want it? If Grace didn't keep it, then somebody else must have it."

"Unless it died." Josh's comment was sobering. They were just theorising with no proof of anything and no way forward without a lead.

"Well, to date, there have been no babies abandoned in the South Wales area during the last two weeks. Perhaps we need to check new-borns given up for adoption."

"We could be wasting time," said Josh. "Until we know where she went, we're scuppered. I mean she could have gone to London or North Wales or further afield. It's a pity her mother or stepfather didn't ask more questions."

It was true but didn't help. Things were going nowhere fast, and they were stuck. Mandy was sitting gazing into space, deep in thought when Josh spoke.

"I've written up the interview with Nia Jones. Is there anything else tonight?"

Mandy raised glazed eyes. "Huh. Do you really think, knowing what we know now, that Grace Mathias would be involved in blackmail?"

"Seriously? Not a hope."

"When she gets pregnant, she hides the pregnancy. Goes off somewhere and has the baby secretly. Just abandons it? No. Doesn't ring true. There's something else here and I'm not getting it." She stretched and yawned. "Tomorrow is a new day. Let's hope we get some gem out of all this shit."

* * *

The snow had started in earnest as Mandy drove home although it didn't seem to be sticking. A white Christmas wasn't on the cards, according to the forecasters although who could trust the weather? She couldn't remember the last time it had snowed enough to disrupt things. Over ten years ago at least.

The lights were on downstairs, but it was quiet when she entered her hall. Unusual. Joy liked to have music playing all the time. Maybe she was having a nap or Tabitha was trying to do homework. Mandy heaved off her coat and boots and pushed open the door to the lounge. Joy was on the sofa, staring into space. She turned when she became aware of Mandy's presence. The look on her face spelt trouble of some sort. Mandy's stomach flipped.

"What's the matter, Joy? Where's Tabs? Nothing's happened to her?"

"She's fine. Upstairs doing her homework and texting that Daniel boy I expect." Her expression was flat, emotionless, as if every word was an effort. "It's the baby." She cradled her stomach and bit her lip, eyes glistening. "There's something wrong."

"What? Have you seen the doctor? What's wrong?"

Joy swallowed and then gulped air, "I had a routine appointment today. The doctor couldn't detect a heartbeat. I'm having an emergency scan tomorrow. She said… she said…" The tears started; soft sobs gave way to heaving cries as Mandy folded her twin into her arms. She was at a loss. What could she say to make things better?

"Does Tabitha know there's something wrong?"

Joy shook her head. "No. I didn't say anything. I told her I was a bit tired and needed to rest. She made me a cup of tea and went upstairs."

"You don't want her to see you in a state. She'll think I've been horrible to you. I'm sorry, sis. I'll go with you tomorrow. There's nothing Josh can't deal with. Now, let's clean the snot off your face and I'll make us something to eat." Joy opened her mouth to protest but Mandy stopped her. "No. I'm not listening to any excuses. You need to eat. Nobody can function without proper nutrition. Scrambled eggs on toast won't kill you."

With a weak attempt at a smile, Joy sagged back into the sofa while Mandy went to the kitchen to prepare the food. Dealing with a missing baby and now the possibility that there was something wrong with Joy's pregnancy. All too much to think about. They'd deal with whatever needed to be done tomorrow. And someone would have to tell Tabitha.

She watched Joy pick at the egg, moving it around on the toast, now and then putting a morsel in her mouth.

"Come on, sis. Eat it before it gets cold. I'm going to sit here and watch you until you've cleared your plate."

"You're bullying me."

"For your own good. And mine. Last thing I need is you fainting from malnutrition. Eat."

With a sigh Joy made more effort and managed to swallow most of the meal before pushing the plate away. "I can't stomach any more. What do I tell Tabs?"

"Nothing until we know what's going on. Time for bed."

CHAPTER TWENTY-TWO

DAY FOUR

When she woke the next morning Mandy was aware of an unusual silence. God it was cold. She shivered as she pulled on her robe and slipped her feet into slippers. Six o'clock. Still dark as a cave. She padded into the kitchen to fill the kettle. A mug of green tea was essential. It was too early to ring Josh to tell him she'd be in late. The blind in the kitchen was up and she could see why things seemed quieter than usual. An inch or more of snow had fallen in the night, muffling everything and covering the ground in a pristine sugar coating. It was quite beautiful but also a nuisance. She could walk to work, no problem, and the main roads should be gritted. Joy's appointment was after nine-thirty so there was time for a bit of a thaw once the sun came out.

She lay down again on the sofa-bed, cupping her mug of tea in her hands to warm them. A noise on the stairs alerted her. As the lounge door creaked open, she was surprised to see her sister.

"I didn't expect to see you for another hour. Tabs still asleep?"

"Yes. I think so. I couldn't sleep. It snowed in the night."

"Tell me something I don't know." Mandy passed her mug to her sister. "You look ghastly. Drink this. I'll go and get another one."

They sat in silence, cwtched up together on the sofa-bed, like they used to do when they were younger, before life and all the problems got in the way.

"Do I really look ghastly? I feel dreadful."

"You're a bit tired and strained. It shows. Natural to feel crap under the circumstances. It's bloody freezing and the middle of the night. It's not as though you're going clubbing and on the pull."

"Ha ha. As if. Stop hogging that blanket." She pulled the blanket over more and wrapped it around her knees. Noticing Mandy's pensive expression she said, "What are you thinking about?"

"Joy, tell me. If a teenager got pregnant and no one knew about it, except maybe the father, what would she do after the baby was born? I mean, you were in your twenties having Tabs, but you never told us who the father was. I'm just wondering in what circumstances would someone give a baby away?"

"I suppose if it was prearranged in some way." Joy tilted her head as she thought about it. "If the father wanted the baby and it was going to ruin the girl's life if she kept it. I often wonder if my life had been different if I'd given Tabs up for adoption. It wasn't easy, you know."

Mandy had to restrain herself from saying something she might regret later. Joy had walked out on her responsibilities to her daughter just as Tabs reached adolescence. It wasn't exemplary behaviour. Then she remembered the appointment later that morning and Joy's vulnerability.

"You don't think she would leave the baby somewhere and hope somebody found it? If she was alone when she gave birth, for example."

"God, Mand, the last thing you'd want is to be alone giving birth. I know it happens, but it wouldn't be a choice. The pain. I don't think a teenager would cope without support." A shudder passed through her. "I'd better go and have a shower and get ready. You don't think we'll have a problem getting to the hospital, do you?"

"We can walk if the roads don't clear, but there's a thaw starting. I can hear a drip somewhere. It's not going to lie for long."

As her sister left, Mandy pondered what she'd said. Who was with Grace when she gave birth? She rang Josh. He sounded half-asleep.

"I'm going to be in late. Hospital with Joy. Explain later. Have another look at Grace's diary. See if there's anything. I think we'll have another word with Ashley later. She was hiding something. I'm sure of it. And chase up Stefan's DNA results. See if they match."

* * *

She didn't need to be told her sister was nervous at the Early Pregnancy Assessment Unit in the hospital. She could feel it too. The uncertainty was leading to a feeling of dread she never felt entering the mortuary. At least it was brighter and smelt cleaner.

A nurse came out with a clipboard. "Joy Wilde."

Joy and Mandy stood. The nurse looked from one to the other.

"I'm Joy. I'd like my sister to be with me."

"Of course. I'm Kim. Follow me, please."

They were taken along a corridor to a room with no windows and artificial lighting. The nurse checked Joy's particulars, ensuring they matched the form and then asked her to lie on the couch while she prepared the ultrasound equipment. Another nurse was in the room at a screen in the corner.

The examination took less than five minutes. The results devastating. As they left the hospital, they were both silent, Joy clutching a letter explaining next steps.

CHAPTER TWENTY-THREE

Josh flicked through the pages of the diary. Olivia was still scrolling through social media. She was making notes of dates and events and the corresponding payments into the bank account. Helen was also making lists of people who had contributed to the GoFundMe page. Some people made generous donations, over a hundred pounds or more, including the local councillor, while others had contributed five pounds or less. It all added up to a considerable sum gathered over the last couple of years, even discounting the regular anonymous payments. Grace would have been well suited as a marketing and fundraising manager with her impressive track record.

"I don't get it, I don't." Olivia sat back in her chair and pushed her owl-like specs up her nose. "I've gone back a couple of years. Lots of photos of Grace and friends; pictures of animals; books she's read; films she's seen; parties and all the stuff you'd expect. Then the fundraising starts and it's as if her life ends. Look here, now. Nothing on there, except all the events organised; photos of people who helped; those giant cheques you see with lottery winners and stuff; she's even got stuff in Cardiff Life. Odd it is."

"Cross reference and put it up on the board," said Josh. "We know that after the so-called days away in Bristol with her friends she deposited large amounts of cash in the bank. Do any of those dates tally with events? Even up to a couple of weeks before? Helen, anything struck you as odd? Same names coming up on a regular basis?"

"A few, but not big donations. Regular monthly payments of ten pounds from a few people, Gwen Long is one. She's the neighbour who has helped out. I think she knew Eleri's grandmother."

"All the diary gives apart from the various events are a number of smiley faces and scribbles although the initials CR come up on a regular basis. It's a two-year diary and the entries with CR start about eighteen months ago."

"Can I have a look at it?" asked Helen.

Josh passed it over. "I didn't think anybody used paper anymore," he said. "Everything on the phone. That reminds me. Anything come from her phone records?"

"I'm checking through all the numbers. Regular calls to friends and various people linked to the events. No calls at all on certain dates," said Helen.

Josh cross-referenced. "The dates she was supposed to be in Bristol, but we don't know where she was. We definitely need to speak to Ashley and Sunil again. If this monthly thing has been going on for well over a year, they must have some inkling," said Josh.

"These dates marked in the diary. They're every twenty-eight days."

"Regular as clockwork. Why? Have you spotted something, Helen?"

"Josh. You're a married man. Think. Why would a woman mark her diary every twenty-eight days?"

A flush spread over his face as he made the link. Olivia laughed. "Oh, you've embarrassed him now, Helen."

But Helen was too busy examining the diary again, flipping over pages, backwards and forwards. "Here. Sad face. Then nine months ago a happy face. That's when she knew she was pregnant. She was happy about it."

"If she was happy, why did she conceal it? Even after the birth? It's not making sense."

"And look," said Helen, pointing, "halfway between the faces that's when she met CR. She would be her most fertile then. It looks as though the pregnancy was planned, deliberate. But no baby."

"We need to find out who CR is. Check through the donors on the GoFundMe page. Anyone with initials CR should be of interest to us. Maybe we've got something here."

"What have you got?" Mandy plodded into the room and flopped down into a chair. She felt grey, drained of all colour and energy.

"Are you alright? Joy? The baby?" asked Josh. Helen and Olivia were quiet, unmoving, watching her.

Mandy's throat felt tight when she spoke. "It seems the baby has died. Joy will have to go back and they'll deal with it then." She was aware she sounded cold, unfeeling which was far from how she felt but she needed to keep it together for everyone's sake.

The background sounds in the room, muffled voices along the corridor, a telephone ringing somewhere in the building seemed to fade into the distance somewhere. Mandy sat, face rigid, unable to say any more. Helen put a hand on her shoulder. "You need a nice mug of green tea. It's not a good way to start the day."

"A dead baby is never a good thing," added Josh, just as Superintendent Withers entered the room. Josh's remark startled him.

"Dead baby? You've found the Mathias infant?" The overpowering smell of his aftershave made Mandy want to gag.

"No. It's my sister. I've just come back from the hospital. They told her the baby is dead in her womb."

"Ah. I was going to... I can speak to you again. Should you be here? Don't you want to be with Joy?" Withers had a concerned look on his face, despite the grumpy tone.

"She doesn't want me there. She says she needs space to get her head around it all. I'm better in work. Focus on something else."

Withers held her eyes for a moment. "If you need time, let me know. Losing a baby, even an unborn one, is traumatic for everyone. My wife lost our first at thirty weeks. It took quite a time to get over it. You've a good team here. They know what they're doing." With a noise somewhere between a grunt and a cough he left again.

"Blimey. Was that praise?" Mandy gave a faint laugh. 'I wondered what he wanted to talk to me about. Let's get up to speed. What have you got?"

CHAPTER TWENTY-FOUR

"There's a clue in the diary. It looks as though the pregnancy was planned. We think CR could be the initials of the father."

"Good work. Any idea who CR could be?" asked Mandy.

"Just starting to do that," said Josh. She flipped through the diary as Josh pointed out any significant entries. "She planned the pregnancy. Look." He indicated the smiley faces.

"It's not making sense, is it?" said Mandy.

"Three possible on the donors list," said Helen.

"There's people mentioned on some of the social media stuff too. Want to see if any of them are the same?" asked Olivia. "I've got Christopher Robin–"

"Like Winnie the Pooh?" asked Mandy. "That has to be a piss-take."

"No, it's true. He's a bloke about thirty or so, looking at the photo. He organised a race and picnic to raise funds. They did well out of it," said Olivia.

"Okay. See what you can find out and add him to the list for a face-to-face. What else? Who else?"

"Christopher Robin is also on the list of donors," said Helen. "Have you got Callum Rosser and Caradog Roberts there, Olivia?"

"Yeah. I was thinking about the councillor. He's done an awful lot for her, hasn't he? His surname's Roper. What if CR stands for Councillor Roper?"

"What's his first name, Liv?" asked Josh.

"Gwyn."

"And a G might look a bit like a C." Josh checked the diary and passed it to Mandy. "What do you think? Her writing's a bit scatty at times."

"Put him on the list. I propose we pay a visit to each of these and ask them for DNA samples. Helen, get us a list of addresses. Josh and I are going to have a little chat with Ashley again. It might help us to know what she isn't telling us. If we can squeeze it out of her."

"Did you want us to follow up on any of these names, boss?" asked Olivia.

"A bit of digging won't go amiss. Check their telephone numbers with the numbers on Grace's phone. We've got a list, haven't we?"

"Yeah. I got it. No probs."

"Should we ring before we go to Ashley's house?" asked Josh.

"No way. I'm not giving her a chance to avoid us. Come on, let's go before the bloody snow starts again."

CHAPTER TWENTY-FIVE

Ashley's mother opened the door to them, flushed face and worried eyes, as she indicated for them to enter. They followed her down the hallway with its tiled floor to a room at the back. In summer it would be an attractive place to sit but in the winter it all looked a little sad. The polished floors in the room were a honey colour, and an old fifties-style fireplace was the centrepiece of one wall with a cheery log fire burning in the grate. A faint waft of woodsmoke gave a feel of country pubs.

A tub chair sat by the French doors, but Ashley was curled on the duck-egg blue sofa, a checkered rug over her knees. She raised bleary eyes to meet them. They declined the offer of hot drinks, Mrs Rivers left and Mandy perched on the sofa beside Ashley while Josh removed a cushion and wedged himself into the tub chair.

Ashley regarded them, dark shadows under her eyes from too little rest and too much crying. Despite her empathy with the girl, Mandy knew the sooner they got answers the better.

"We know you've been hiding something, Ashley. Perhaps you've thought about things a bit more and you can help us now." She waited to let that sink in. "It's too late to do anything for Grace, but it would help her mother, and us, if we could understand a little more about what's been going on. We still don't know where the baby is, although we believe it may be alive."

If the infant had been abandoned somewhere they would have expected to have found it by now. Distraught mothers, underage or otherwise, were inclined to leave their newborns where they would be discovered – hospitals or shopping malls. No body meant there was a strong chance the baby was being looked after. The diary also gave them hope. What they needed was more information.

Ashley didn't seem inclined to say anything. Mandy coughed and with a warning glance at Josh said, "Perhaps if we reveal what we know to you, it might help. This is all confidential, of course. We won't ask you to sign the Official Secrets Act," she smiled, "but it can't be shared. Do you understand?"

At last, they had her attention. A whispered 'yes'.

"We know that Grace met someone. This someone had money, possibly influence, to help Grace to raise those funds for her mother's treatment."

Ashley, wide-eyed and alert, rolled her lips together. She said nothing.

Mandy carried on. "We also think this person was responsible for the pregnancy and is likely the father of Grace's child. If we are correct, then the baby is probably safe, but we still need to find it. Do you understand what I'm telling you?"

"Yes." Ashley swallowed, her eyes darting beyond Josh to the garden.

"Is there anything, anything at all, you remember that could help us? You've already told us about the weight loss and weight gain which bothered you. Did Grace confide in you? Did she mention anyone? Even if it was only a name? Or a hint of something. Think. It could be vitally important."

Ashley blinked at her. A minute or two passed and the smell of vegetables cooking drifted in from the kitchen. At last, Ashley roused herself.

"It may be nothing…"

"It all helps."

"I can't remember exactly when," Ashley gazed into space, "not long after the fundraising stuff started, I think. Grace was very excited. She said she'd met someone, and it was all going to be alright. She could do something to make a real difference to someone's life, not just her mam's. She was like that, Grace was. Always put herself last." She sniffed. "I feel awful we didn't see each other for months. Maybe she needed somebody to talk to and I wasn't there."

As more tears threatened Mandy asked, "Do you think she confided in Sunil?"

"No. She was protective of him. I'm sure he didn't even notice when Grace was stick-thin." She plucked a little at the blanket. "He's a little self-obsessed at times. Do you want me to ask him? I might be able to find out more than you. He would freeze if the police turned up at his door. His Dad's very strict. He didn't approve of Grace as a girlfriend. God, if he knew the truth about Sunny."

"Indeed. Have a quiet word with him. If you think he's held anything back, then let us know. We can arrange to meet somewhere neutral."

"I'll text him now and see if he wants to talk later. I'll tell you if he's noticed anything or if Grace said anything to him."

They left the warmth of the house and out into the road again where a heavy sky and a keen wind resulted in a dash to the car.

"Not much there," said Josh "apart from delicious smelling soup."

"Soup?"

"Best thing on a day like this."

"How do you know it was soup?"

"Smelt like it. Wishful thinking." He blew on his hands,

"You need to invest in a pair of gloves," said Mandy.

"You're right. Whoever Grace met it was a secret. Not something she could share with her friends. How does anyone keep something huge like that to themselves?"

"Tell a stranger?"

It was a thought. Would Grace say things to a stranger? Things she didn't want known but found it hard to keep hidden?

"Let's see what Olivia and Helen have to tell us about our suspects. If we have a shortlist, we can get DNA samples and see where that takes us."

"Nowhere fast. It takes at least two days to get anything back from the lab."

"We can ask for fast-track. That reminds me. Toxicology from the PM should be back and maybe, if we're lucky, Stefan's results. It would be good to be able to eliminate him. He's a decent bloke."

CHAPTER TWENTY-SIX

"Anything more?" asked Mandy when they got back to the office. Josh disappeared to heat up a couple of sausage rolls he'd picked up on the way, after begging Mandy to stop at the local Tesco.

"Yes. Rishi rang," said Helen. "The toxicology report confirms his theory. She had a small amount of opiate in her system, consistent with taking the painkillers. In normal circumstances it wouldn't have mattered, but the drowsiness coupled with the extreme cold led to hypothermia." She swallowed. "It will go to the coroner, but the verdict is likely to be misadventure, not death by suicide. I'd better go and tell Stefan."

"It doesn't make anything better. She's still dead. At least they know it wasn't deliberate." Mandy shook her head. "A small compensation, I suppose."

"We got the list here, boss. Addresses and phone numbers." Olivia waved a sheet of paper. "Want to have a look?"

"I did a bit of checking, like you asked. Put them in order. Think Mr Caradog Roberts can be discounted as the father. He gave a big donation at the beginning, then a tenner a month." Olivia prodded the list. "See here, he's living in a retirement home, up in Caerphilly. My sister has a friend who works there. Want me to ask her if she knows anything, like?"

"Wouldn't that be against the rules for the friend? Confidential information?" asked Josh.

"Technically, 'suppose. But everybody knows everybody there. I'll check the records. Find out how old he is. Don't seem the most likely though, do he?"

"No. Who else on your hit list – apart from Christopher Robin? Callum Rosser. Isn't he a rugby player?"

Olivia laughed. "Not this one. Sells double glazing. In his fifties, I reckon. Likes the gym and stuff. He sponsored the first event Grace organised. Offered first prize of a new front door if they could get over five thousand in sponsorship. Loads of photos of him hugging her. Good publicity for him too. His company boomed after."

"He won't object to a little chat and a DNA sample, I'm sure. Good work, Olivia. We'll see Christopher Robin tomorrow, but I think it won't do any harm to visit Mr Rosser this afternoon."

"And there's the councillor…"

"We'll have to use a softly, softly approach with that one. I've come up against Gwyn Roper before. He's no pushover and a bit up his own arse. Let's see where we get with the others first."

* * *

Callum Rosser's factory and showroom was off Rover Way. The photograph Josh pulled up on his phone looked typical of a unit on an industrial estate. When they got there, it was as expected; grey and anonymous with huge doors leading to the factory floor under a sign with Adam Windows and Doors – C. Rosser.

"Adam Windows?"

Josh shrugged. "Letter A comes up first in a search? Don't suppose it matters. It's the right place."

Mandy swung the Juke into a space outside a door marked Trade and they got out. The place was busy with a couple of vans loading up out the front while the view of the warehouse floor showed at least a dozen men engaged in the various stages of window making. Huge sheets of glass were propped up on a trolley and a row of wooden tables supported windows and doors in various stages of production. It was noisy with the machinery, men shouting instructions and music blaring. The smell of solvent was strong, probably why the front of the warehouse was open to the elements, even in mid-winter.

"Business looks brisk. You'd expect things to be slow in December, wouldn't you?" said Josh, eyeing up the work going on.

"Cheaper to buy in the winter maybe. Don't fancy it myself. I mean who wants a bloody wind blowing through the house this time of the year? Come on. Let's find Callum Rosser and see what he has to tell us."

The trade entrance led to a small room with a counter and shelving behind with boxes of what looked like handles and other fitments. A bell pinged as they entered, and a sheepish looking lad emerged from somewhere to the side. His eyes narrowed, not in a friendly way, as he looked at them.

"Mr Rosser about?" asked Josh.

The lad sniffed and then called, "Cal. Pigs here for you." He disappeared again.

"How did he know?" asked Josh.

"Shifty little buggers like that can smell a copper a mile away." Mandy grinned. "I expect he's just relieved we aren't after him."

Callum Rosser appeared. He was about Josh's height with smiling grey eyes and a little goatee beard a similar colour. They showed him their warrant cards which didn't seem to faze him as he kept the same pleasant expression on his face. "What can I do for you, detectives?"

"We're investigating circumstances surrounding the death of Grace Mathias. I believe you knew her?"

The smile faded. "Yes. I sponsored one of her events. I can't believe she's gone. And Eleri. It will finish her off. From what I've heard she's not doing too well anyway."

Mandy didn't comment on Eleri's health. Josh got down to business.

"Perhaps you'll tell us why you gave such generous sponsorship?" Josh consulted his notes. "A new composite front door, fully fitted by specialist firm Adam Windows and Doors. That's some prize. Worth a bit. Generous in the extreme, I'd say. What did you expect in return?"

Callum sighed. "It was for Sîan, really. When I saw that Eleri was ill and Grace was doing everything she could to raise cash for treatment, I thought 'why not help?' We'd had a good season and stuff like that is always good publicity for the firm. Bit of a no brainer. Helping everybody."

"Sîan?"

"Eleri's sister. We went to school together Sîan and me. I had a massive crush on her. We lived next door at the time. The grandmother ruled them with a rod of iron. I'm not surprised Sîan scarpered."

"So you have a strong connection to the family?" Mandy asked. "There was a bit of friction there at one time I believe."

"Back in the day. Sîan walked out and never came back. She kept in touch with me for a bit. She cleared off to London and then north. She had a little kid too. A girl. Rose or Ruth or something. I suppose she might have half a dozen by now."

"There was some sort of family dispute too, I heard."

"I have no idea what went on. I went travelling after A levels and lost touch with Sîan after a time. Never thought I'd end up back in Cardiff doing this lark." He nodded towards the workshop.

"You donated quite regularly to Grace's page."

He flushed at the remark. "Yeah. Good business. If someone said they'd come to the firm through seeing my sponsorship I put ten percent of the profit from the sale into the fund. Seemed fair. We got quite a bit of free publicity from it."

Callum Rosser seemed guileless. Hard to believe, though, that someone would be so generous because of a crush he'd held for Sîan as a teenager. He met Mandy's eyes with sincerity. Painting himself as a generous donor to Grace's page had made good business sense for him. The place was booming, and he looked like a man with few financial worries.

"When was the last time you saw Grace?"

"Dunno. I usually tried to make an appearance if there was something going on. Park the van up. Bit of advertising. When was the last big thing?" He frowned and looked into the distance. "Race around the lake in September maybe? Want me to check the calendar? Or there'll be photos on our social media page. The missus comes with me and does all that social media stuff."

Now for the tricky bit. Mandy counted to five before asking, "Do you mind if we take a sample of your DNA for elimination purposes?"

The smile dropped from his face as he considered the request. "DNA? What elimination purposes? I thought Grace's death was an accident. You don't think somebody did her in?" His mouth dropped open.

"We are not looking for anyone in connection with the death but there are some complications. We're trying to establish what happened in the last year or so and interviewing a number of people who played a significant role in Grace's life. DNA sampling is part of that investigation. I can assure you, that samples will be destroyed once we are sure there is no link to this matter."

"I see."

Although he didn't look too thrilled with the procedure, Callum allowed Josh to take a sample. He cheered up as they were leaving.

"If you ever need windows or doors, I'll give you a good deal. Don't forget that."

"Businessman to the core," said Josh. "I don't think he's our guy though, do you?"

"No. Interesting though. Must have had a helluva crush on Sîan. Wonder where she ended up. Some family row too. It's always useful to find out family history."

CHAPTER TWENTY-SEVEN

Mandy was deep in thought as they drove back towards the centre of the city. Time was passing and they were no further along in the search for the missing baby. DNA results took a couple of days so nothing until then. Someone was keeping a big secret.

"Penny for them?" Josh interrupted her thoughts.

"Not worth a penny. I'm just very worried. That poor girl. Whoever she was shielding deserves a solid kick up the arse. How could they leave her like that?"

Josh just shrugged and wiped the inside of the fogged-up window. "Let's see what Christopher Robin has to say to us."

The primary school, where Christopher Robin taught, was a solid red brick building with high windows and scaffolding outside. Like many in the city it had been built in the Victorian era and maintenance was an issue. School had just finished so they waited until the stream of parents and children abated before making their way through the playground to the main entrance. A teacher stood on guard with a couple of children whose parents were late arriving to pick up their offspring. She was tiny in stature, smaller than some of the older pupils who had just left. Mandy flashed her warrant card and asked where to find Mr Robin.

"You'll have to sign in. There's a book–" She broke off as a harassed looking woman with flushed face arrived, panting. "Here's your Mum now, you two. Off you go." She waved at the parent and then turned to them again. "Follow me. I'll sign you in and give you visitors' passes."

They followed her into a little office, signed the book and then asked where they could find Mr Robin.

"Chris will be in the hall." She pointed down the corridor. "Room at the end. He takes a music class after school. Recorders. Awful din. I'm sure he'll be glad of an excuse to pause for a few minutes." She gave them a curious look but didn't ask any questions. Their visit would cause gossip in the staffroom.

Teachers and assistants were busy packing up with a general clatter of noise and the occasional peal of laughter. They passed a cleaning lady who was spraying tables in the corridor with a lavender-scented polish. She ignored them, unconcerned about their presence and too busy to care.

The hall was a surprise. A prefabricated building added at some point. It was light and airy. At one end a small group of children were making what purported to be music while a fair-haired man conducted them. As they entered a couple of the musicians stopped playing. One boy said, "Sir. Sir," and pointed. Christopher Robin turned to face them. His blue eyes were hidden behind enormous tortoiseshell frames. A dirty blond fringe flopped over one eye. He was short and slight, dressed in blue shirt and navy trousers, with polished loafer style black shoes. Smart. Professional. The music stopped as he made his way down to them.

"Mr Christopher Robin?"

He nodded and then frowned as Mandy and Josh introduced themselves and produced their identification.

"We just need a few words." Mandy glanced at the group who were now chatting loudly to each other.

"Give me five minutes, please. I can't leave this lot unattended. You're welcome to take a seat." He indicated low benches, probably used for PE. They lowered themselves on to a bench and Mandy stretched her legs out. They watched as Christopher regained the attention of the group and put them through their paces. He was patient but firm, quashing any possible misbehaviour with a stern look or warning finger. But he'd known Grace as a child. Was he a likely suspect?

CHAPTER TWENTY-EIGHT

"What a job. Give me criminals any day," Josh muttered under his breath.

Mandy suppressed a chuckle. "Possible criminals of the future," she said in a low whisper.

The five minutes seemed to stretch until at last, Mr Robin said, "Okay. Enough for now. Practise that piece over the week and let's see if you can make something that sounds more like music and less like a cat howling next time." A few giggles followed and then the children lifted their things and filtered out. Christopher Robin followed them with a quick, "Just got to check they are being picked up." He returned moments later.

"Right. Sorry you had to suffer that, "said Mr Robin with a smile. "It's a new group and most of them are tone deaf. Why did you want to speak to me? I haven't done anything wrong have I?"

"Now why would you think that?"

"Police don't usually pay social visits so there has to be a reason." He seemed unconcerned, smiling at them in a friendly fashion.

"We'd like to talk to you about Grace Mathias."

His eyes clouded. "Tragic. I taught her in Year Six. Bright as a button. Emotional intelligence too. She was always the champion of the underdog. I've seen her face up to bullies in the playground, defending someone less fortunate than herself. The fact she was shorter than many of them didn't stop her. There was something about her. Jelly baby outside but tougher on the inside."

An interesting description. Mandy raised an eyebrow. "What do you mean?"

"She looked like an angel, had the disposition of one too. But an inner strength. If Grace Mathias was your friend, she'd do anything for you."

"Was she your friend? Did she do anything for you? Why did you become involved in her fundraising?" asked Mandy.

"She came to the school and asked if she could distribute leaflets about one of her fundraising events. A swimming challenge. I was on playground duty and recognised her. We had a chat and she told me about her mam. It was a shock." His face assumed a serious expression. "Eleri was always one of those lovely mums, full of smiles. Devoted to Grace. One of the school governors too."

After a bit of mental arithmetic Mandy asked, "So you weren't her teacher when Eleri remarried? It must have been hard for Grace to share her mam with somebody else."

Christopher laughed at that. "Not Grace. If ever there was a girl overflowing with love, it was Grace. Always saw the best in everyone."

Josh took over. He had his phone out and scrolled through until he found the details he was looking for.

"We've noticed you became more than a little involved in Grace's campaign. Not only did you get sponsorship for her you also gave a regular donation to her page. Why's that? Bit odd. Former pupil and all that." He squinted at Christopher, suspicion in his voice.

It didn't seem to faze him. "Two reasons. First because I knew the family and I wanted to help. Second, a very good friend of mine died last year with a similar condition. I couldn't do anything to help him, but I could help Grace and Eleri. I didn't even know there was treatment available when my friend was ill."

It all seemed sincere enough, but they still needed to get a DNA sample. With a nod to Josh, Mandy looked Christopher in the eye. "Grace's death was unfortunate but there were circumstances leading up to her death that require further investigation. We've been taking some DNA samples for the purposes of elimination in our enquiry. Do you have any objection to giving a sample? Simple test. Take seconds."

"My DNA? What for? I'm not altogether happy about that."

It would be much easier if they could give the real purpose, but she wanted to keep the reasons hidden, for now at least.

"We're trying to find a link to someone important in Grace's life. We just need to find a match." It was vague and she hoped she wouldn't have to say any more.

"The most important person in Grace's life was Eleri. You don't think someone killed Grace, do you? The news said—"

"No-one is suspected of killing Grace. I can't divulge the circumstances, but I can assure you the samples will be destroyed as soon as we have eliminated you from the investigation. I repeat, no foul play was suspected in Grace's death. You are not under suspicion for anything like that."

A voice shouted, "Night" and a door slammed somewhere in the building breaking the tension, as they waited for Christopher to decide.

CHAPTER TWENTY-NINE

"I don't understand but I've nothing to hide. What do you need? A hair? Fingernail clipping?" asked Christopher.

Despite herself, Mandy smiled. "You obviously don't watch much crime drama, or too much of the old stuff. We swab the inside of your mouth. DS Jones will do it. Takes a couple of days, or usually more, to have results back. We'll be in touch when they come through."

He still looked unsure. "I wish I knew what this is about."

"Do you have children?" asked Mandy.

"No thanks. I get enough of that at work. My partner, Guy, and me decided we'd have a dog instead. Much less bother. Except the seven am walks." He gave a rueful grin.

"You're probably right," said Mandy as thoughts of Tabitha and Joy entered her head. Next door's cat was enough for her without a fluffy friend.

"Don't forget to sign out and drop your badges off," he reminded them as they left. "I'll be the one to get into trouble if you don't. Health and safety and all that. Rules and regs."

"Thoughts?" asked Mandy when they were outside.

"Don't think it's him. Do you?"

"Not after the remark about the children. I'm sure after a day of dealing with unruly kids that last thing you'd need is a crying baby at home. Can you find your own way back? I want to pay a social call."

"Social call? Didn't know you did social."

"Oh, very funny. I do have friends – just not a lot of time to see anyone. And I've got Joy waiting at home too." The thought of her sister had an instant sobering effect on Mandy and her shoulders slumped.

"Who are you going to visit?"

"That old boy. The one that found Grace."

"Mr Davis, without the e?"

"That's the one. He said he'd seen her before. Passed the time of day. I thought I'd pop in to see him before I go home. Take him some food. Check he's okay and ask a few questions. He might remember something else."

"All heart, aren't you? Joining the Sali Army next." In mock despair he said, "It's fine. I can fight my way through the cold and sleet. Don't worry about me." ·

"Come with me if you can face it. Patience required, not that I have much to spare."

"Think I'll brave the elements."

As Mandy made her way to Robert Street she thought again about the babies. Grace's baby and the dead baby inside her sister. A difficult conversation faced her when she got home and the trip to see Mr Davis a distraction. Procrastination. What she expected to glean from him she had no idea. Just a hunch. Police work didn't deal in hunches but sometimes she allowed herself to follow her gut. Mr Davis could know something he wasn't even aware of.

CHAPTER THIRTY

Mandy stopped at a corner shop and bought some tins of soup, chocolate biscuits and, on a whim, a Bara brith. Their Gran used to make Bara brith and give them wedges of it, thick with butter, maintaining it was good for them, all that fruit and sugar. Nan Betsi didn't do much these days. Too busy basking in the Spanish sun with Mandy's parents.

There was no sign of light when she knocked on the front door with its tarnished old-fashioned brass knocker. Mandy knocked again. Then, a faint light and sounds from within. A reedy voice asked, "Who is it?"

"It's DI Wilde. We met at the cemetery. After you found Grace."

More shuffling and the sound of a chain rattling. He opened the door a fraction and peered out. Mandy held her warrant card where he could read it and stood where the streetlight illuminated her face. With a grunt Jeff Davis unhooked the chain and opened the door.

"Come in. Come in. You must be perished. I'll put the kettle on."

He shuffled along the hall and Mandy followed. The layout was much the same as her own house except the two reception rooms remained separate. He led her into the back room where a gas fire was burning. Two fireside chairs sat either side, a small television on a table in the corner and a gateleg table leaned against one wall. It all looked neat and tidy although estate agents would have described it as needing modernisation. Mandy handed over the carrier bag full of goodies. The reaction was immediate.

"How kind of you. What a lovely thing." He pulled the items out one by one placing them on the table. "And Bara brith. My absolute favourite. You'll have a cup of tea?" Although framed as a question there was going to be no refusal.

"Lovely. Weak with no sugar or milk, please." No chance of green tea here. She expected Jeff Davis had never heard of such a thing. Declining her offer of help he shuffled into the small kitchen just visible through a glass door and busied himself putting on the kettle and rattling cups. Mandy took in the faded curtains, wedding photographs of a much younger Jeff and Lily, his late wife, and the folded newspaper on the chair. When he came back, he had a tray with two cups and saucers and a teapot, plus milk jug and two china plates with thick slices of the bara brith. Lily had trained him well.

"I don't get many visitors, so this is a real treat."

"Did someone come to check up on you after your ordeal?"

"Indeed. That lovely constable and now you. I'm struggling here by myself. They said social services might provide me with some help but… let's just say I don't want just anyone tramping around, do I? Interfering and looking at private things."

He passed her a mug of steaming tea and a plate with the fruit loaf.

"How well did you know Grace? You said you'd seen her there before." Mandy nibbled on the slice of Bara brith he'd given her. It tasted good, the spicy aroma reminding her of childhood and happier times.

"We met a few times. I like to go up to do my bit at the cemetery. I'd spoken to the young lady quite a few times. Since my Lily left me, I need to get out every day. If I don't go and stretch my legs, I don't feel right." His eyes turned towards the wedding photograph. "Lily and me, well, we used to go everywhere. When we were young it was on the bikes and then we'd walk. In the end she was too poorly to walk far. The cemetery was like a trek to Everest." He turned away from her, but Mandy spotted his eyes watering. He slurped his tea.

"What did you talk about? With Grace."

"This and that. She was a good listener. She told me she loved the peace of it. And the history. She liked thinking about all the lives of the folk buried there. She had a favourite spot." He took a shuddering breath. "That's where she was when I found her."

Mandy put a hand on his arm. "It was awful for you, for anyone. Especially as you knew Grace."

"In the summer sometimes, we sat on the benches and had a picnic. She'd bring sandwiches or cake. We'd have a little chat. I asked her to come here once but... Young people are so lovely. I'm going to miss all that." He sighed and took another sip of tea. "Gracie was so happy in the summer. Springtime she looked a bit peaky but when the sun came out it was as though she was glowing from the inside."

"Good memories."

"Yes. It's important to hold on to those memories. It's all we've got left, isn't it? I've got some lovely memories of my Lily." He gestured towards the photograph. "That's her when we got married. A real beauty. Fell for her the first time I saw her. She had on an orange coat, and it was as though the sun was reflected in her."

She needed to get him back on track before he went too far down memory lane. "Do you think there was any particular reason Grace was happy? Did she talk about anyone or give any reason?"

He was eating as he contemplated the question, turning the food and his thoughts around at the same time. "She didn't mention any names, but she did say something about meeting someone and it was going to change lives."

"Who? Did you know about her mam? The illness and her fundraising? Was it something to do with that?"

"Oh, she told me all about it, did Gracie. Proud of how she'd raised the money and knew she was soon going to get to the total they needed."

It was a puzzle. What had Grace planned? Is that where the ten thousand came into play?

"This person she met, did she say where or when?"

Jeff looked a bit puzzled, squinting at her as he tried to recall. "It would have been a while back. More than a year. Maybe a year. I'm not so sure. All the days are the same." He heaved a sigh. "She was excited. What did she say now? I wish I could remember. A piece of jigsaw. That's it. She said a piece of jigsaw and she was going to join all the pieces and make it bigger and better. Never been great on jigsaws, me. How about you Inspector?" He held her hand a little too long for Mandy's liking, looking at her in a speculative way, his eyes sweeping her figure. She stood up and shook her head. It didn't make any sense. This was certainly a puzzle though, with more than a few pieces missing. Leaving Jeff to his memories she headed back to the car.

She was still churning things over when she got home. No sign of either Tabitha or Joy. Her phone bleeped. 'Just at Kelly's. Home soon.'

Well, at least she knew Tabitha's whereabouts. Joy? Mandy tiptoed up the stairs. Maybe Joy was asleep. The emotional trauma this morning had been enough to knock anyone, and Joy must feel dreadful. She tapped on the bedroom door. When there was no reply, she opened it. Joy was lying on the bed. At the creak of the door, she turned, and Mandy could see her sister's tear-stained face. Without a word she gathered her in her arms, like she did with Tabitha, and rocked her. Sobbing, Joy tried to speak. The words tumbling over themselves interspersed with heaving breaths.

"I didn't know how much I wanted this… but it's too late… I've made a mess of everything… I've spoilt everyone's lives." She moaned. "Yours, Mam and Dad's, Tabitha's. I … I've done awful things… hurt you all."

"Stop. That's enough." Mandy pushed her sister away until she could see her face and make eye contact. "Tabitha will be home soon, and this performance will distress her." Mandy knew she sounded stern and unfeeling but the last thing she needed was her sister in meltdown.

"Will… will you tell her?"

Passing the buck again. Suppressing her frustration Mandy nodded.

"Yes. I'll do the dirty deed. What happens next with you? What did the letter say?"

Joy swallowed. "I have to go in tomorrow afternoon if I don't start bleeding before then. They've drugs to get… expel the… foetus. It's before twenty-four weeks so not even classified as a baby." The tears started again.

"Go and wash your face. I'll tell Tabitha what's happened, but she'll want to see you. Sort yourself out or you'll frighten her. Will they keep you in?"

She shook her head. "No. Unless the drugs don't work or there are complications. You'll be with me, won't you sis?"

"Of course."

The crunch of the front door closing warned them Tabitha was home. "Bathroom," hissed Mandy as she straightened herself out and prepared to pass the news to her niece.

CHAPTER THIRTY-ONE

DAY FIVE

Olivia was whistling as she shed her coat, scarf, beanie and gloves and settled down to the computer. Her specs had steamed up after coming in from the cold, so she blinked, removed them and was rubbing them on her jumper to clear the lenses. Mandy wondered why she didn't opt for contact lenses, like most young women. Then, Olivia wasn't like other young women. She didn't really give a toss about appearance. Her attraction was her brain. Razor-sharp.

"Chirpy this morning," said Mandy.

"Yeah. I went up to see my sister last night. Snow up there on the tops of the hill already. I'd forgotten how we'd get snow in Caerphilly when it was just wet in Cardiff." She paused and seemed to be having an inner debate. "She was working. My sister that is."

Mandy wasn't sure of the significance of the comment.

"In the old folks home."

The penny dropped and Mandy grinned. "I see. Did you happen to see Mr Caradog Roberts by any chance?"

"Well, now that you ask," Olivia's eyes were twinkling. "He just happened to be in the lounge, so we had a little chat."

"I thought those places were like Fort Knox. You have to sign in and out and say who you're visiting."

"Yeah. Becca, my sister made me do all that. She said he never had visitors, poor dab, so it would do him good. Lovely old boy, too."

"Not our CR, though."

"No way. He'd never met Grace, but you'll never guess – he used to have the hots for her great-nan about a million years ago."

"What? Eleri's gran? The one who brought her up?"

"That's it. He knew her when she was a girl. Said she was a looker. Then she had the two girls to look after, and he'd moved on by then. He's always had a soft spot for her. He remembered Eleri too."

"So why the donations?"

"It's a bit sad, it is. He's got no family. When he saw the appeal, with the councillor and all, he realised he knew them. Decided he could afford to give something to help Eleri. And the photos of Grace reminded him of his first love. Romantic, innit?"

"Sad that all Grace's efforts have ended in tragedy. We can rule any involvement with him off the board. Oh God, you realise what this means?" Mandy groaned.

"What's happened?" Josh had entered, followed by Helen, both of them red-cheeked from the cold wind.

"Olivia went to visit Mr Roberts last night. Another one off the list which means–"

"We're back to the councillor as a suspect. What's the problem?"

Mandy tilted her head towards the Super's office. "Withering won't like it. Political clap trap. I'll need to talk it through with him first. If I can persuade him that it's his idea, we'll have an easier time of it."

They could see the Super in his office, drinking his coffee and reading a file. Mandy considered how to approach the subject. Telling herself that he also wanted the case sorted sooner rather than later, she braced herself and knocked on the door. He looked up, seemed surprised at first and then beckoned for her to come in. His overcoat hung on a peg near the radiator and his hair was still damp. Already the air in his office felt oppressive with the stale smell of clothing drying, like a dead dog in the corner.

"Problems? How's your sister?"

The station was like a beehive, everybody buzzing around and gossip rife. The question was unexpected, although kind.

"It's confirmed that the pregnancy has failed so she has to go back to the hospital later to have the drugs to dispel the foetus." Calm. Matter of fact. No betrayal of her feelings.

He scrutinised her face, peering over his gold rimmed specs before grunting, "Family is important. It's easy to forget that in this job." Mandy guessed he was thinking about his divorce and the fallout from putting the job first.

"It's the Mathias case I'd like to talk to you about."

"Something turn up?"

"We have a bit of a conundrum, sir. We have Grace's diary. Every month she's put the initials CR. When we correlate the dates with deposits into her fund, CR appears around a week before a substantial deposit."

He stroked his chin, pondering the topic. "Do we have any idea who CR is?"

This was it. Give him the information and let him make the links. Mandy tried to school her face into a bland expression.

"We've checked all the donations. We've identified some men with initials CR who gave large or ongoing donations. Apart from one old chap who's in an old folks' home, we've secured DNA samples. We can check those against the sample from the retained placenta and ascertain paternity if any of them match."

"Do you think the baby is alive?"

"I hope so, sir. I wanted your advice. Councillor Roper may be a CR too. He was very supportive of Grace's endeavours to raise money, donated generously and also ensured she had the publicity. Ongoing publicity."

The Super's eyes narrowed and both hands were now flat on the desk. He pulled his lips together as he contemplated the issue.

"Bloody politicians. Seize every opportunity to show how wonderful they are to the public. There's reasonable suspicion so I think you should ask him for a sample. I'm sure he won't object. If he's got nothing to hide that is." He almost smiled. Withers wasn't a fan of the local councillor.

"You think it's a good idea?" She forced her face into what she hoped was a bland look and waited while the Super weighed up the options.

"Yes. Go for it. Do it discreetly though. I don't want a political storm blowing up because you jumped in with your size nines."

"Size sevens." Mandy's lips twitched as he raised an eyebrow. "Don't worry, sir. We'll be nice as apple pie."

CHAPTER THIRTY-TWO

She gave a thumbs up to the team. "Josh, you're coming with me to the lion's den. Councillor Roper and charm offensive. Where are we now? What else is going on here?"

"I'm going through all the photographs and trying to identify everyone in them. Just in case we missed anyone, like." Olivia pushed a strand of hair behind her ear and blinked.

"I'm off to see Stefan. I promised him I'd keep him informed, even if there was nothing to report. He needs to feel we aren't the enemy," said Helen.

"Good. When you come back, check the numbers on Grace's phone against her contacts. See if they're genuine. She could have put a false name to cover up whatever she was doing or whoever she was seeing. Longshot but no stone unturned. Okay? Let's hit the road, Josh."

The wind had dropped a bit. It was still biting cold, so they wasted no time in making their way down to County Hall. They'd been told Councillor Roper had a meeting at ten, so they wanted to catch him before then. The building was built in the 1980s by the old Bute East Dock. It had low slate rooves and Mandy always thought it looked like a pagoda. It lacked the grandeur of City Hall, but to her eyes it had a certain charm. Inside much of the council business took place although it was also used as a conference and wedding venue. No sign of any weddings today.

She swung the Juke into a parking space in Atlantic Wharf and, flashing her ID at the security guy, made her way into the main reception area with Josh in tow. She spotted Councillor Roper and, ignoring the reception staff, rushed over to where he was about to disappear through a door.

"Councillor Roper. A word, please."

He swung around to see who was calling him. He didn't look quite as his professional photograph on the council website. Recognisable though from the social media posts. He looked like a farmer, rosy cheeks, overweight and sandy brown hair, thinning on the crown. A little over five ten Mandy reckoned. He seemed an affable man, smiling at them, no doubt thinking they were some of the people from his ward.

Mandy produced her badge. "Detective Inspector Wilde. Detective Sergeant Jones. Is there somewhere we can talk?"

"I've got a meeting in fifteen minutes. Can it wait until later?"

"It won't take long. Is there somewhere a bit quieter perhaps?"

A stream of people passed them, sporting badges. A banner at the door announced a conference on Climate Change. The building would be flooded within minutes.

With a resigned sigh he said, "Follow me," and led them through to a room overlooking the water.

"How may I help you, officers?" His voice was high-pitched, the voice of a little man. It didn't suit this burly figure. Mandy wondered if he had to shout to be heard in meetings.

"We are investigating the events leading up to the death of Grace Mathias. Trying to understand various aspects of her life."

He looked crestfallen. "Such a terrible shock. After all that poor child did to try and help her mother. I must go and visit the family. I should have done so already but it's been so busy."

"You gave Grace a lot of time and support."

"Yes indeed. Part of my role. My commitment to those in my ward."

"Do you give the same commitment to everyone, or just the pretty ones?" It was a glib remark and Mandy realised she shouldn't have phrased things in such a blunt form when she saw the reaction.

Gwyn Roper coloured. "What are you implying, Inspector? What exactly are you trying to find out?"

"Grace was seeing someone called CR on a regular basis in the last year of her life and a little before. We think CR was giving her money. A lot of money. We're trying to find the person concerned by a process of elimination. We're speaking to those people with initials CR we know she had contact with in the last year or so."

"I don't understand. My first name is Gwyn. Why me?"

"Did Grace call you by your first name?"

"No. She always called me Councillor." His eyes narrowed. "Oh, I get your drift. You think I'm this mystery man. I can assure you my only connections with Grace were professional. Just helping someone in my ward, as I told you." He puffed himself up, an indignant expression on his florid face.

"Then you won't mind giving us a sample of your DNA, sir. So, we can eliminate you from our inquiries."

"My DNA. Most certainly not. I don't know what little game you are playing Inspector Wilde, but I do know that I have an important meeting. My dealings with Grace were always professional. I have no idea why you need a sample of my DNA so unless you have a rock-solid reason you are prepared to share with me, I think this meeting is over. Good day to you."

He rose with more speed than expected for a man with a weight problem and stormed out of the room. Mandy looked at Josh.

"That went well," he said. "The Super will be pleased."

CHAPTER THIRTY-THREE

They were silent as they left County Hall. Without the sample they couldn't be sure Gwyn Roper wasn't involved. What caused him to almost implode at their request? It was out of proportion.

"We can't force the issue unless we have evidence and we've only got a vague suspicion he might have been involved with Grace," said Mandy.

"Perhaps we need to look a little deeper into his background. Financial checks. See if he's been paying out big sums of money on a regular basis and who to."

"You can make a start on it. I've got to go to the hospital with Joy later on."

There was a silence before Josh asked, "How is she?"

It was a question Mandy didn't want to think about. Joy had stopped crying and put on a brave face for Tabitha. She'd withdrawn once Tabitha had gone to bed refusing to talk about anything and giving monosyllabic answers to Mandy's questions.

"God knows, but the next few days aren't going to be pretty. I just hope she can pull herself together for this play Tabitha's performing in. She needs to concentrate on the child she's got instead of the one she isn't going to have."

"That's a bit harsh, isn't it?"

"You don't know Joy. The idea is better than the reality." She bit her lip. "That's not a nice thing to say, is it? I'm just a bit wound up about it all. Worried about Tabitha. Worried about Joy. And this missing baby of Grace's…"

"It's a weird one that's for sure. It doesn't add up."

"Nothing in this bloody case does." She thumped the steering wheel.

The rest of the journey back to Central station was in silence. Each left to their own thoughts.

Olivia was still trawling through photographs and ticking off lists. Helen was absent. Josh settled down to check out Gwyn Roper's financial records and Mandy had a look at his profile on the council website. His photograph didn't hide his florid complexion or his bushy eyebrows. There was no information about his wife and family, so she'd look elsewhere for that. She scrolled down. Attendance at Meetings, Declarations, Register of Interests, Training. Nothing of significance, full attendance at all meetings, usual declarations and then she clicked on the Register of Interests. He ran an IT consultancy firm. It was useful to have those skills and probably lucrative. She made a note to look it up with Companies House before she carried on reading his profile. Interesting. He was a Governor at the primary school where Christopher Robin was a teacher. She made another note. Could be nothing. Coincidence or wheels within wheels.

Lost in the research Mandy wasn't aware of Withers until he was breathing fire down her neck.

"What the hell did you say to Councillor Roper? I've just had twenty minutes of him threatening to make a formal complaint about police invasion of privacy."

Swivelling around in her chair to face him she took a breath. "We asked for a sample of his DNA. He got on his high horse and refused. End of story, sir."

"According to him you were rude and overbearing."

"I don't think that's true. We were totally professional and polite. I think he was upset because he's hiding something."

"I agree," said Josh, leaving his seat and walking over to where Mandy seemed pinned to her chair. "When we asked for a sample of his DNA, he went apoplectic and stormed out. DI Wilde did not act out of turn. I can support her statement. We did not harass him. And he's definitely hiding something. We're looking into his background now, sir."

Withers looked surprised. Josh stood firm. When the Super spoke again, his tone was more measured. "I've calmed him down. For now. I explained the situation and he's thinking about it. I agree. His reaction is a bit over the top. Politicians. Damned nuisance. Carry on."

"If anything comes up in his financial records, we'll have something more substantial to approach him, sir."

Withers held his look then nodded. "Right. Keep me informed. Good." He turned and left.

"God. What brought on the act of bravery? Standing up to him to defend me. Whoa." She shook her head, grinned. "I never thought I'd see the day."

"It wasn't fair. Roper is hiding something and blaming us for doing our jobs. He's a nob."

"Agreed. Let's see what we can find to give us a bit of leverage."

The next thing Mandy wanted to look at were minutes of committee meetings the councillor attended. Had he been involved in anything of interest? Anything controversial? Her phone beeped. Text message from Joy. *Hospital rang. Go in at four. Okay?* It was already creeping up to half past three. Mandy shut down her computer reluctantly.

"I've got to go to the hospital. If anything of significance comes up, let me know. I'm surprised Helen isn't back." She looked at Olivia.

"She sent a message while you were out. Sorry, forgot. The school rang. One of her boys had an accident," said Olivia.

"Nothing serious I hope?"

"Nah. Little one had a bump on the head. Helen says he's a bit of a drama king. Likes attention. She's had the doctor check him out. But she had to take him home."

"Right. Let's hope we make some progress with this lot. I should be back tomorrow."

"It's your rest day," said Josh.

"Damn. I forgot and we're still on the 'no overtime' regime. Unless, of course, there's a body."

"Careful what you wish for."

* * *

Joy was peering through the blinds when Mandy arrived home. She waved. A minute later she appeared wrapped up against the cold and carrying a small case. She dropped it into the back seat before settling down beside Mandy in the front.

"What's with the suitcase? I thought it was a simple in and out."

"So did I, but the nurse said to bring an overnight. Just in case. You won't have to stay. Someone needs to be with Tabitha. She's a bit fretty. I didn't want her to come to the hospital with me."

A bit fretty meant Tabitha was rolled into a ball on the sofa, crying and pulling at her hair. Mandy concentrated on driving the short distance to the hospital. The cold snap had passed, and intermittent showers left the road wet with puddles forming at the kerbs. They left the car in the carpark and crossed to the main building. The wind had dropped so the temperatures, still in single figures, seemed almost balmy in comparison to the previous few days. Mandy carried Joy's suitcase as they made their way to the ward, their footsteps squeaking on the vinyl floor. A couple of people did a double take as they passed, but Joy didn't notice, her lips pressed together and steps firm and deliberate.

"Joy Wilde. I was told to report."

The nurse behind the desk looked from one to the other and blinked. She probably thought she was seeing double through tiredness at the end of her shift. She checked the list.

"I'm glad you've brought your case. There's been an emergency so a bit of a wait, I'm afraid. Follow me." She turned to Mandy. "You'd best go home, lovely. She could be here all night. We've got your number. We'll let you know."

Dismissed. Joy grabbed her in a bear hug then followed the nurse without a backwards glance. Mandy bit her lip.

Despite her callous words to Josh, she felt some empathy with Joy. How could she not? Her twin was part of her life.

It was a surprise when she got home to find everything quiet. The lounge lights were dimmed, although she'd seen flickering lights through chinks in the shutters indicating the television was switched on. Mandy abandoned her boots and crept to the door. No sound of crying. The poor child had worn herself out. If Tabitha was asleep, she needed to just let her rest. Without a sound, she opened the door and peeped around.

"What the hell?"

CHAPTER THIRTY-FOUR

The couple on the sofa disentangled and jumped apart. Mandy couldn't believe it. Tabitha and Daniel Levin. Both dishevelled and red-faced. She knew Tabitha had a crush on Daniel. She knew they spent a lot of time rehearsing their parts for West Side Story. She knew, so why was she surprised?

"I'd better go now." Daniel tucked his shirt in, pulled on his sweater which was on the floor along with his shoes, and stood up.

"Yes. I think you'd better." She stood to one side to let him into the hall and while he hastily pulled on his coat, she glared at him. "I'd just like to remind you that my niece is just fifteen and from what I've just witnessed you're in danger of forgetting that."

"Sorry. I didn't… I mean…"

"Just go and be aware. If you harm a hair on that girl's head, I may not be responsible for my actions."

She could feel anger rising as she balled her fists at her side. Daniel almost fell over her boots as he made a swift exit. Mandy turned to see Tabitha right behind her, at the bottom of the stairs.

"How dare you? How could you embarrass me like that? I'm not a child." Tabitha's jaw was set and stiff with anger.

"I'm trying to protect you. Boys like Daniel feel privileged. They think they have the right to–"

"You don't know him. He's not like that. How can I face him at drama club when you've made such a fool of me?" Tears filled her eyes.

"Tabs. I didn't mean to upset you. I'm just looking out for you."

"Well, don't bother. I can look after myself. You're not my mother so stop acting like you are."

She ran up the stairs and slammed her bedroom door leaving Mandy standing dumb- founded in the hallway. She felt as though someone had kicked her in the gut. Tabitha had never spoken to her like that before. She didn't know what to do and could feel herself crumbling inside. "Many a truthful word is spoken in anger," her mother used to say. And it was true. Mandy opened the kitchen cupboard and poured herself a large gin from the bottle kept for special occasions. This was no celebration, but she'd had a shock and felt she needed something. She wanted to forget the last few minutes. Upstairs all was silent. At some point exhaustion took over and she slept.

At about three, the darkest time of the night, she woke. A sharp pain gripped her lower abdomen. It seemed Joy's miscarriage had started. Bloody Couvade Syndrome. She padded upstairs, intent on finding the paracetamol and a hot water bottle in the cupboard on the landing. Tabitha's light was on. Should she? The bathroom door creaked as it opened. Mandy gripped her middle. She needed those painkillers. She rattled around in the bathroom cabinet and then jumped as a shadowy figure appeared in the doorway.

"I'm sorry. I didn't mean it." Tabitha was pale and red-eyed.

"I know you didn't." Mandy opened her arms. Tabitha threw herself into her aunt's arms and sobbed. Faint with pain and fatigue Mandy cradled her until the crying ceased. "Hey. Come on. You need your beauty sleep, and I don't feel too good."

The crying stopped. "Are you sick? Have I made you sick? I didn't even ask. Did they keep Mam? I'm sorry."

"Hush. It's all okay. They've kept your mam in overnight, but the drugs are working. I'm having sympathy pains." She doubled up as a wave of pain hit. "The benefits of being a twin. Sharing everything."

Tabitha helped her get into the bed where Joy had taken residence since October. She filled the hot water bottle and then cuddled up to Mandy.

"Do you forgive me?"

"Nothing to forgive. I stepped out of line. I'll apologise to Daniel at drama group."

"No way. Did you see his face? He was terrified." She giggled.

Mandy closed her eyes. Bloody teenagers. A breed apart.

CHAPTER THIRTY-FIVE

DAY SIX

When her Oasis ringtone woke her just after dawn, Mandy thought it was Joy, but Josh's voice pulled her from sleep. A glance showed her five missed calls. The gin mixed with the painkillers must have knocked her out.

"What's up?"

"Report of youth with a knife on the loose. Threatened a delivery guy then hoofed it. We need to find him before he does any damage."

Although she still felt as though she'd been in a rugby scrum, Mandy dressed in a hurry and swallowed more painkillers. She looked like hell, dark shadows under her eyes and grey-tinged skin. Tabitha was sound asleep, so she scribbled a note.

Got to go to work. Ask Kelly's mam to give you a lift to drama. See you later. Love you.

She drew a big smiley face and a heart. Maybe it was better if she didn't see Daniel.

* * *

By the time she arrived at the scene Josh was questioning people, mainly early morning workers. No-one had seen the lad or didn't want to get involved more like.

"CCTV?" asked Mandy.

"We're on to it."

The delivery driver was standing to one side, smoking a cigarette.

"Want to tell me what happened?" Mandy asked, careful to stand out of the way of the spiralling smoke.

"Told the boss, here already." He took another drag, inhaling deeply and holding the smoke in his lungs before blowing towards Josh.

It was the sort of assumption that raised Mandy's hackles and did nothing to enhance her mood. Giving the man a frosty look, she said, "I'm the boss here and I'd like to hear it all again, please. If you don't mind too much, sir."

He glanced at Josh and then back with a shrug. "Whatever."

Mandy waited while he took another drag from the cigarette.

"I stopped the van here as usual and started unloading when I see this kid, mask over his face, taking a knife to one of the tyres. I yelled at him and took a step forward and he says, 'Don't come near me or you'll get it instead.' Then he scarpered. Bloody tyre needs sorting, so I rang in. I need a crime number to give my boss otherwise they'll dock my wages."

"And the lad? See where he went?"

"Up there – main drag. No way was I following him. Not with a knife. Probably on something too. Dangerous like."

"Description?"

"About five four, slim build."

Mandy sighed. Not much to go on.

"Clothing? What sort of knife?"

The driver shrugged. "Dunno."

"Sounds like a kid to me." Mandy looked him up and down taking in the beer belly and stocky build. "And you're a big bloke.""

"What you trying to say? I'm afraid of a kid? The driver spat to one side. "I'm the bloody victim here and you'd better remember I pay your wages. Bloody pigs."

Mandy gritted her teeth. Today wasn't the day when she could put up with this crap. "I'm saying that you aren't very observant." She turned her face away before muttering under her breath, "Plus, you're an arrogant prick."

"What the hell? I heard what you said. You can't talk to me like that. I'll complain." His face had gone red, his nostrils flaring.

"See if I give a damn."

She walked away, her fists clenching and unclenching. Idiot. Whatever sort of a knife was used it hadn't made much impact. She looked around. Josh was talking to a middle-aged man with a large dog, Mandy rubbed her eyes. The city was beginning to come to life with delivery trucks and commuters bustling around. Rumbling noises in the background. A watery sun crept between roof tops bringing little warmth. The ground was damp as the morning frost melted. The street was clear. God knows where the lad gone but they'd have to follow it up. A kid with a knife, possibly high on something, was not what was needed in the city centre during the morning rush.

Pointing towards the driver she said to Josh, "You'll have to deal with that dickhead. I just want to thump him.

Tell him how to get his bloody crime number and take a formal statement. And leads? Thoughts? Possible direction?" Her brain was foggy, like the light mist that was gathering.

"Dunno, boss."

"We need to find him. Quickly. Anybody see anything at all to help?"

Josh shook his head then added, "Although the nearest camera is offline, we can look at the cameras in the neighbouring streets. See if anyone looks suspicious."

"Lots of kids these days carry knives. That's the problem. This sounds more like vandalism than gang related." Mandy glanced over at the driver who was glaring at her. "Unless it's some sort of initiation ritual or dare or something. God knows. The older I get the less I understand what goes on in the mind of bloody teenagers."

Her phone rang. She listened. "Another teenage drama. Girl missing. She's in foster care with her kid sister. The foster mother went to wake her this morning, but her bed's not been slept in. Last seen at nine last night." Mandy glanced at her watch. "Nearly twelve hours. I've sent Helen to the home. We'd better get back to the station and set things in motion. You can sort neanderthal man out first."

CHAPTER THIRTY-SIX

Withers was waiting for her.

"There's been a complaint already today, Wilde. Mr Barry Pugh says you insulted him. What the hell have you been doing? Barely nine o'clock and already rubbing people up the wrong way."

"He's a jobsworth, sir. Big bloke with two brain cells working alternate days. Some kid tried to slash his tyres and then ran off. All he wanted was a crime number so he could make an excuse for not doing much work if you ask me."

"I didn't ask your opinion on a member of the public. I asked you what you did to warrant a complaint." Spit was gathering at the side of his mouth and his eyes had narrowed. He was so close Mandy could smell the sourness of last night's wine on his breath.

"I may have called him a prick." Despite standing tall, Mandy could feel her heart pounding.

"Well, he's complained and it's not the first time we've had a complaint about your cavalier attitude. If it happens again, you might find yourself on a disciplinary. I can't have all this going on with upstairs," he nodded towards the roof, "considering how we monitor behaviour in our teams. Haven't I got enough to contend with? Just do your job and don't step out of line. There are plans afoot which could threaten all of us."

"Sir."

What plans? Despite Withers raging at her, Mandy's thoughts strayed to Tabitha and Daniel. Her stomach was still contracting sending spasms of pain which she tried to ignore as Withers changed tack.

"I'm seconding a couple of DI Blake's team to you for a couple of days. DS Gregory and DC Fraser. I've told them to report to the incident room and familiarise themselves with the Mathias case." A cough. "Now this missing girl. What do we know?"

"Amy Johnson. Thirteen. She's in foster care with her little sister. Last seen nine o'clock last night. Her bed's not been slept in."

"I'll get on to the news people. Put out an appeal for her. Do we have a photograph? Anything that could help find her?"

"Helen's with the foster mother now. She'll send a photograph and any relevant information. I'll pass it on to you."

* * *

Helen was trying to calm the distraught foster mother. Cerys Swain was pacing up and down, glancing every few minutes at the clock on the wall and then her phone. The house was an ordinary semi and the room they were in had flowered wallpaper, magazines piled on a coffee table and a big box with toys stacked in one corner beside a large screen television. Through the window Helen could see a swing and climbing frame. Cerys was a pleasant-looking woman with laughter lines around her eyes and mouth and an ample figure. Her light brown hair was uncombed and she kept pulling at it. Helen persuaded her to sit down while she sent the photograph and description of Amy to the team.

"Does Amy have a mobile phone?"

"Yes. I've tried ringing but it just goes to voicemail. She's not answering texts either and now it's not doing anything. Switched off." There was a hint of hysteria in the woman's voice.

Helen kept her voice calm and measured. "It's probably just a flat battery. Kids these days use their phones all the time, streaming, music and videos. It soon drains the battery."

She didn't look convinced, wringing her hands and pulling on her wedding ring.

"I believe you also foster Amy's sister?"

"Yes. Bella. She's a bit of a handful. My neighbour has taken her to school today. She wanted to know where Amy was. She likes her big sister to walk her to school. I've had to tell her a lie. Said Amy had to go in early for a test." She bit her lip. "I don't like lying. These kids have had so much thrown at them. They need, truth, love, and security. I feel bad about it."

Helen touched her hand. "She'll understand. Now, do you have any idea where Amy might have gone? Friends? Does she have relatives? Favourite places?"

"She's a quiet girl. Subdued, you know. She was beginning to open up a bit. The girls have only been with me three months. Amy said very little and Bella, well, that's a different tune. Exhausting."

"Does she go to the local comprehensive?"

"Yes. I got the feeling she was finding it hard to fit into school. You don't think she's run away, do you? Or," she put a hand to her throat, "been abducted? You hear so much these days." Her eyes filled with tears as she considered the possibilities." She grabbed Helen's hands. "You will find her, won't you?"

Helen was careful not to make promises she couldn't keep. "We will do our best. Her description will go out on the media with an appeal for information. I think you should have someone to stay with you. Do you have a relative? Neighbour?"

Cerys nodded. "My neighbour's coming back after she's dropped Bella and explained the situation to her teacher."

Helen took a card out of her bag. "This is the number to ring if you remember anything or if Amy comes back and I'll update you on progress."

CHAPTER THIRTY-SEVEN

As far as Mandy was concerned the incident room was overcrowded. DC Sam Fraser was a steady hand, but DS Richard Gregory was a different prospect. Short, stocky with his shirt straining to contain a beer belly and an attitude towards women, he was the last person she wanted. Mandy got them up to speed on the missing baby and teenager.

"Seems a waste of time looking for the baby. Might as well chase ghosts. As if we don't have enough to do." DS Gregory's voice boomed.

"Our first duty is to preserve life. Unless you know where the body of Grace Mathias's baby is concealed then I suggest you keep your opinions to yourself. We believe the infant is still alive."

Richard Gregory turned to Sam Fraser. "DDD at work." Even though it was spoken in a lower voice, Mandy heard.

"Perhaps you'd like to share that comment?"

"Come on, Mandy. It was a joke."

She said nothing but fixed him with a stare until he blinked and looked away. "A word after this meeting, please, DS Gregory."

The rest of the briefing passed without incident. Mandy assigned their tasks and dismissed them. As

Richard turned to leave, she stopped him, closed the door.

"I think an explanation is needed. I'm your superior officer and expect you to remember it. Any more comments on my family or stupid nicknames will not be tolerated."

"Ah, come on Mandy. We all know your old man was dodgy. DDD. Dodgy Derek's Daughter is what we called you when you started. Just before the old bugger scarpered off to Costa del Crime." He laughed.

"That was a long time ago. My father was never charged with anything illegal." The laughter stopped as Mandy closed the gap, towering over him. "I don't like your attitude and if you so much as breath too heavily I'll have you on a disciplinary. Understood?"

Gregory stepped back, a mixture of fear and antagonism in his eyes.

"Yeah, Mandy. I get it."

"Another thing. Only my friends call me Mandy. You can call me boss or ma'am. Now get out there and do your job."

As DS Gregory left, he slammed the door behind him. Mandy was furious. How dare he rake up her past like that?

* * *

Withers prepared a statement to read to the press and, with unprecedented speed it was set up to go out at midday. They were all aware how in a missing person's case the first few hours were vital in the search. Josh had

171

returned with the statement from the driver and the same vague description he'd given to Mandy.

"That guy's not very happy with you."

"Tell me about it. Withering is threatening to demote me if I insult any more members of the public. There's something afoot and Mr Bloody 'I pay your wages' has made a formal complaint."

Olivia was scanning the city centre CCTV footage in the hope they could track the lad with the knife. It revealed little, just the city centre becoming more congested as people commuted to work or came in to do early morning shopping. Then eagle-eyed Olivia gave a little cry.

"I think I got something." She pointed at her screen. "Look here. This is our knife carrier I think." The shadowy figure, wearing a puffer jacket with a hood pulled low over his face, turned down into Charles Street. A few minutes later, a similar figure emerged in a hurry, long hair flying in the wind and a jacket or coat over their arm.

"That looks like a girl," said Mandy.

"I know, if you look closely, you've got the same build and," she zoomed in, "same white trainers. I think our lad could be a girl. With the hood up you can't tell." Olivia grinned and peered at Mandy over the top of her owl-like specs.

"I think you're right. See if you can find out where she goes. Check the other cameras in the city centre. If she thinks we're looking for a lad, she may not be so cautious. We might find her before she gets into any more trouble."

"See if you can get a close-up of her face," said Josh.

"It's a bit grainy, isn't it?" said Mandy. "I wonder if there's a way of enhancing it."

"Yeah. I can try," said Olivia. "My little friend in the lab showed me. There's an app."

Mandy smiled. "One day he'll find out you've been leading him on. Then we'll have trouble."

"Nah. I keep him stocked up with chocolate biscuits. Smoothing the wheels, like. Besides he enjoys showing off. He's cool as long as I make the right noises to show I'm dead impressed."

They laughed. The telephone rang. Josh picked it up and mouthed to Mandy that it was for her. Tod Blakeney, the reporter. She put it on speakerphone.

"Got an exclusive for me, Mandy?"

The familiarity made Mandy's hackles rise. "I've told you before. It's Inspector Wilde to you. Only my friends get to call me by my first name."

A sort of chuckle was the response. "I'm up for getting more friendly if you are." The chuckle became more suggestive. It was obvious he was winding her up.

"Get–"

"What can you tell me about this knife attack in the city centre?"

That stopped Mandy from slamming the phone down. How the hell had he found out about it so quickly? In an icy voice she said, "No comment." After one complaint already today, there was no way she was going to risk any further misdeeds.

"Oh, come on. It's not a state secret, is it? I've spoken to the delivery guy and the other witness."

Other witness? Shit. What other witness? Her silence told the reporter what he wanted to know.

"You didn't speak to the woman then? Reckons she saw it all."

"If you have evidence then it's your duty to give us the relevant details. The name of the person you spoke to and their contact number."

Another chuckle. "I knew it. She told me the police hadn't spoken to her. Waitress working in a café nearby. Saw a figure approach the van and then run off again. Always best to ask around, Mandy."

Ignoring the deliberate use of her name again she said, "We need the name and number for this witness, please."

He rattled off the details and Josh scribbled it down while Tod carried on talking.

"Did you want to know what she told me?"

God. If she had her hands on the little weasel, she'd squeeze the details out of him. She forced out a "yes" through gritted teeth.

"My witness said it was a young girl. Slight build. Long dark hair. She reckons she's seen her in town before with a bunch of other girls in school uniform." He told them the name of the school.

"Clothing?"

"All in black except white trainers. Standard teen gear." It fitted the description of the figure they'd seen on CCTV.

"Young?" asked Mandy.

"Didn't I tell you that? Yes. She guessed early teens. Hard to tell these days, isn't it?"

It took an effort, but Mandy realised she needed to express her thanks, even if the words stuck in her throat.

"It's good to know you're doing your duty like a good citizen, Tod. Thank you."

"Pleasure. I scratch your back, you scratch mine. Any juicy snippets?"

Was it worth the risk? Withers was going to be issuing a statement anyway. Mandy took a breath before saying, "Superintendent Withers will be on the news. Missing schoolgirl. Amy Johnson."

"Thanks, Mandy. Gives me a head start. I'm working on something I may need your help with. Drink sometime?"

The audacity of the man. Mandy saw a grin spread over Josh's face as he waited to hear her response.

"I think you'd better invest in one of those long handled plastic forks to scratch your own back. Not interested."

She ended the call, muttering, "prick" under her breath.

"He's got the hots for you, our Tod. You need to nurture him, like Olivia and her lab boy. Take him for a drink or a meal. Buy him flowers and chocolate."

"Piss off, Josh. I'd rather go out with a boa-constrictor. Much more attractive. I wonder what the little shit is working on now. He's got a nose for trouble. Let's hope he doesn't bring it here."

Her mobile buzzed. A text from Joy.

Complications. Got to stay in another night. Can you bring in clean stuff at visiting time? Ta sis.

CHAPTER THIRTY-EIGHT

"Okay. Problems. I suggest we prioritise finding Amy. Chances are she's just skiving off school but as her bed hasn't been slept in it's not a good sign. We need to speak to her teachers and see if there's any clue there. Josh, you can follow up on that. Give the school a ring." Mandy started writing tasks on the whiteboard. She drew a line down the middle of the board. On the other side she wrote **Knife Attack** and a description of the figure they could see on screen.

She turned to Olivia. "Any clue where our little knife bearer is likely to be?"

Olivia was peering at the screen. "She hasn't gone into the centre. It looks as though she headed towards Bute Park. No. Wait a minute now. She went into a coffee shop near the castle."

"Time?" Mandy asked.

"Forty minutes ago."

Mandy groaned. "Not much chance of her still being there. I'll go down and talk to the owner or whoever is on duty."

Another note on the board. "Josh, when Helen gets back see if she's got anything useful from the home. Contact Social Services. Her social worker could be a source of information. List of possible places she might

176

go if she wanted to escape, anything in the background. Has she run away before, relationship with the little sister. You know the drill. She can't just have vanished."

"Unless..."

"Let's not go there just yet but keep it all in mind in our search. Olivia there'll be a stream of calls after Withers makes his statement so make notes. Richard and Sam can help by following up any leads. I'm going to see if I can catch the little ratbag with the knife. He or she may have intended vandalism, but we can't have someone with a dangerous weapon loose in the centre."

Mandy headed towards the coffee shop. Olivia had fast-forwarded the CCTV, but they hadn't seen the figure coming out again. However, there was an entrance at the side so the suspect could have made their escape that way.

The warm fug inside the café was welcome. The shrill noise of the grinder and the aroma of freshly brewed coffee mixed with the chatter and sweet smell of pastries. The place was full. No empty tables. Mandy scanned the room, looking for a lone figure. At the back, huddled together in a corner sat four teenage girls, hunched over their phones and giggling. Three were in school uniform and the fourth dressed in black with a puffer jacket rolled into a ball on the bench beside her. The group didn't notice as Mandy approached.

"No school today?"

Three of the girls looked up.

"What's it to you?"

"I'm looking for someone." As Mandy looked under the table, she could see a pair of white trainers. The owner kept her head down. It was impossible to see her face. Pulling out her warrant card Mandy said, "I think one of you has a knife, so I'd like you to empty your bags and pockets –now."

"What? You can't just–"

"I'm a police officer and I have every right."

The mouthy girl paled and gave a panicked look towards her friends. "I haven't got a knife."

"But you've got something you don't want me to see? Drugs perhaps? Stolen goods? Started the day with a bit of shoplifting perhaps?"

She could see she'd hit the mark. The girl shifted in her seat.

"I think I need to speak to your friend here. You three can go. I'd like your names and addresses before you leave. And don't lie. I know which school you go to."

"I've got the knife." The girl in the corner raised her head and met Mandy's eyes. It was a face she recognised instantly.

CHAPTER THIRTY-NINE

"Amy. We've been looking for you."

Amy slumped further into the corner as the other three paused and stared at her. Then, in unison, they stood. One girl scribbled on a piece of paper and passed it to her. Three names and three mobile numbers.

"We've got to get back to school now." She put a hand on Amy's arm. "Will you be alright, Amy? Come over after, yeah?"

"Sure. I'll be fine, Rach." She attempted a smile, but her eyes were anxious as she watched them leave. Rachel gave a tentative wave.

Thirteen and scared was the impression Mandy had of the young girl in front of her. How the delivery guy saw her as a threat was beyond belief. There was no doubt the missing teen and the knife attacker were one and the same.

"We need to have a little chat. First, I'd like you to give me the knife, please."

Amy shrugged. She pulled a knife out of her pocket and passed it across the table. It was a small pocket-knife, less than six centimetres long. The blade, when opened was tiny. It looked like something found in an expensive cracker. Mr Barry Pugh had exaggerated his fear. She wondered if he would press charges when confronted with this doe-eyed girl.

"You'll have to come to the station with me, I'm afraid. Carrying a knife is an offence, although a folding pocketknife with such a small blade is permitted–"

"Will I get it back? My Dad gave it to me before he had the crash. He was going to take me fishing. It was to cut the fishing line."

"At the moment it's evidence. We need to see what happens. You've been accused of vandalism. Trying to slash tyres. You can tell me all about it later. Now, I need to let my colleagues and your foster mother know you're safe."

Mandy took out her mobile and rang the station.

"Call off the searches. Two birds with one stone. Well, it's one bird only. I'm bringing Amy in now. Could someone get her foster-mother as a responsible adult for an interview? Explain the situation to her." She half-smiled at Amy as she finished the call.

"Cerys will be furious." The anxious look was back. "She's got enough problems with Bella. My little sister's a demon. She misses Mam."

"Mrs Swain is out of her head with worry. She thought you'd been abducted. Now, do you want anything to drink on the way back? Have you eaten?"

Amy shook her head. "Eleri, that's the mouthy one, got me a hot chocolate. I didn't have enough money. I'm starving."

Mandy took her over to the counter, ordered a hot chocolate and toasted teacake and passed them to Amy. She kept a close eye on the girl, half-expecting her to make a run for it. The lure of the food seemed to work though. Mandy was rewarded with a smile.

"Can't have you fainting before we have our chat now, can we? You've a lot of questions to answer young lady."

Amy devoured the teacake in record time, trotting alongside Mandy on the way to the station. They were both surprised to see Mrs Swain in the lobby. As soon as she saw Amy, she hugged her.

"God, Amy. You scared the life out of me. Where have you been all night?"

"I couldn't sleep. I got up about three when everyone was asleep. Walked around for a bit, but it was cold. I sneaked into the train station where it was a bit warmer until–"

"You've no idea how worried I've been. I had to tell Bella you'd gone to school early for a test, but she knew something was up." She unfolded her arms and held Amy's face in her hands. "I know I'm not your mam, but I do care."

"I… I suppose you're going to send me back to the children's home now, aren't you?"

"No way. You and that naughty little sister of yours are with me until your mam is well enough to look after you again."

It was the catalyst for a stream of noisy sobs as tears flowed down Amy's cheeks. Cerys Swain stayed calm holding the girl close and stroking her hair. It was genuine affection.

Barry Pugh strode into the lobby at that moment and glowered at Mandy.

"Well, where is he? That detective guy told me to come in and identify him. I'd like to give the little toerag a good hiding." He sniffed, all bluster and bigmouthed, holding his chest out as if facing up to an opponent in the boxing ring. "Suppose it's best to let the law deal with him."

"Are you able to identify the young lad who was so aggressive towards you?"

"'Course I can. Where is he? Identity parade or something?"

Before Mandy could respond Amy spoke. "I'm sorry. It was me. I didn't mean any real harm. It was a dare. I'm sorry."

A look of disbelief crossed Barry Pugh's face. He started to turn red around the neck, coughing and pulling at his collar as he surveyed the slip of a girl, long hair tumbling around her shoulders and eyes swollen from crying.

"You her mam?" he asked Cerys.

She shook her head. "Fostering her and her sister. Her mam's in hospital. Her dad was killed in an accident a while back."

Barry was conflicted. He made a sound somewhere between a grunt and a sigh. "Well, I don't recognise the lad who threatened me. Don't suppose I'll be wanting to charge anyone here today. Best I get back to work, innit?" With a nod towards Cerys he said, "Look after her. My mam fostered. Ain't easy. Good luck to you both."

"And the damage to your vehicle, sir?" asked Mandy. "Do you want us to continue to investigate the incident?"

"Guess It wasn't too bad after all. Might have been a nail or something causing that. But you tell me if you find the lad with the knife. Okay?"

Before any of them could reply he'd left. She'd still have to caution Amy, but Barry Pugh had done the decent thing.

Mandy was aware of the delicacy of the situation. Amy was vulnerable.

"Your sister's a bit of a show-off then?"

Amy looked at Mandy and shrugged. "She misses Mam. Cerys is very good," sneaking a sideways look at her foster mother, "but Bella, well Bella's the baby, 'suppose."

"You know what you did was wrong?"

Amy looked at the floor, her lips pressed together. Cerys put an arm around her.

"I'm afraid I have to caution you. It's a formal procedure and it will go on your record. Those girls are not your friends if they're encouraging you to do things they know to be wrong. It must be hard," Mandy lowered her voice, "to try and fit in."

CHAPTER FORTY

As she was leaving for home, she spotted Tod Blakeney hovering outside the station. She ignored him even when he called after her. But he wasn't deterred.

"Seems our little knife thrower turned out to be something and nothing." He dashed after her and caught up as she neared her car. "I've another little morsel of information you might be interested in. A bit of gossip about a certain councillor."

Now that was something. It stopped her in her tracks although she played it cool. "Why on earth would I be interested in any gossip you've dug up while playing your dirty little games?"

"I'm just doing my job. I happened to be in County Hall the other day when you were talking to a certain councillor."

"I talk to a lot of people. It doesn't have to mean anything."

"Oh yes. You just wanted a little chat with Gwyn Roper because your drains are blocked, or about your refuse collection. Do me a favour. I did a bit of digging myself. Interesting. You'll be reading about it in tomorrow's paper. Unless you want a preview over drinks?"

She ignored the invitation and said, "If you've got anything that could be pertinent to our inquiries you need to tell me."

"How could I do that when I don't know the nature of your enquiry?" said Tod. "Maybe one day you'll realise I'm not muck raking and we'll come to an arrangement."

Open-mouthed, Mandy watched as he sauntered off, humming the theme tune to *The Pink Panther*.

* * *

As she entered the hallway, Mandy could hear giggling. Her heart sank. Not Daniel again. She coughed as a warning before entering the room. Two pairs of eyes met hers. Tabitha and Kelly. Relief. Tabitha still looked a bit sheepish.

"Good joke?" asked Mandy.

Kelly's guileless blue eyes met hers. "One of the lads made a video at rehearsals this morning. Hysterical." She passed her phone to Mandy.

The footage was shaky and the sound unclear, but it was Daniel singing "Maria." Four couples were dancing in the background, but one lad lost his footing, fell over, crashed into the makeshift scenery which clattered and fell off the stage with a crash. The boy who had fallen had somehow ripped his trousers, revealing bright red boxers. Slapstick humour. Mandy tried not to smile, failed, and passed the phone back to Kelly.

"I don't suppose Ms Thomas thought it was funny."

"She had a paddy," said Kelly, unconcerned. "And we've got extra rehearsals this week."

"Plus, an essay to write and a maths test for school." Tabitha reminded her. They groaned in unison and then laughed. A car horn sounded outside.

"That's Mam. Gotta go. See ya." Kelly grabbed her coat, pulled on her boots and dashed out of the front door.

The house seemed quieter. Unsure what to say to her niece, after the row last night, Mandy made for the kitchen. "I'll drop you up to see your mam for visiting after tea. What do you want to eat?" There was no reply. Mandy turned.

Tabitha was pulling and twisting at her sleeves, covering her hands. "I'm sorry. About what I said last night. You're the best ever."

"What you said was true. I'm not your mam. I know you're sensible, but boys are a different thing. You just need to be careful."

Tabitha nodded. "Did you find the boy with the knife? It was all over the news."

"It wasn't a boy. It was a girl. Just thirteen. She was very frightened. She did it as a dare and it all got a bit out of hand." Mandy rubbed a hand over her eyes. "It's been quite a day."

Tabitha's eyes were like saucers. "Thirteen? Oh God. That's scary. Carrying a knife."

"Plus, we stopped a couple of lads who seemed to know us. Just be extra alert, okay?" Mandy hesitated. "Teenagers can be unpredictable. In many ways."

CHAPTER FORTY-ONE

DAY SEVEN

Joy was weary when Mandy collected her from the hospital the next day. Tabitha had another rehearsal, so Mandy dropped the girls off before she whizzed up to the ward. On the way back from the hospital there was silence in the car. They didn't need to speak.

Lost babies. Mandy tried not to dwell too much. As the days progressed there was less likelihood to finding out what had happened to Grace's baby, or even if it had been born alive.

By the time Joy was settled in bed with a hot water bottle and painkillers it was time to collect the girls again. She called into one of the local supermarkets to get some treats for the evening. An attempt to entice Joy to eat. The headline on the local newspaper made her stop in her tracks. THE DOUBLE LIFE OF LOCAL COUNCILLOR. Byline Tod Blakeney. The sneaky swine. He'd warned her, of course, and she hadn't taken the bite. Now she'd have to buy the damned newspaper to find out what it was all about.

In the end it was all smoke and mirrors. The police had been questioning Councillor Gwyn Roper. Was it anything to do with the rumours last year that he'd been having an affair with a secretary, a single woman with a young child?

Why would the police show interest unless he'd stepped over the line? Was the child his? How come the woman in question had received a promotion and no longer worked with Councillor Roper? Speculation. Bloody rubbish. A big fuss with little substance. No doubt she'd get it in the ear about it from Withers. If anyone had seen them talking it could have been misconstrued. She didn't need any more of this shit.

Daniel gave her a wide berth when she went into the hall. Not surprising. Ms Thomas asked if any parents were willing to help with costume changing, make-up or selling raffle tickets on the night. Only two days to go and the excitement and adrenaline in the hall was palpable. Mandy volunteered to sell raffle tickets. It seemed the easy option until she found out she also needed to collect and display the prizes. As if she didn't have enough to do.

* * *

DAY EIGHT

Josh was looking pleased with himself. He'd coped well with taking charge, collated the statements from everyone and had already written up the report. Amy would be given all the support needed, from her family as well as social services.

"Did you see the paper yesterday?" Mandy asked Josh. "Tod Blakeney has been raking up muck again. Maybe that is why the councillor was so defensive."

"Could be. We still need a DNA sample. The other samples are in. No match."

"So, Mr Roper is our favourite for CR. If he's not going to co-operate, we need to find a reason to ask again. I'm going to go through the rest of the information on the council site. See what you can dig up about his family background and the identity of this other woman."

What else did they need to do? Tod had stirred things up, but it could make the councillor more on his guard. They needed to move fast.

"Olivia, let's get a warrant rushed through and check through Gwyn Roper's financial records, please. We've got reasonable grounds for suspicion. He's got an IT business so he may be adept at hiding things. You're the one most likely to root it out if that's the case."

"I was wondering about Grace's phone records," said Helen. "If she wanted to keep CR secret, it could be in her contacts list but disguised as someone else. I mean, I've got my bank details under the name of a girl I was in school with."

"Good thinking. She must have had some way of contacting this person. It wasn't through work as she did a variety of temporary jobs over the last year or so." She turned to Richard and Sam. "You two check her employment history. Go and talk to people she worked with. Anything seems odd make a note and follow it up. Her mam came first for most of that time. It's bizarre. Lying to everyone, hiding the pregnancy seems at odds with everything we know about her."

Richard Gregory snorted but was silenced by a look.

"You're right," said Josh. "She's almost saint-like. Altruistic in the extreme according to everyone who knew her."

"No-one likes to speak ill of the dead," said Helen.

"Don't see why we have to go out in the cold and talk to people." Richard again. "Can't we just ring around? Get the list and ring the bosses. Quicker." His expression was sour, lips curled in disdain.

Mandy inhaled before replying in a measured tone. "Because, DS Gregory, as you are aware, when you visit a place of work the boss is the least likely to know the employee personally. So, what do you do? Ask around. Talk to other workers. Find out more about the victim."

"I've got the list here. I'd already thought it could be an avenue to explore." Sam said.

"Thanks, Sam."

Mumbling under his breath Gregory picked up his coat and followed Sam out.

"God." Olivia looked relieved to see the back of the two detectives. "What's got into him? Glad he's not working with us on a permanent basis."

"Likes to throw his weight about too," said Josh. "He's been trying to tell me how to do my job. Sam's okay though."

"I feel sorry for Sam. He's not being given the right example to follow." Helen said, shaking her head.

"We just need to remember we're on the same side, allegedly. I'll try to keep them out from under your feet as much as possible and hope we solve this bloody case sooner rather than later."

They settled to their tasks. Everything checked, shifted, checked again. The councillor seemed too good to be true. Appointments to several committees; patron of a couple of charities; school governor; member of several other groups. A common thread seemed to be helping refugees or the homeless. All commendable unless it was linked to his business. Did he have an eye towards making a profit from any of those contacts? What a pity her antipathy to that bloody reporter stopped her from finding out more. Mid-morning, Mandy stretched and went to make a cup of green tea. Olivia and Helen were still glued to their screens. Josh glanced up as she passed.

"Anything?"

"Some info on the business site. He's not big on social media but his wife is all over it. She's tweeted a response to the allegations in yesterday's paper. Have a look." He swivelled his screen so Mandy could read it.

@ceri_roper

Some people have nothing better to do than start rumours. I've been married to Gwyn for nearly 30 years. No gutter press reporter will damage my marriage with innuendo.

"Not pulling any punches, is she?"

"No children. From reading between the lines, it was a conscious decision. She's got her own recruitment business. Called Second Chance. Specialises in people who've been made redundant or decided to switch careers."

"I'll remember that next time I've had enough of this crap," said Mandy.

A shadow of a smile crossed Josh's face.

"I think I've got something," said Helen. "Could be nothing but there's a number here with no registered name."

"Under contacts?"

"Maisie."

"Nobody has mentioned a Maisie. School friend?"

Helen shook her head. "Not mentioned before. I've tried ringing but it's switched off. No response."

"Maisie? Ask Stefan. Ashley or Sunil might know if he doesn't. Maybe we've got something here." It was the injection of hope they needed.

Later, with a warrant for examining the councillor's finances in hand, Olivia set to work. "Something by here. Mr Roper moves money around a bit, so it wasn't too obvious first time but look here now. Big cash deposits from his business account every month. Five hundred here and there. Same on joint account with his wife. Over the last six months, total twelve thousand."

"And it's a similar amount to the money going into Grace's GoFundMe page. Bingo. I think we've got a link. We can have a little chat with our bumptious councillor. Wipe that superior look off his face."

The shrill sound from her office phone stopped Mandy from saying anything else. She was grinning as she answered. The desk sergeant had another surprise for her.

"DI Wilde. Councillor Roper is here. He'd like a word. He's in the foyer."

"Well, speak of the devil."

CHAPTER FORTY-TWO

Mandy sneaked a peek at Withers' office. The door was shut and there was no sign of him. Fortunate. She prepared for a confrontation, as she went downstairs to meet Gwyn Roper. They weren't quite ready to pull him in for questioning and she'd need to be careful not to annoy him any further. The last thing they needed was another complaint.

Expecting him to be bombastic and blustering on about invasion of privacy or something else, Mandy was surprised to find the councillor looking awkward, almost hangdog.

"DI Wilde. Is there someone private we can talk?"

She took him to an interview room, got the councillor a glass of water and invited Josh to join them. Whatever Gwyn Roper had to say it was pertinent to the case, she was sure of it.

The councillor sat and undid his tie and top button. He looked more florid than before, and Mandy wondered if he had high blood pressure. No-one spoke for a minute. The radiator gurgled in the background and somewhere a door slammed shut. He coughed, leaned on the table and said, "I suppose you've seen the latest that snivelling little bastard Blakeney has raked up?" This was a side to the councillor that surprised them. He almost spat the words.

There was no point in denying it. Everyone in Cardiff would have seen the story or a version on social media.

"What can I do to stop the little shit? Apart from break his legs?" There was real anger behind the remark. More than the newspaper article warranted.

Mandy tried to diffuse the situation. "It's innuendo. Surely as a councillor you've had plenty of experience of dealing with journalists. It's no big deal, is it?"

"My marriage will implode, and my job too, if he digs up any more dirt." He trailed a hand through his hair and put his head in his hands.

"Perhaps you'd better tell us the whole story. I gather, from your reaction, there's some truth in his allegations." Josh took over. "I doubt if there's much we can do to stop his paper printing the story."

Councillor Roper sat upright and stared at them both. "What about blackmail? Can you stop that?"

It was as if everything in the room came to a standstill. Mandy inhaled. This was the last thing they expected. Should they record the conversation? Josh glanced towards the recorder. She shook her head. Best not destroy the flow of words.

"Is Tod Blakeney blackmailing you?" she asked.

Despite her dislike of the reporter, she didn't think he'd stoop so low.

Once the councillor started to talk there was no stopping him. "No not him. It's her, mouthing off to the press. I told her. No more. I can't afford it. My wife is beginning to get suspicious after she found an envelope full of notes in my desk. This newspaper shit hasn't helped. For God's sake I did my best to get her the job. I can't help it if they didn't appoint her because she's a bloody bird brain, can I? I need you to speak to her. Tell her to give me the skirt. She could have put the deposit on a house with the cash I forked out in the past fifteen months. It has to stop. I told her. Blakeney was her way of warning me, I suppose."

He was gabbling. No sign of the aggression when they'd approached him in County Hall. Or the pure anger when he'd first come in. From what he said and the snippets in the newspaper they could guess. Gwyn Roper had been playing outside the marital bed.

"Blackmail is a serious offence," said Josh. "We'll need details. The person's name, address. Plus, we'll have to take a formal statement from you."

"Just get the skirt back, will you? It's her proof. I won't press charges."

"If it's established that the person in question has been demanding money from you it may not be your call. The skirt?" asked Mandy.

He was sweating, they could smell it. He looked exhausted too. "The one and only time anything of a sexual nature occurred. And boy, have I paid for it. Big time."

"Bit of a Monica moment?"

To Mandy's surprise Gwyn Roper appeared to be blushing, his neck and ears burning red. She'd guessed correctly.

"At least you won't face impeachment, although it could lead to your dismissal from the council," she said.

"I'm going to resign before they push me out. One little loss of control and…" His voice trailed off.

"Is that why you refused to give us a DNA sample?" asked Josh.

"Yes. I panicked. I thought it was to do with her. I don't know what I was thinking. I'll give you a sample now if you like."

Josh left to get a kit. Slumped in the chair, Roper looked a broken man. She felt sorry for him. Her investigations into his background hadn't brought up anything sinister and, in fact, he'd supported several worthy causes in his time with the council, including Grace's fundraising. It would be a shame to see him dismissed. The blackmail accusation would have to be followed up, of course. It was a serious offence. It looked as if the money had nothing to do with Grace either. And, if the DNA brought up a negative result, which she now suspected it would, they were back to square one with the case. So frustrating.

"It's looks as if our good councillor is not CR," said Mandy when they went back to the office. "Back to basics. Let's see if we can do anything with the odd telephone calls. Ask if anyone knows this Maisie. Helen, you can contact Ashley and see if we can get her and Sunil together. We need to be sensitive. Sunil's parents are not keen on the police calling and he's a bundle of nerves at times. Josh and I will have another chat with Stefan."

"I'm still doing the social media stuff," said Olivia.

"Any word from the other two?"

"Nah. Probably in the pub."

"Yeah, knowing Dick – Richard. Carry on with it. It's like looking for a particular grain of sand on Porthcawl beach. If anything seems odd, make a note."

CHAPTER FORTY-THREE

Ashley seemed surprised at being contacted again but agreed to ask Sunil to come over to her house. As they'd been friends for years his parents wouldn't have to know the police wanted to speak to him. Poor kid had enough to deal with. Helen regarded them both. They seemed a bit strained. Not unexpected. Teenagers thought themselves immortal so when someone their age died it was a body blow to confidence. Ashley had chewed her nails to the quick. When she answered the door, she looked startled.

"DC Helen Probert. We spoke on the phone." Helen showed her ID and smiled at Ashley.

"I was expecting the other one. The tall one. DI Wilde." She seemed to relax a little when she knew Mandy wasn't going to be involved.

"DI Wilde is busy, so she sent me. Just a couple of questions. Is Sunil here?"

"Yes. Come through to the back room."

Sunil was sitting on a bean bag by the patio doors. He stood when Helen entered the room and shook hands with her. His face was open, dark eyes sincere. Helen warmed to him. She perched on the sofa, Ashley beside her, and positioned herself so she could see both their faces.

"We've got a bit of a mystery and I'm hoping you can help." Helen thought approaching them in this way might make them feel more relaxed. The two young people nodded.

"We've been checking the numbers on Grace's phone. She had quite a few contacts. Many of them were linked to her fundraising activities. However, we have someone called Maisie. Have you any idea who Maisie is? Perhaps someone you were in school with?"

The pair exchanged bemused glances. Sunil said, "We all went to the same school. I don't remember anyone called Maisie. Do you, Ash?"

"No. We had a Daisy in reception. I remember because in the summer we used to make daisy chains and drape her in them. Do you remember Sunny?"

His face lit up. "Yes. I'd forgotten all about her. Pretty. Blonde hair and always smiling. They moved, didn't they?"

"Yes, before we went into the juniors. England, I think."

"Any of the mothers called Maisie?" asked Helen.

"We only knew the mums by the kids' names or their surnames. I only know Grace's mum is called Eleri because of the fundraising. She was always Mrs Mathias before then. I can't think of her in any other way."

Helen could believe it. When she was at home, she was just Mum. The boys' friends always called her Mrs Probert.

Ashley looked at Helen, unsure then, in a whisper. "How is… she? Grace's mum? Would she know Maisie?"

With a shake of her head, Helen said, "Mrs Mathias isn't very well, I'm afraid. I don't think she can be questioned." She cleared her throat. "The number on Grace's phone is unobtainable."

"Like a burner phone?" Sunil's eyes lit up.

"He watches too much telly," said Ashley with a smile. "Well, too many crime dramas. Burner phone. Grace." She rolled her eyes.

Helen stood to leave. "If you remember anything you think could help then please let us know. If there was anyone hanging about at events in the last year, or any remarks Grace made—"

"Perhaps it was someone at the cemetery," said Sunil.

"What do you mean?"

"Grace loved it there. She said it was so peaceful and she could think. It soothed her mind. We'd sometimes go for a walk with her. She was fascinated by the names on the headstones." He shook his head, smiled. "She wouldn't be ringing a dead person."

"We'll let you know if we think of anybody," said Ashley as she followed Helen to the door.

A gust of icy air blasted them when the door was opened so Helen dashed to her car.

CHAPTER FORTY-FOUR

Every time Mandy saw Stefan, he seemed to have diminished a little more. His eyes seemed to be sunk deeper in his head and his misery was like an invisible cloak around his body. The smell in the house was overwhelmingly clinical now; disinfectant, bleach and the heavy odour of death approaching. Mandy was more aware than ever that their presence was an intrusion. He seemed to have lost all vitality, beckoning them in without a sound and padding down to the back of the house. The door to the sick room was ajar and a soft voice, the words indistinguishable, floated in the air. Someone was in with Eleri.

"The nurse is with my wife. She had a turn for the worse this morning." He almost fell into a chair and put both hands to his head. "It's so hard." His voice was breaking, emotion overtaking him.

Mandy leaned forward, her voice low and sincere in tone. "I'm so sorry. I know we're intruding, but we may have a lead. Did Grace ever talk about someone called Maisie?"

A frown creased his forehead. "Not that I remember. She wasn't a secretive girl. At least I didn't believe she was until all this. Now I don't know anymore. How could she?" He swallowed. "I didn't tell Eleri about the baby. I thought if you found the child it might be a comfort. It's dead too, isn't it?"

"We don't know. No body has been found. We're working on the theory that whoever is the father has the baby. But we haven't been able to find him."

"But you have DNA?" Something like anger sparked for a second in his eyes.

"No match yet. We were asking about Maisie as there's a contact on Grace's phone we haven't been able to trace. The number is unobtainable."

"I don't understand. Why are you telling me this?"

"We think Maisie could be a cover for the man who fathered Grace's baby. I know forensics have been, but I wondered if you would mind me looking again at Grace's room?"

He shrugged. "Do what you want."

"Thank you. DS Jones will make you a cup of tea. I won't be long."

Mandy crept up the stairs to avoid making too much noise although she suspected Eleri was not aware of much. What she hoped to gain by entering Grace's room again, she had no idea. Maybe sitting in the room would somehow provide an inkling into Grace's state of mind.

It was just as she remembered. Either forensics had been sympathetic to the family situation and put it back as it was, or Helen had tidied up after them. What did she think she could find. A picture? A number scribbled on the back of something? She turned over photographs and checked the numbers on the list pinned to the board, comparing them to the unknown number. Grace's notebook had nothing about Maisie. She sat on the end of the bed. "Who's the father, Grace?"

Once again Mandy was struck by the extreme neatness of the room. Grace had few possessions. The shelves held a dozen or so books. Mandy picked up a slim volume of poetry, disturbing the pile and a paperback dropped to the floor. Daphne Du Maurier. Of course, the teacher said she was doing a project. As she picked it up to return to the shelf, a slip of paper fell out. No doubt it had been used as a bookmark. She did the same thing herself, using old envelopes or supermarket receipts to keep her reading place. This was something else. It was a bus ticket from Cardiff Bus. She checked the date. Two weeks ago. About the same time as Grace was supposed to be away in Bristol. The days they knew, or suspected, when she had given birth.

CHAPTER FORTY-FIVE

Josh made a cup of tea and sat and listened as Stefan talked. Most of it was unloading his fears and sorrows. He thought he'd return to Poland when everything was sorted. Eleri had made a will before they were married and hadn't got around to changing it. He knew the house was left to Grace so what would happen now? Complications in life. Eighteen-year-olds didn't think about making a will. He knew what sort of a funeral Eleri wanted as she was organised, expecting death. But Grace? She wasn't religious. What should he do about it all? They were questions Josh couldn't answer so he listened, making a sympathetic sound now and again to let Stefan know he was engaged.

As soon as Mandy entered the room, he could tell she'd found something. He raised his eyebrows and had a barely perceptible nod in response.

"Do you use Cardiff Bus, Mr Nowak?"

"The bus? I used to, sometimes. Not for a long time now. I don't go out much since Eleri became so ill. A bit of shopping, the pharmacy, the doctor." He shrugged.

"So, this bus ticket is most likely to be Grace's? I found it being used as a bookmark. I don't know how the forensic team missed it."

"Does it tell us where she went?" asked Josh.

"Not in so many words. Easy to find out with a couple of calls. It has the route number for starters. We'll need to get back to the office." She turned to Stefan. "DC Probert will call in the morning. We promise to keep you informed if we find anything. Apologies again for the intrusion."

They almost bumped into the nurse who was leaving Eleri's room. She waited for them to pass, indicating she needed to speak to Stefan.

"We'll let ourselves out," said Mandy, eager to escape.

"Do you think this will help?" asked Josh, examining the ticket as they were driving back to the station.

"No idea. We've got precious little else to go on. Let's find out where the bus goes and the route it takes."

"What's with you and Richard Gregory?" Josh asked.

"It's that obvious, is it?"

"Yeah, since that first day and some quip he made. I thought you were going to throttle him. I didn't get it, but the air is decidedly chilly when he's about."

Mandy sighed. "It's one of the reasons I send the two of them out to do some of the groundwork. He's been around since I was a newbie. You once asked me why I joined the force."

"Yeah, I remember."

"It was an act of defiance. My Dad sailed a bit close to the edge with some of his business dealings. He was well known to the police as Dodgy Derek. Richard Gregory called me DDD. Dodgy Derek's daughter. He thought it was funny."

Josh was silent as he digested her words. Mandy glanced sideways at him. It wasn't the sort of information she usually shared with colleagues.

"Of course, it was better than his nickname." She laughed. "He didn't like being called Dickhead and he was the same grade so could do nothing about it."

Josh grinned. "No wonder he looks as if he's chewing wasps every time you give him an order. It explains a lot."

As soon as they got back to the station Mandy fired up her computer. The first piece of information on the ticket was Route 30.

"It's the Newport bus. Why Newport? It doesn't make sense. But then nothing about this case makes sense." Mandy scratched the back of her head.

"Unless she took a bus to Newport and then on to somewhere else? Like Bristol?"

"No. I don't think she spent the weekend with her friends. Those two seemed genuine enough. What did you think, Helen? Any progress there with Ashley and Sunil?"

Helen shook her head. "Precious little. Sunil came up with the theory of a burner phone."

"Interesting. Wonder why he said that?"

"Ashley just said he watched too many detective dramas." She smiled. "She also said the man could be someone she met in the cemetery. Grace liked it there."

"We know she's always been keen on the peace and solitude of the cemetery but it's not really the spot for romance, is it? Let's look at the route the bus takes and see where it stops. According to the ticket it was issued at Customhouse Street. The boarding stage for City Centre. It doesn't say where she got off."

They flicked open the map on the Cardiff bus website and groaned.

"About forty stops. Anywhere between here and Newport bus station."

"Royal Gwent hospital," said Josh. "She was pregnant, wasn't she? Could make sense."

"So, she finds herself pregnant, registers with a doctor in Newport and gives birth there." Mandy thought about it for a moment. "What about the weekends away? A check-up at the hospital would take, how long? An hour? Two at max with waiting time. Not days."

"Can we find out?"

"You know what hospitals are like. Confidentiality is key. You'd have more luck getting into a nun's knickers. We'll need a warrant, I suppose, unless..."

Everyone stopped as Mandy hesitated. "The press often finds out stuff by different methods."

Josh glanced at the others then back to Mandy.

"You're not thinking what I think you're thinking?"

"Our little friend Tod Blakeney might be able to smooth talk somebody. Then again, he can't be trusted. Births need to be registered within a certain time though, don't they?"

"Forty-two days in the district where the birth took place," said Helen. "I know because we were so busy after the second baby arrived, we almost forgot. Over a month before we gave him a name. My mother was not impressed."

"Okay. We have a vague idea, within a week, of when Grace had the baby. If we look at births registered in that time frame, we might find her or be able to speak to the mothers who were in hospital at the same time."

"Bit of a long shot," said Josh. "Lot of legwork for a baby who might have been stillborn."

"Stillborn babies still need to be registered. Helen, give the Newport Register Office a ring and see if they can help, please. Any birth registered to Grace Mathias in November. Births are public records so ask for a list of registrations from the latter half of the month."

As Helen made the call Josh rubbed a hand over his eyes and yawned. "Do you think this baby is still alive?"

"Until we find a body we must hope. We owe it to Grace to find her child – alive or dead."

CHAPTER FORTY-SIX

DAY NINE

Forty-seven births had been registered in the last two weeks. As they didn't have an exact date for the birth, they had to assume it was sometime in the week Grace had been away. Wherever she had given birth, Newport or somewhere in between, it was unlikely she had travelled back to Cardiff on the same day.

Mandy contacted Cardiff Bus and arranged to interview the driver when he'd finished his shift after lunch. It was the evening of Tabitha's performance, so, as Josh had proven himself to be capable of leading the team, they would have to do without her if anything turned up – like a dead baby.

"Anything to report?" Mandy asked the team.

"Nothing from any of her work placements – so far," said Sam Fraser, flicking open a notebook. "Pleasant, friendly, quiet, helpful. No-one knew much about her apart from the fundraising stuff."

"Okay. Continue with those enquiries. Someone may have noticed something."

"I've got the list of registered births and checking through now," said Helen. "I thought I'd check for a Maisie anywhere, either mother or baby name."

"Good."

"I might have something, now," said Olivia. "I've been going through all the photos and trying to put names to faces. Lot of people get tagged. It's taken forever, but I've an idea."

"Spit it out."

"What if CR is a woman? We've looked at all the men thinking we're looking for the father. What if CR and Maisie is the same person? It's a bit crazy but, I don't know. We don't seem to be getting anywhere, do we?"

"Carry on. Bit of lateral thinking. I like it," said Mandy with a smile of approval. "If we start looking for a woman, do we have any candidates who potentially fit the bill. Initials CR?"

"How or why would a woman be involved?" asked Josh.

"I've been pondering why Grace would give away a baby. Only way I can think of is surrogacy. I thought about it right at the beginning but thought she was probably too young to contemplate that. It's quite an undertaking. Plus, they don't usually like potential surrogates under twenty-one." She waited while the team digested the information. "If Grace was a surrogate for someone it would explain why everything was kept so secret."

"Of course," said Josh. "And everyone says how Grace was so altruistic. She'd do anything for anyone. What did Ashley say? She'd give her right arm to save her Mum. Makes sense."

"Don't forget the money. If she was carrying a baby she got paid when she handed it over." Mandy put a hand to her forehead. "Bloody hell. We've been looking at this from the wrong angle. Well done, Olivia. New line of enquiry."

The morale of the team seemed to lift. Now they had two lines of enquiry. Helen found the register of births yielded little to follow up at first glance but with initials CR added to the list she found three names. Olivia added two more to it. People involved in fundraising activities.

"There's something else that's a bit odd, like." Olivia was flicking back and forth through the social media photographs.

"What is it?"

"I've got a woman who is in several of the event photographs but there's no trace of her on any platform so no idea who she is, now."

They clustered around Olivia's desk and peered at the screen.

"Look. She's here," click on the mouse, "and by here," another click, "and in this one. But she's not been tagged by anyone. It's odd."

The woman in question was unremarkable in appearance. Short dark hair, hazel-coloured eyes and a fresh complexion.

"Could be anyone. Bit of a coincidence though. Three photographs. Wait a bloody minute. Look who she's standing beside." Mandy pointed at the screen. "One of our suspects. Well, well."

"Our teacher. Christopher Robin." Josh grinned. "Do you think he has something to do with it?"

"I certainly do. Many gay couples want children and the only way for him, and his partner would be to find a suitable surrogate. Where does he live? Anywhere on that bus route?"

Josh checked the address. "Sorry. Going towards Pontypridd. Doesn't mean he wasn't involved. I'll print out the photograph."

"Back to school for us and then off for a chat with the bus driver." She turned towards the others. "Helen and Olivia can you two follow up on the lists you've got? Contact them and go and have an informal chat. See what you come up with. Take a photo of Grace in case anyone recognises her."

"Most new mums meet at antenatal classes, but she may have spoken to someone if she was at the hospital at the same time," said Helen. "We'll get on to it and let you know if there's any progress. I want to try and pop in to see Stefan later."

Mandy and Josh pulled on their coats and headed out, Mandy whistling. Outside the cold snap had given way to a warmer front. Rain. Heavy drops splashing into puddles and damp which seemed to seep into bones. God, she hated these dank winter days.

The school seemed noisier than last time they visited with singing from a couple of classrooms and excited children squealing. Christmas decorations were strung across windows and along the corridor. Somewhere in the building someone was baking gingerbread and Josh sniffed in appreciation.

"Hell's bells. It wasn't like this when I was in school," grumbled Mandy as a couple of small children dashed along the corridor and almost collided with the detectives.

Christopher Robin had been alerted to their presence, frowning as he greeted them. "I don't have long. My teaching assistant will let them run riot and the rest of the day will be a write-off. What was it you wanted to see me about?"

He took them to what looked like a stockroom. Boxes lined one wall, each balanced precariously on top of the other. It had the musty smell of a place not much used. They perched on tiny chairs and Mandy could see Josh trying not to laugh as she attempted to crouch her tall frame into the space.

"We've been trying to identify this woman," said Josh, showing Christopher the photograph. "She's standing beside you and talking to you."

Christopher studied the photo, staring at it before handing it back. He shrugged his shoulders.

"It was taken at the fancy dress race in May last year. Your partner was running, I believe," said Mandy.

"Yes. Bless him. He came in second from last." Christopher smiled. "Dressed as a dinosaur. Oh. Wait a mo. Now I think I remember. Some woman said perhaps he should have had trainers on instead of dinosaur slippers. Could be the one in the photo."

"Can you remember anything else about the conversation?" asked Josh.

"Hardly a conversation. I asked her if she knew anyone in the race. She said her partner. That's about it."

"Did she say what her partner's name was or give you her name?"

He shook his head. "Sorry. It was twenty seconds a long time ago and a lot has happened since then."

"Do you have children?" asked Mandy.

"No. And I don't want any. As I say to anyone who asks, I get enough of children in the day job without facing that at home as well." He laughed. "My class has probably gone wild by now. I'd better rescue the teaching assistant. Christmas and young children combined means overexcitement and tears."

They rose and he reminded them to sign on the way out of the school again, before dashing along to his classroom.

"Do you believe him?" asked Josh as they got back into the Juke.

"I think I do, but we'll check him out anyway. We need to go back to the list of participants in that race and check them all and their partners. A new baby on the scene for any of them could be the one we are looking for."

"Any chance of a pit stop before the bus depot?" Josh's stomach was rumbling again.

"We've got time to grab something. Suggestions?"

"I know a place where they have home-made cawl with chunks of sourdough and cheese."

"Direct me to it. I forgot to bring my lunch with me this morning. Joy will have it. Nothing wasted."

"How is your sister?"

Mandy sighed, long and loud. "I wish I knew. Super quiet. Withdrawn, fragile and pale as mist. Tabitha's performance is tonight so I hope she can pretend to show enthusiasm for it. I'm selling bloody raffle tickets."

CHAPTER FORTY-SEVEN

The driver, Joe, didn't look happy to be talking to them after his shift. The manager ensured they had a room where they could be private. It was one of those anonymous offices with magnolia walls, an ancient desk with a computer and shelves of files. The whiteboard behind the desk had names and numbers scribbled into a grid. Similar to the office in the station in many ways. The man was overweight, smelt of cigarettes and had a cauliflower ear to one side of a grumpy face.

After introducing themselves and explaining the nature of their business, Mandy tried to establish some rapport with him.

"Used to play rugby, did you? Wales doing alright now, aren't they? Josh here used to play. Not sure his wife approves though." She indicated Josh with a flick of her head.

He seemed to relax a bit. Mandy indicated for Josh to take over, so he took out a copy of the bus ticket.

"We're hoping you can help with this, sir."

The guy grunted.

"This ticket could be a very important lead in a case we're trying to solve. Now we know that you were the driver," he pointed to the number, "and this is the trip ID. Can you pull that up on the system for us, please?

You see we're trying to find out where this young lady may have been going to." He showed him the photograph of Grace. "We may need the CCTV as well."

The driver pulled out a pair of cheap supermarket specs from his breast pocket to examine the ticket. He smiled at the photo.

"S'easy. I remember her. Young. Reminded me of my niece, Zara. Didn't look too good last time I saw her though." He checked the date on the ticket. "Yeah. Would have been the same day."

"What do you mean?"

"I drives to Newport regular. Picked her up in town a few times. Like I said she looks like Zara, so I remembers. And polite. Always says please and thank you. Smiles too."

Mandy could feel her pulse accelerating. It was better than expected. If he remembered Grace, could he remember where she got off the bus?

"Are we able to see the CCTV of that journey? Is it still in the system?" asked Mandy.

"Usually kept three to six weeks. Depends. You'd have to make a formal request for that, love."

Josh was smirking. Mandy stiffened. Not many people got away with calling her love. The driver was oblivious.

"We'll do that. It's important we see the footage, so we know where she got off."

"No worries, love. I can tell you that. Dog and Bone at Castleton. Told you. Not the first time I seen her on the bus. Always got on at the city centre and off at

Castleton by the pub. Sometimes see her going the other way too. Back to Cardiff, like."

"How often did she travel on that route? Would any of the other drivers be likely to remember her?"

"Dunno 'bout that. Different shifts see."

Not much point in trying to talk to other drivers if he could give them the information they needed.

"Did you see anyone with her? Or when she got off? Did you see where she went?"

"I just drives the bus, love. She always got on alone. Once I drop a fare I don't bother where they go. Although," he paused, his face scrunched up as he tried to recall something, "last time she looks a bit pale and no smiles. On her phone. Texting. Looks as if she was in pain. Strained, you know? And when she gets off there was a car parked by the stop. Bit unusual that."

"What make? Model? Colour? Did you see if there was someone inside?" asked Mandy.

"Blimey, love. I'm driving the bus. More interested on what's on the road." He winked at Josh. "That's right. Ain't it, buddy? Keep on the right side of the law."

The information could be nothing or it could be vital. If Grace got off the bus at The Dog and Bone, did someone meet her there? Where could she have gone? Who did she know?

"We'll need to see that footage if it's still available. Let's see if it can be sorted as soon as possible." She gave a faint smile. "Thank you for your time, sir. You've been really helpful."

"Tell the boss, love. Maybe I'll get a bonus." He grinned, displaying crooked tobacco-stained teeth.

When they were outside again Josh said, "You know who lives less than a mile from the bus stop?" He showed her the map on his phone.

"Bloody hell. The teacher. Nia Jones. But her baby is months old. Can't be the link. Can it?"

"One way to find out."

"No time now. Tomorrow. I've got to get home. Tabitha's big night. She gets to kiss Daniel on stage. At least there he can't get up to anything in full view of the audience."

"You hope."

CHAPTER FORTY-EIGHT

Joy was dressed and ready to go when Mandy got home. She'd made an effort to put on makeup and try to tame her hair. Like Mandy, the slightest dampness in the air resulted in frizz.

"You're cutting it fine, Mand. I thought you said you had to sort the raffle table and sell tickets."

"We got a break. Fingers crossed." She glanced at the clock on the shelf. "Oh shit. You're right. Five minutes. I'll just get changed. Kelly's mam collect Tabs? How was she?"

"Yeah. They left forty minutes ago. Tabs was nervous but excited as well. I hope it goes alright."

"It will."

She dashed upstairs, opened a couple of drawers and found a red jumper. Her black trousers would have to do. Respectable enough. She yanked off her top, wiped her armpits with a flannel, sprayed on deodorant and pulled on the red jumper. With a quick brush of her hair, she bounded downstairs again. Joy had her coat on waiting in the hallway.

"Right. I'm as ready as I'm going to be. You might have to take one side of the hall to sell tickets while I do the other." As an afterthought she asked Joy. "How are you feeling?"

"Like death warmed up. Stuffed full of painkillers."

"Hell sis. Don't fall asleep when the lights go down."

* * *

As they were entering the hall Mandy spotted a figure lurking in the shadows. She couldn't be sure but to her it looked like the lad they'd caught on Wellfield Road; the one who had made veiled threats. She made a mental note to check out what had happened after they'd been charged and to keep a discreet eye on his movements. The threats could have been bravado but best to be safe. Inside the utilitarian space of the hall had been transformed. It was lit by fairy lights along the edge of the stage and they had managed to hang drapes. Already it was almost full, most seats taken and whispered conversations taking place. A couple of younger children whimpered. As they entered a few people glanced their way and then did a double take. It always made Mandy chuckle to see the reactions when they went out together. Ms Thomas spotted them and approached in haste. She looked from one to the other then made up her mind and addressed Joy.

"You must be Tabitha's mother. I've reserved a seat for you near the front, by Daniel's parents." She turned to Mandy. "Inspector Wilde. I've sorted the raffle table already. Tickets, please. A pound a strip."

She passed Mandy a tin with some change and a wad of raffle tickets before disappearing behind the scenes again. Joy smirked and went to find her seat while Mandy set to her task. With her height and no-nonsense approach, she had little difficulty selling tickets and the tin filled with notes in a short time. Daniel's mother glared at her but Jacob, his father, put a twenty-pound note into the tin and declined the raffle tickets. A show of wealth. Did he expect a round of applause? What a prick.

At last, an announcement that the show would start in five minutes left her free to take the seat beside her sister. The hall lights dimmed, and the show began. As they watched Mandy felt a glow of pride. Tabitha was a different person on stage. The shy, self-effacing teenager changed into a confident performer with a lovely voice. There was a certain chemistry between her and Daniel, the kissing scene raising a few oohs and aahs from the audience. At the end they had a standing ovation from the proud parents. The raffle raised over two hundred pounds for a local children's charity and Ms Thomas was pink with happiness.

Afterwards, filled with pride, Mandy and Joy hugged Tabitha. They were all high on adrenaline. Joy had been out earlier and bought a bottle of Prosecco so they celebrated, Tabitha included, with a glass of bubbly when they got home.

"No more rehearsals with Daniel," said Mandy, watching to see Tabitha's reactions. Her phone had been beeping non-stop. "Is there going to be a party?"

"Yeah. Next Saturday during normal drama club time. I'm down to take cheese and biscuits."

Another ping on the phone.

"Daniel again," said Joy, with a wink. The evening out had lifted her low mood.

"I've finished with Dan." Tabitha glanced up as both sisters gasped. An unexpected bombshell especially after what looked like a passionate kiss onstage earlier. It didn't look as if they'd been acting that bit.

"He's too big-headed. His friend Luke's much nicer. He's asked me to go to the cinema with a few others on Saturday afternoon, after the party. That's okay, isn't it?" She looked from Joy to Mandy and then back again, unsure who would give permission.

Mandy bit her lip and looked away. Not her call.

"Of course, Tabs. Mand, you know this Luke boy, don't you? Is he suitable? Good enough for my daughter?" There was a teasing note in her voice as she looked at her sister.

"He's a nice kid. Dad's in the force."

"So that's okay then." Joy said.

"Thanks Mam." Tabitha blushed and, gripping her phone, left them to go to the privacy of her room.

"Makes me feel old, my daughter dating already."

"Come on. You were out with boys when you were just fourteen. Told Mam you were going to choir practice." Mandy laughed. "Do you think she believed you?"

Joy sniggered. "I doubt it, but probably easier to let me go than put up with the tantrums."

"Thankfully, your daughter has not inherited your temper."

"I hope she's got your common sense. I couldn't cope with a moody teenager."

Mandy opened her mouth to say something and then changed her mind.

CHAPTER FORTY-NINE

DAY TEN

Nia Jones was surprised at the call from the police but agreed to speak to them again.

"Come about eleven. I usually put him down for a nap then, so we'll have peace to talk."

Mandy hoped that was true. The sounds of a screaming infant down the telephone line were strident enough without experiencing it close at hand again. They were examining the map of the area and identifying other places within a mile of the bus stop when Withers came in.

"Have you got a minute, Wilde?

Her heart sank as she tried to think of anything she'd done to step out of line. Not the councillor again she hoped. That little fracas should be smoothed over by now. What was it?

"Close the door." Withers sat down behind his desk, took off his gold-framed specs, rubbed his eyes and then replaced them. He put his hands on the desk, fingers steepled, and seemed to hesitate.

"Sit down. There's something I need to tell you, Miranda. I've been trying to do so for a few days but there never seems to be the right time."

Bloody hell. Serious stuff. Using her first name. He was the only senior officer who called everyone by their surnames. She sat and waited, stomach churning, while a nerve in his cheek twitched.

"The boys upstairs," he rolled his eyes towards the ceiling although they both knew the higher-ranking officers were not in the building, "have decided that we need closer relations with other forces."

Mandy tilted her head and raised an eyebrow. Where was this going?

"In a bid to understand how the different divisions work we are having a DCI from North Wales seconded to us in the New Year."

An interesting development. "Does that mean I'm going to be sent up to north Wales?"

"I suppose it could be a possibility. They wanted to send me up there, but I dug my heels in. I'm within a couple of years of retirement and all these fancy ideas don't help with what's happening on the ground." He sighed. "Just more damned paperwork."

"Do you miss being in the thick of it, sir?"

"More than you know. But it's only part of the story." His eyes seemed to be examining her face as he continued, "The DCI they're sending to us is Lucas Manning."

The colour drained from Mandy's face. She could feel it flowing to her gut which started churning again.

"I wanted to give you the news before it becomes common knowledge. He'll be joining your team and considering your past," he hesitated, "association with DCI Manning, I thought you needed forewarning."

She'd never seen the Super at a loss before. So, under all the bluster was a decent bloke. Lucas Manning. Imagine Withers remembering. Then he'd been around at the time. Witnessed all the drama.

"It was a long time ago." Her voice sounded strange to her ears. Almost a whisper and with a definite croak. "Our break-up was messy but mutual." She'd been lucky Lucas hadn't pressed charges. "Our paths haven't crossed since."

"I'm aware of that, Miranda. A lot can happen in sixteen years and people change. If you need support while he's here, come and speak to me." He coughed, seemed almost embarrassed by the conversation. He'd been a sergeant at the time. Tasked with dealing with the fallout.

"I'm sure I'll be alright, sir. Thank you for the heads-up. When does he start?"

"First of January, although he may appear before then to make himself known to the team." He cleared his throat, his tone becoming less conciliatory and sterner, as normal. "And I don't expect trouble while he's here. Any hint of conflict between you and DCI Manning and I won't be leaping to your defence."

"Yes, sir."

The conversation over, Mandy stood and left. Typical. He'd give his support if she didn't give him grief. In the corridor she leaned against the wall. Once, a long time ago, she thought she had a future with Lucas. She tried not to think about it. She had work to do.

"Right, Josh. Little trip out? See Mrs Jones?" They grabbed their coats and headed out into the chill December air.

"What did the Super want? You looked a bit shaken when you came out."

"New initiatives. I expect he'll tell the team in the next few days. They're sending a DCI from North Wales to shadow us. A matter of co-operation or some such shit. He'll be with our team for a while after Christmas."

"How long? Do we get a chance to go up there and experience life in the north?"

"God Josh, you make it sound like a foreign country."

"Far as I'm concerned it is. I wouldn't mind it, though. Lovely scenery and stuff. Make a change from the city."

"And full of fields of sheep and rural communities who hate strangers. Fresh air and small villages. Give me the city any day. The countryside is over-rated, especially at this time of the year. And if it snows."

"We're just not geared for it. In Toronto they have underground walkways so you can get around the city."

Mandy shook her head. "You're a mine of bloody useless information. Now, let's see if Nia Jones can shed some light."

CHAPTER FIFTY

Somehow, they managed to get lost on the way to the farm. Mandy was deep in thought and overshot the turnoff. She realised when they came to an unfamiliar group of houses clumped together on the main drag.

"Bugger. I'm not thinking straight. I'll have to turn around."

The road was too narrow to do a three-point turn with ease, so she drove on a few hundred yards until she got to a farm gate and was able to swing around and retrace their journey.

"You seem a bit distracted, boss."

"Sorry. A lot going on. Here we are. Turn here at the blue house. I don't know how I missed it. Why the hell didn't you tell me?"

"You'd passed before I realised. I didn't know there were other houses up here. Could Grace have been visiting someone in one of those?"

Mandy considered it. "Bit of a trek from the bus route but worth looking into. Get on to Gregory and Fraser tell them to check it out. Afterwards we'll go to the pub and ask if they have outside CCTV. There's a chance she wasn't visiting Nia Jones at all."

As he waited for Gregory to answer the call Josh said, "Do we know what colour or make of car Nia Jones, or her husband, drives? I know we didn't see much from the bus footage but worth considering."

"I think we're on a wild goose chase here, but you never know. They'll have two cars, I'd imagine. She travelled to school from here, so she'd need her own vehicle and he's probably got a car. He's not likely to go everywhere by tractor, is he?"

Josh briefed Gregory as they approached the track leading to the farm.

The farmhouse was bathed in winter sun, the off-white render turned pale golden, and the surrounding trees silhouetted against an unexpected clear sky. It would be short-lived, more rain and sleet were forecast, but more welcoming than the snow flurries they'd experienced last time.

A silver Volkswagen was parked near the house and the dogs were there again. A barn door was open, and a man could be seen working inside. He nodded as they passed, not pausing or showing any further interest.

The dogs barked and Nia appeared almost at once calming them and inviting Mandy and Josh in. The warmth from the wood-burner was welcome and Nia, without asking, put on the kettle. Something was on the Aga, bubbling away. No sign of the baby.

As if aware of their thoughts, Nia said, "He's asleep. Just gone down. He's sleeping through the night now, thank God." They sat while Nia bustled around, made a pot of tea and buttered some scones before sitting down with them at the table. Mandy declined the scones, but Josh wasted no time tucking in.

"Was that your husband working in the barn?"

"I expect so. Tall, bulky, green jacket and blue beanie?"

Mandy nodded.

"He'll be trying to fix the tractor. It's got a bit of a leak somewhere. Nothing serious but he's fussy about keeping everything in tip-top condition."

"Anyone else work here?"

"We have help. No-one permanent. Depends on the budget. That's my job now. I'm busy getting the stuff together before the tax returns. It must be in before the end of January. Our accountant retired last month so I'm left holding the baby, in more ways than one. Now, how can I help you?"

If there was one thing Mandy prided herself on it was judgement of people. As she looked at Nia Jones and her open face, she couldn't believe this woman knew anything about Grace's missing baby. On the other hand, this was the only known link to the journey Grace made before she gave birth.

"When did you say you last saw Grace Mathias?"

"In the summer. After the exams."

"Not since then? She didn't come here about a week before her death? End of November?"

Nia glanced from one to the other, puzzled. "No. I'd have told you."

Josh held her look for a moment. "Did she confide in you? Ask any questions you thought unusual in any way? Or talk about people she knew?"

Leaning back in her chair Nia studied the beams on the ceiling for a minute. "I'm trying to remember our last conversation. She asked if it had been a difficult birth.

229

That struck me as a bit odd from a teenager." Nia paused. "And how I'd felt about the baby after he'd been born."

"You thought this was strange?"

"Inspector, I taught teenagers. They are mostly egocentric. It's all me, me, me." She laughed. "Grace was always more perceptive, more empathetic, sensitive. With some of the others I taught I'd have thought those sorts of questions highly unusual but with Grace not so much. It's only in retrospect it seems a little peculiar."

"Did Grace know anyone else here? Your husband, the people in Bluebell Cottage or any of the workers for example?" asked Mandy.

"Not that I'm aware of." She only came a couple of times. Even if she saw anyone on the farm it would have been at a distance. They're always busy."

"If she came when you weren't here?" Josh was persistent.

"I'm nearly always here. And it's not the sort of place you drop in on spec, is it? Bit too out of the way."

With the realisation they were not getting anywhere Mandy changed direction. "Your neighbours. Who lives close by and what do you know about them?"

As she took a sip of her tea, Nia narrowed her eyes in concentration. "Ian and Rachel live in Bluebell Cottage. Then, up the road a bit there are three houses. Glen and Mary, retired couple, have lived there forever. Phil and Paul moved in about the same time as Ian and Rachel and the third house is empty. Bit of a problem with damp rot which the landlord is trying to sort out."

Josh was making notes. "Would any of those people have known Grace?"

"I doubt it. Why would they? There's no connection as far as I know. Why do you think she came here?"

"We found a bus ticket dated the week we think she had a baby. She got out at The Dog and Bone and was picked up by someone in a dark car. What sort of car do you drive?"

"The silver Volkswagen outside is mine. Craig has a battered pale blue Peugeot he uses if I need the Volkswagen. As I told you, I haven't seen Grace for months. Have you asked at the pub?"

"Next stop," said Mandy, rising to her feet. Josh swallowed the remains of a scone and dusted the crumbs off the front of his coat.

CHAPTER FIFTY-ONE

Mandy brooded as they left the farm. Every time they thought they had something it slipped away. Like chasing wraiths. A car was parked outside Bluebell Cottage, and they had a glimpse of a pale face surrounded by dark hair getting out of a grey Focus. If there was no luck at the pub, they would have to start door to door again along this lane and the other side of the road to Marshfield. The Super would not be happy. Manpower cost money.

At the pub the girl behind the bar looked a bit concerned when they showed their identification and asked for the manager. A portly man, red-faced and blustering, appeared from the cellar where he'd been changing a barrel. He didn't look too pleased to see them either.

"Who's been complaining now?" were his first words.

"Why do you think there's been a complaint?"

He looked a bit abashed and cleared his throat. "There's always some bugger kicking off about something, isn't there? We had a noisy lot in last night. Some bloody stag do. Thought it was that."

"We're here on a different matter, sir. Do you have CCTV for the outside of the building?" She knew they had cameras but sometimes they were dummies put up to deter would-be criminals and vandals.

"Yes. Carpark and entrance."

"What about towards the bus stop? Would it show people getting off the bus and which way they turned?"

"Might do."

At last. If they had a positive sighting of Grace and whoever picked her up from the bus, they would have something to go on.

"We'd like to see the footage from a couple of weeks ago, please." Mandy told him the time and date.

He took them through to a small back room, a storeroom of sorts, piled high with boxes of crisps, soft drinks and crates of bottled beer. To Mandy's surprise there was a sweet smell in the room, and she grimaced as her boots stuck to the floor.

"Dropped a bottle of alcopop," he said when he noticed her expression. "Sticky bloody stuff."

He showed them the operating system, found the right date and left them to it. There was one chair, so Mandy sat down while Josh leaned over her. The quality of the recording was poor, so blurred it was impossible to distinguish much at all.

"That has to be Grace." Josh pointed at a slight figure descending from the bus. She turned away from the pub and out of the angle of the camera.

"Bugger. We can't see the car the bus driver told us about or who was there to meet her." They watched again to make sure. Mandy heaved a weary sigh. "We'd better get back."

"I want to have a word with Rishi. I'll drop you at the station first. Follow up where we are. See if anything hits you. What are we not seeing?"

"Dunno, boss. There's something niggling me but I'm not quite sure what. Bit of a bind, isn't it?" He sighed as he wiped the condensation off the inside of the window. "Maybe we'll never find the baby."

"I know what you mean. A series of leads all ending up in Shitsville. I don't want to leave it as an unsolved case, especially if we're having a bloody DCI from North Wales breathing down our necks in January. It would be nice to get a clean slate on the case before then."

The traffic was heavy. It always got worse in December. Christmas shoppers descending on the city centre like the proverbial plague of locusts. Bumper to bumper and second gear most of the way. Mandy swung into Cathays Park, dropped Josh and headed off to the mortuary. The car park was busier than usual. Not even visiting time. She had to circle to find a space.

Rishi was sitting reading something on a screen and eating a sandwich when she got there.

"God, Rishi. How can you eat in here? I mean it bloody stinks for a start, and you're surrounded by the dead."

He looked surprised. It obviously didn't strike him as odd. "Well, at least I do not have to share my food, unless you would–"

"No bloody way."

With a grin, Rishi said, "This is not a social visit I take it. How can I help?"

"Grace Mathias. From the evidence do you think she had help during the birth? I mean she didn't just go off somewhere, have the baby and dispose of it?"

"No. It is my belief that she had not just assistance but help from someone trained in medicine. The fragment of placenta left in the womb was small. Enough to create severe pain but easily missed on examination. There was also evidence of an internal tear that may have been stitched up."

"She was stitched up by a doctor? So, she was most likely in hospital."

"Or a midwife. Midwives are, in many cases, more competent at dealing with the birthing process," said Rishi. "The birth could have taken place in a hospital or in someone's home with a midwife in attendance." He took another bite from his sandwich. Mandy's stomach turned. How could he?

"We're trying to find out about births through the register. We thought she had attended at The Royal Gwent. Attempting to get anything from a hospital is impossible, due to privacy issues. We've no idea when or where Grace gave birth, and we can't get a court order without a substantial reason."

"A conundrum, Inspector."

"Too bloody right. Thanks, Rishi."

Mandy was glad to get out into the crisp December air. Even in the hospital there were signs of the festive season. She spotted a porter with a Santa Claus hat as she made her way back to the car park. A harassed mother with a screaming child passed and her thoughts turned to Joy. Her sister seemed subdued. Not unexpected considering the trauma she'd endured. Tabitha was like a mother hen, fussing over her mother.

CHAPTER FIFTY-TWO

Helen was not at her desk and Olivia seemed less chirpy than usual. No sign of Gregory or Fraser.

"Where is everybody?"

"Here, boss." Josh emerged from the kitchen, mug in one hand and tuna wrap in the other. Helen's gone to the Mathias house. Eleri died an hour ago. She's gone to see what she can do to help Stefan." The others are checking out the people in those houses we passed.

"Poor bugger. Double funeral." It was a sobering thought. "Does the Super know?"

"Yes. He came to find out how things were progressing." Josh sat down, slurped his coffee and took a bite from his wrap.

"Into a black hole at present. I suppose I'd better go and have a word. Anything to report, Olivia?"

"Still going through the list of runners and checking them out. They weren't in any order, like. I'm about halfway through." She tucked a strand of hair behind her ears as she peered at Mandy. "Some I've been able to talk to. It was a big race. Takes time."

"Keep at it. Seems our only lead for now. I'd better go and see Withers. Tell him about our journey to nowhere."

She went and knocked at the Super's office. A gruff, "Enter" was the response. Withers was jabbing at the keyboard with two stubby fingers, eyes wrinkled in concentration. He didn't even look up. "Any idea how to export data in Excel?"

Despite everything, Mandy had to smile. It seemed everyone these days had to be computer literate and the Super was old school. She offered a few instructions and a few clicks followed. It seemed to do the trick as he mumbled his thanks and turned his attention towards her again.

"The Mathias case. I believe the mother died this morning. DC Probert has gone to offer support. Sad case." He clasped his hands together. "What progress?"

"We are assuming the baby is still alive. It's possible Grace was acting as a surrogate for a childless couple. As the usual age for a woman to act as a surrogate is twenty-one things would need to be conducted covertly. Agencies won't accept anyone under that age. Hence the secrecy."

Withers thought about it. "And the money was her payment?"

Mandy nodded. "There is absolutely no evidence to suggest she was involved in anything dodgy like drug dealing or sex work. She was altruistic in nature. Everyone we've spoken to has attested to her kind and caring nature."

"Not so altruistic if she had ten grand stowed under the bed." He sounded disbelieving. Hardened by years seeing the worst in people.

"The money wasn't for her. It was to get her mother medical treatment in America. Hence all the fund-raising efforts. There was only a slim chance of success. Unfortunately, Eleri Mathias was sicker than they realised. Too late."

Withers seemed to consider before he responded. "I suppose if she did act as a surrogate the child would be safe. With both Grace and Eleri Mathias dead, I wonder if perhaps the investigation needs to be wound down. It's been a couple of weeks. DI Blake has asked when he'll get his officers back. I gather Gregory's been moaning about wasting time."

"DS Gregory is a–" Mandy stopped, pressing her lips together.

"A–?"

"He's disruptive and unprofessional. Constantly making snide remarks and undermining my authority. I can do without him. I feel sorry for Sam Fraser. Gregory's an appalling example of negative policing."

Withers peered at her over his specs and grunted. Non-committal. Then, "I'll tell DI Blake he can have his men back." A smile. "You can tell Gregory and Fraser we no longer require them."

"We can't give up."

"I didn't say to give up, but I think, as all we have are theories, we give it a few more days. After the weekend I'll keep it on review in case anything comes in pertinent to the case. There's plenty of other work. The Roper blackmail case for example."

Of course, the bloody blackmail case. She'd shoved it to one side in the search for a baby who could be dead.

CHAPTER FIFTY-THREE

Helen was pale when she returned from the Mathias home. God knows how Stefan was dealing with it all. What would happen to him now?

"What news? How's he coping?" asked Mandy.

With a shrug Helen replied, "Calmer than I expected. I suppose he's been preparing for Eleri's death for a while. He's organising Grace's funeral and I'm trying to help with the details. It's going to be a miserable Christmas for him."

Mandy's thoughts turned to her sister again. Joy hadn't been in a good place since the termination. She needed something to give her a different focus. A purpose. But what? Then it came to her. A way to solve two things. The old boy who had found Grace was lonely. If she could get Joy around there to call on him, it would make her realise how lucky she was. Bloody genius. She decided to ring Joy straightaway. Sort it.

Joy's voice was flat when she answered the call. Ignoring the lethargic response, Mandy pretended exasperation.

"Hey sis. Can you do me a favour? There's this old boy in Robert Street. Jeff Davis. Lives alone. I told him I'd call in but things here are a bit frantic," she surveyed the quiet office, "and I don't think I can do it. He was a bit shaken up. Yeah. The one who found the body. Take him some biscuits or something will you? Just half an hour chatting. Go on. It's not going to kill you, is it?"

Josh, who was nearby, could hear the over-dramatic sigh before Joy said, "Okay. What number?"

Joy's job in the Spring as a care-worker had brought out her empathetic side. She'd enjoyed the work until lover-boy had called. Mandy had visions of her sister training to be a nurse or social worker. People could change, couldn't they?

"How's it going, Olivia?"

"Mmmm, getting there, I think. Few more phone calls should do the trick. One or two don't seem to have a media presence so it's a bit harder then."

Mandy started sifting through things again. She picked up the book where they'd found the bus ticket. A novel by Daphne Du Maurier, *My Cousin Rachel*. Nia Jones said Grace had been a Du Maurier fan. Mandy remembered reading *Jamaica Inn* a long time ago. Smugglers in Cornwall as she recalled. Maybe she'd read it on her day off. Or watch the film.

There was something itching in the back of Mandy's head. She turned to Josh.

"Any ideas? My gut feeling is still that Grace's baby is alive. So who has it? And where? We thought she'd given birth in the hospital, but we know she got off the bus on the way to Newport and was probably in labour. If you wanted to keep a birth secret, but safe, what would you do?"

"You'd be prepared. A doctor on hand to deal with any complications; equipment for the baby; somewhere quiet so the neighbours wouldn't be suspicious. I don't know."

"Grace knew this was going to happen. From her diary entries she was prepared. If, as we suspect, CR was the person paying her, then CR is the parent. We've been thinking father, but it could be the mother. Equally it could be a gay couple wanting a child. Grace was the provider, the egg donor and incubator and, in return, she had the money to enable her mother to have the treatment." Mandy shook her head. "Imagine how she must have felt. In pain after the birth, parting with the baby and all for nothing. All too late to save her mam. Poor kid."

"Wonder what she'd have done with the money if she'd survived."

"From what we know of Grace she'd probably have set up a charity to help others. I can't imagine her blowing it on an around-the-world trip. I daresay Stefan will do something about that when he gets his head around it."

Glancing at the clock Josh grabbed his coat. "Gotta go. We've got an appointment. Lisa will kill me if I'm late."

"Well, if you're not in tomorrow, we'll know why." She yawned. "Think we could all pack in for today. My eyes feel as though someone put sand in them."

* * *

The lights were on when Mandy got home and music was playing, subdued and soothing melodies. Some sort of piano thing. Not Joy's usual choice. Her sister was in the kitchen, cooking and a welcoming spicy smell filled the air.

"Where's Tabs?"

Joy had both hands in a bowl of something doughy, "Upstairs. Doing her homework, I hope."

"What are we eating? Smells good."

"I've made a spicy lentil and squash stew. This mess is supposed to be dumplings but it's more like playdough." She grinned. "I went to see your old boy, Jeff. He's a bit touchy feely but I distracted him talking about music. Lent me his CD of piano music. He used to play and says it soothes the soul. It took me a while to find something to play it on. I've been in your attic. No bodies I'm glad to say." The raucous laugh that followed made Mandy laugh in response. Joy's mood had improved. "I told him I'd call again. He needs support. He's lonely."

"We've contacted social services. Fingers crossed but everything is so stretched these days. Did he tell you about finding Grace?"

"Yes. He's still so upset about it. He says he used to talk to her a lot. Share confidences. He'd tell her about his wife and Grace talked about her mam. Seems she'd been in touch with some other relatives too."

Mandy reacted to that. "Other relatives? What other relatives? He didn't mention relatives to me. He said she'd met someone and was happy. Bloody hell. Relatives changes the tune a bit."

Joy's bottom lip jutted out. "Didn't say. Just she'd seemed happy about it all but wasn't sure about her mam's reaction."

"Do you think it was genuine? His comments, I mean. He hasn't said anything about relatives before."

"He's a bit forgetful." Joy shrugged. "Bit of an old devil too. I don't know if he was being honest or not. You'd have to ask him yourself, I suppose."

CHAPTER FIFTY-FOUR

DAY ELEVEN

It was still dark when Mandy left the warmth of her house the next morning. She shivered as she scraped the thick layer of frost from the windscreen. The weather forecasters were predicting snow for Christmas, but Mandy couldn't remember the last time there'd been a white one. She was on duty on Christmas Day anyway so they were not having their celebrations until the evening when, she hoped, she would have finished for the day. Joy had asked Jeff if he had somewhere to go on the day. It turned out he had a niece in Bristol who was coming to get him on Christmas Eve, and he was staying with her family until after Boxing Day. It was a relief. In all conscience she wouldn't have been able to leave him on his own for the day. What about Stefan? Had Helen found out his plans? Poor guy.

Richard Gregory was heading towards the station door at the same time as Mandy caught up with him.

"You're back with your usual team again today. We're continuing the investigation, but you aren't required."

He sneered. "Told you it was a waste of time. Chasing ghosts. Think you'd have more sense DDD."

"How DI Blake puts up with you is a mystery."

"He's a good bloke. Knows his stuff. Not into the lost baby crap."

"You're lucky. A few more days listening to your guff and undermining my team and you'd be on a disciplinary."

"Oh, I'm so scared." He waved both hands in front of him, mocking her.

"One day you'll cross the line and when you do, I'll be there to take you down."

As he moved closer she could smell his breath reeking of stale booze, anger vibrating from him. She stood still. Unmovable. Unafraid.

"You'd better watch your back, DI Wilde. I'm coming for you. I don't like being threatened by a–"

"Woman? I'm your superior officer and don't you forget it. Dickhead."

She pushed ahead of him, shutting the door in his face. Leaving him in the cold.

A sense of merriment instead of the doom and gloom of the previous day seemed to have descended on the team. Josh, Helen and Olivia were all beaming.

"Lisa's had the all-clear. The lump's benign." Josh sounded thrilled and relieved and had obviously shared the news with the others.

When had she missed the news that Lisa had a lump. Had Josh told her? This was huge news. Had he been more edgy lately? Not that she'd noticed.

"I didn't know anything about it. When did all this happen?" Mandy shook her head. Brain fog.

"He didn't want to say anything as he thought you had enough to deal with. Your sister and all that." Helen's voice was soft, almost apologetic.

"I'm responsible for your welfare as well as cracking the whip," said Mandy. "I know I can be a right cow at times but bloody hell, I hope you can come to me with worries and problems. We all have shit in our lives."

Josh looked at the floor. "I didn't want to talk about it. Helen wheedled it out of me. She was here when Lisa rang to say she had to go and have a biopsy. I was panicking and she talked to me. I wanted to share the good news with her."

"Right then," said Mandy. "Good to know all's well." She rubbed her hands together. "Back to work and the search for Grace's missing baby. We've got a couple of days before Withers says we have to slow it down," she raised a hand to stop Olivia saying something, "but we've a possible new lead. Jeff Davis says Grace mentioned a relative. Now, as far as we are aware the only relatives are Sîan Mathias and her child – or children. We know she had one child, but she may have had more, married, changed her name or whatever."

"Olivia, carry on with the social media and following up on that aspect." She turned to Helen. "Go and see if you can get anything from Stefan. Old photographs, any letters, postcards, any past addresses for Sîan, whatever he can remember."

As Josh fired up his computer Mandy sighed. She'd need to do something about the bloody blackmail thing but first she wanted to concentrate on what felt like a last-ditch attempt at solving the mystery of the missing baby. Could the HOLMES system help? Unless Sîan had been involved in an incident it was unlikely.

"Think I've got something." Olivia's eyes were staring at her computer as she flicked from one screen to the other. "There's the woman we've been looking for, see here," she pointed then scrolled, "And by here. No tags on social media and we know she spoke to the teacher bloke but in both these pics she's beside this other guy. Look here." She clicked and scrolled again. "We haven't got a tag on him either so no social media presence," she shook her head as Mandy tutted, "but there are only three unaccounted names left on my list." She waved a sheet of paper in the air. "He's gotta be one of these now."

"Do we have contact details?"

"Nah. Just nicknames, I think. Somebody taking the piss. M.Y. Balls, C. U. Swoon and Harry Upp." She smiled as she peered over her specs. "Preferring to remain anonymous."

"I thought they paid a fee or something to do the run. How does it work? Sponsorship?"

"Yeah, sometimes. We might be able to get bank details from Grace's bank if they did it by transfer, like."

"Olivia. You're a genius. We'll see if the bank will give us the contacts."

"Doubt it. Confidentiality and all that code of conduct stuff. We might need to wait and get a court order," said Josh. "Plus, if they weren't keen to give their real names, they may have paid cash on the day. I don't suppose Grace would have denied them the chance to run and donate if they just turned up."

He was right, of course. Any bank would dig their heels in and wait for the paperwork. She'd have to speak to the Super if they couldn't find out by other means.

Where to start with the search for Sîan? They could contact the DWP. With a National Insurance number, they could find her. They didn't even know where she'd gone when she left Cardiff. Maybe they needed another word with Callum Rosser. He knew more than anyone else and maybe he'd remembered something in the interim. They rang to make sure he was at the warehouse before heading out. He sounded positive on the phone and told them he'd found something which could help their search.

Mandy was quiet on the short journey, her mind as frizzy as her hair as she pondered over the case.

"Penny for them, boss."

"What? Sorry, Josh. I'm away with the frigging fairies. We could be on a route to nowhere again. We haven't much to go on, have we? Hunches and rumours. A young woman who should be alive and looking forward to the rest of her life. It's too bloody depressing. There's something about the festive season makes stuff like this seem worse."

Josh sucked a mint and grunted. She wondered how he was feeling about it all. Lisa's health? They weren't even sure if Grace's baby was alive, yet here they were chasing around the city in the hope of a glimmer that would lead them on the path to the truth. Every day Mandy dreaded news that a baby's body had been found. The dogs hadn't found anything in the cemetery, but the infant could have been buried anywhere, by anyone who knew Grace was pregnant.

CHAPTER FIFTY-FIVE

They could see Callum waiting for them as they approached. He was dressed for the weather, a body warmer under a waterproof coat. Although the morning had been frosty the air had warmed to above freezing with just the damp greyness and heavy air of the shorter days of winter. Not long until the winter solstice. A whiff of woodsmoke reached them and Mandy sniffed. It was easy to forget this industrial setting was fringed by housing.

"DI Wilde. DS Jones. Come into the office." He led them through to a small room off the showroom where a laptop was flanked by filing cabinets and shelving. A whiteboard on the wall indicated who was on duty and where fittings were taking place that week. Callum went to his chair behind the desk while Mandy and Josh perched on two metal fold-up chairs which were far from comfortable. A fan heater in the corner expelled dry air, taking the chill off the room.

"I'm glad you contacted me again," he began, opening a drawer and removing an envelope. "After I spoke to you last time, I got to thinking and had a rummage about in some old stuff at home. I'm a bit of a hoarder, see."

Mandy raised an eyebrow and turned her head to survey the pristine office with a look of disbelief. "Really?"

He laughed. "This is work. It needs to be organised. At home it's different. My wife goes spare with me because I won't throw anything out. It goes in the shed eventually. I've two sheds now."

He paused and Mandy was forced to smile. His expression was earnest and the image of two sheds stuffed full of odds and ends amused her.

"You've found something of interest in your shed then?" Josh shifted forward in his seat, nodding towards the envelope.

"Yes. It took a little time, but I found a postcard I had from Sîan years ago. I kept it as it had a picture of Liverpool, the Liver building, on it. I've always wanted to visit Liverpool but never made it yet. How stupid is that? It's only up the road a bit really. I've been to New York but never Liverpool."

He took a battered postcard out of the envelope and passed it over to them. On one side was a photograph, taken from the Mersey ferry they assumed, of the Liver building. One the other side a message.

Hi Callum.
Liverpool at last. Wish you were here? I'm heading
further north in a few days. Got a seasonal job in
the Lake District and then I'll see what happens after.
Maybe I'll meet a millionaire. Ha ha.
Sîan xx

"Did you hear from her again? It's a long time ago."

"There was a parcel with a tea towel a year or so later with a label saying, Made in Scotland. No note or anything but I thought it was from her. We used to argue over whether the Loch Ness monster was real or not. Another place I haven't visited." Callum gazed past them and smiled as he remembered.

"Did you have an address for her?" asked Josh.

"No. When she told me she was leaving she said she'd keep in touch, but she wouldn't tell me where she was in case the old witch came after her."

"'The old witch?'"

"It's what she called her grandmother. They didn't get on. Eleri was the baby and the favourite, but Sîan was expected to do a lot and resented it. They were aways rowing." He gazed ahead, remembering. "Sometimes in the summer we'd hear them at it in the garden. It wasn't a surprise when Sîan upped and left."

"So, you've no idea where she is now?"

He shook his head, a rueful smile on his face. "Inspector, if I knew I'd tell you. I always thought it was a shame Eleri didn't get to know her sister properly. It was a hard thing for both those girls, losing their parents and being brought up in a strict household. Not easy for the grandmother either but she was a tough old bird."

They had a task in front of them to try and trace the whereabouts of Sîan Mathias. Liverpool, the Lake district and possibly Scotland. Easier to find Nessie than Sîan was Mandy's thought, unless through her work record. If she had a series of seasonal jobs, cash in hand, there was the chance she'd kept under the radar.

As they got back into the Juke they slumped into the seats. Mandy hesitated before starting the engine, deep in thought.

Josh asked, "What next? Where do we start? We don't even know if she married. Her surname could be Macduff, Stewart, Campbell or anything else. Which area did she move to? We haven't a hope."

"We start with the DWP. Employment history. And records of births, marriages and deaths. The National Record of Scotland. See if a Sîan Mathias got married and what the surname was changed to. I wonder how far back we need to look?"

"And if she didn't marry?"

"Good question, Josh. She couldn't drop off the radar completely. It may take a bit of time, but we can find something. I'm sure of it."

CHAPTER FIFTY-SIX

Everything was focused on the search for Sîan Mathias. Helen rang the National Records of Scotland Office and received a voice message to say all offices were functioning on reduced hours and to ring back. Olivia tried the 192 database. Nothing. Their best hope was to request information from the DWP, although a response would be a long time coming.

"I've checked social media," said Olivia, "nobody called Sîan Mathias who fits our profile."

"Stalemate. I suppose we'd better look into our good councillor's blackmail case while we wait."

"I've already got some info on the lady in question. Ms Laura Young." said Josh.

They discovered she was off on sick leave and lived in a flat in Cardiff Bay near Century Walk. The wind was biting cold as they hurried from the carpark to the building. After passing the concierge who seemed unconcerned by a police visit, they made their way up to Ms Young's apartment. It was on the fourth floor and Mandy raced up the stairs with Josh trailing behind. Laura Young wasn't what Mandy expected from Gwyn's disparaging remarks. The plain looking little woman who opened the door was a million miles from the femme fatale Gwyn had described – and the woman with a child in Tod's article. Rumour and innuendo sold newspapers. Once they had shown identification, she invited them into the flat. It was as bland as its owner in shades of grey and white, plain walls and few possessions on display. They'd heard the councillor's side of the story so now it was time to hear Laura's.

She asked them to sit on the pale grey sofa while she sat on the matching chair, looking from one to the other with frightened doe eyes. She wore cream joggers and pink sweatshirt with fluffy pink slippers and pulled at the sleeves of the sweatshirt until it covered her hands.

"Do you know why we are here, Ms Young?" asked Mandy.

"Gwyn." Her whisper was almost inaudible. "What's he said?"

"We are investigating his accusation of blackmail. He's been putting quite a lot of money into your bank account over the past few months. We'd like to know why. Perhaps you might tell us your side of the story."

Laura gazed past them towards the balcony and gunmetal grey sky. She sighed and her whole body seemed to shrink into the chair. She did not look a well woman, black rings under her eyes and hair unbrushed and she was thin, to the point of emaciation. Despite the fact it wasn't long past lunchtime there was no smell of food or evidence of anyone having eaten from what they could see of the kitchen dining area. Everything was pristine, like a hotel room. This was a woman with problems of some sort. She said nothing for several minutes.

"Mr Roper said the payments were connected to a skirt in your possession."

The shrieking laughter which greeted the statement unnerved Mandy and Josh. They exchanged glances, unsure now how to proceed. Was Laura unstable? Perhaps they needed a doctor to attend to her obvious distress. As Mandy was contemplating what to do, Laura stopped laughing and began to cry. She gulped before speaking.

"Gwyn Roper is a dirty old man. He's been at it for years. You know why he was giving me the money. Well, I can tell you." Her voice became louder, more strident. "My sister worked for him for a while. She's the nervous type. He kept pushing himself up against her, making lewd remarks and one day he forced her into a corner and masturbated in front of her. She had nowhere to go. It went all over her skirt." She stopped and took a deep breath. "Ella came home that day in a state. Gave up the job. She became depressed and so anxious she couldn't go out without someone with her." Laura glared at them, cheeks ablaze. "You want to know why he gives me the money? It's for my sister's therapy. It doesn't cover all the costs, of course. It's up to me to do the rest."

"I see. Why didn't she report him?"

"Ella has always been highly strung. It was her first job. She didn't know what to do. I got a job in the offices and watched him, spoke to a few others. He's been at it for years the lecherous bastard. I should have just told someone but who'd believe me? None of the others wanted to say anything to back me up. Afraid of losing their jobs. He told me he'd fix for me to get a better paid job so I could pay more of Ella's treatment and then he said I was too thick. I don't regret anything I've done to protect Ella."

She was animated now, eyes sparking and breathing fast and furious.

"If he wants to take me to court then that's fine. I'd be more than happy to expose his little game."

"He doesn't want to prosecute, but we are duty bound to investigate the matter. Blackmail is a serious offence."

"I never asked him for money. When I told him what his behaviour had done to my sister, he was the one who pressed me to take money." Laura blinked as she looked from one to the other.

"Would your sister be well enough to make a statement about the sexual harassment she suffered in his employ?"

A smile lit Laura's face, making her look less agitated. "Ella is making a good recovery. She's been talking to her therapist about it all and working on ways to move forward with her life. She's always lacked confidence but discovered she's got a rapport with young children. I think she's going to train as a nursery nurse." She tilted her head to one side. "In some ways it's made her stronger. If I was with her, she might be able to talk to you."

"I'm sure it would help clear things up," said Josh. "You may be interested to know the councillor has resigned from his position on the council and all his roles connected to the job."

"Not before time. God knows how many young women he has harassed during his term in office."

"Did he threaten you at any point?" asked Josh.

"What do you think?" said Laura. "Why do you think I'm on sick leave? I stood up to him for so long for Ella's sake, but I've been so stressed I've had to take a step back for now. I'm not strong enough to take him to task for what he's done to so many women. I hope you can do something."

"Unless someone is prepared to take the witness stand the CPS may not be able to do anything about it."

A devious thought entered Mandy's mind. CPS might not want to prosecute Gwyn Roper, but a certain reporter might be interested.

"Of course, there are other ways to take him to task." Letting that morsel sink in they took their leave.

CHAPTER FIFTY-SEVEN

Mandy was whistling as she moved at speed down the stairs. Josh tried to keep up.

"What did you mean by 'other ways?'" he asked. "Should you have said that? You're not on one of your crusades, are you?"

Her raucous laugh filled the stairway echoing off the empty walls. As they reached the concierge's office, they saw a familiar figure. Tod Blakeney. He must have followed them the sneaky bastard. Instead of her usual scowl, Mandy grinned at him.

"Afternoon, Tod. Nice to see you."

An astonished look was followed by a slow smile of understanding. Good. One thing about him, he wasn't stupid, and Mandy would be willing to place bets he'd be knocking on Laura Young's door before they reached the car.

In the confines of the Juke, Josh said, "He'll be up there interviewing Laura now. You know that don't you?"

"Yes. She'll have some justice at least. I hope she makes sure Tod pays well for an exclusive."

Josh shook his head. "And I thought the councillor was devious." He chuckled. "What will you tell the Super?"

"The facts. What else?"

They wound their way through the city traffic back to the station. The threatened showers turned into a storm and the wipers were working triple time to try and cope with the deluge. It was worse inside the Juke, sounding as though seagulls in hobnail boots were dancing on the roof. Drains were blocked and the short trip took them twice as long due to diversions. A car had stalled in the floods near the castle and traffic police were out trying to make sense of the chaos. For once, Mandy felt contented with the day's work. She would give the Super the outcomes and when the front page of the paper told the full story of Gwyn Roper and his misdeeds, well she wouldn't be surprised.

The afternoon was spent on the inevitable paperwork. Nothing from the DWP to follow up yet and all the criminals seemed to be keeping a low profile. Mandy's report to the Super had been illuminating.

Withers couldn't keep his face straight when Mandy reported their meeting with Laura Young and the fact Tod Blakeney had followed them. There was a certain satisfaction after all the hot air and threats the councillor had issued. They didn't have to wait for the morning edition as the evening news was full of the scandal. Whatever Gwyn Roper had been doing over the years had been exposed and he was vilified by his fellow councillors. More details of his misdeeds were promised in the following days. His future as a public figure was in ruins. Mandy hoped Laura and her sister Ella felt some satisfaction. Despite the #metoo movement none of his victims were prepared to be the first to give statements to the police. Laura and Ella's names had been kept secret but there was enough scandal to cause a huge fuss.

* * *

When she got home Joy was full of it. "Have you seen this? I always thought he was a good guy. Turns out he was a bit of a groper."

When Mandy didn't comment she said, "Oh my God. You knew all about it, didn't you? It's not linked to the dead girl, is it?"

"You know I can't tell you anything about work but, yeah, I knew about him and no it has nothing to do with Grace." Mandy sniffed the air. "Smells like curry."

"Right first time. Vegetable Biryani and," she paused for effect, "I made onion bhajis from scratch. Tabs is round at Kelly's."

"And you're feeling okay? Keeping busy at least. I'm drained." Mandy was about to say something about Grace's baby but stopped herself in time. There was no point in opening up that train of conversation. "It's not long until Christmas. We should have the tree up at least. It's in the attic. What are your plans for next year?"

"I wanted to talk something through with you. See what you think."

The good feeling Mandy had all day evaporated with Joy's words. What hare-brained scheme had her sister thought of now? She couldn't keep picking up the pieces all the time. She waited for whatever bombshell was about to land on her lap.

"It was seeing Jeff and how lonely he was made me think about it." Joy bit her lip. "I've been thinking about Mam and Dad in Spain and how it must be difficult for them now they're getting on a bit."

Mandy laughed. "They're having a ball. I don't know how Dad wangled citizenship but seriously Joy, they have the life of Riley. I wish I could retire to Spain like right now."

"But they have Nan Betsi to look after as well. She's beginning to get a bit frail."

"At nearly ninety. No big surprise. What the hell are you getting at, Joy?"

"I'm thinking of going over to sort of look after them. I'd take Tabs as well. I know you've done a lot over the last years–"

"Have you spoken to Tabs about it?"

"No, I–"

Mandy could feel the anger rising. "For God's sake, Joy. You've thrown enough shit at that child. Speak to her first before you decide on her future. She's old enough to know the score. You can't just swing back into her life and decide what's best without talking to her. You buggered off and left her. She could have ended up in care–"

"–If Saint Mandy hadn't stepped into the breach."

"Oh, spare me the bloody criticism. I've done everything I can to cope with you and that chip you've got on your shoulder. I've worried myself sick over you – and Tabs. Try looking at life from the other point of view instead of being so bloody selfish. Mam and Dad tip-toed around you and I had to be the 'good girl'. It was always, 'Don't upset Joy. She's a bit highly strung.'. They don't know you turned into a pothead and then came crawling back. Just as well."

Joy stood nostrils flaring as her temper rose. "You can be a total bitch. They always preferred you anyway. And now you've stolen my daughter too."

CHAPTER FIFTY-EIGHT

DAY TWELVE

Mandy went into work early. She hadn't slept well and was willing to do anything to avoid further clashes with Joy. Nothing had been mentioned to Tabitha although she must have felt the tension between them. Joy was a law into herself – selfish in the extreme. Or was it genuine? Their parents were getting on a bit and Nan Betsi wasn't easy. Probably where Joy got her rebellious streak.

None of the rest of the team had appeared and Sam and Richard Gregory had been recalled to their team, much to everyone's relief. Mandy made herself tea and started to sift through the files. They had followed one dead end after another. It was like a search for the Holy Grail. Did the baby exist or was it dead? The uncertainty was the worst thing.

Olivia was the first to arrive, her owl-like specs steamed up with condensation. The end of her nose was red too and she sniffed.

"Got the cold, Olivia? We don't want any bugs spread around here before Christmas."

"No. It's just my nose and coming in from the cold. I'd give Rudolph a run for his money today." She peeled off gloves and a fair isle patterned bobble hat and unwound what seemed to be yards of woollen scarf. "Our boiler's broken down so I'm glad to get in here today, now." She powered up her computer while she hung up her coat.

Helen and Josh came in together, chatting. Such a good team. Everyone with different strengths and all pulling together. She hoped DCI Manning would see the positive side and not be too critical of their methods. Well, her methods really. Had Lucas changed in the intervening years? He'd always been competitive and too risk averse. It seemed to have worked for him as he climbed the promotion ladder quicker than she had.

The DWP came up with a link. Helen imparted the news. "Sîan Mathias worked for a time in Glasgow. There was a period of unemployment and change of surname. Her last address was in Criccieth, North Wales."

"She got around a bit then. Any other information? The address in Criccieth?" asked Mandy.

"No, and no employment history for the last five years."

"And her new name?"

"Jones."

"You've got to be kidding me? How many people called Jones are there going to be living in Wales? For God's sake." Mandy's exasperation was felt by them all. "I was hoping it was going to be something exotic. Jones. Really." She drummed her fingers on the desk. "Okay, ring the station in Porthmadog and see if they can help us out. Is Sîan still there? Maybe she's ill–"

"Or dead," said Josh.

"Ever the optimist. Re-cap. We can discount all our initial suspects as the DNA results were all negative.

None of those men fathered Grace's baby. If we are looking for a woman is there anyone with those initials or, and this could be nothing to do with it, someone called Maisie."

Josh took up the thread. "We're also looking for Sîan Mathias, now Sîan Jones. We've anecdotal evidence that Grace was excited about meeting a relative."

"It's not much to go on and we've restricted time and manpower so anything you think could be useful, no matter how small, please share."

Mandy took the evidence they had into an empty room and spread everything out in front of her. The paper trail. Could Grace have been involved in something dodgy? Escort to some rich man and got pregnant by mistake? The money would be payoff for her silence. But, the baby? At the centre of it all was the missing baby – alive or dead.

Everything was there from day one of the investigation. The diary. Initials CR. Dates noted. Grace's travel mid-month when she would have been ovulating. The final journey when she could have been in labour. Who? Where? Who knew what had happened and where the baby was now?

Mandy picked up the book from Grace's room where the bus ticket had been used as a marker. She flicked it open and then shut it again with an impatient slap, her eyes skimming the title.

"Bloody hell. Bloody hell. That's it."

She almost ran out of the room, along the corridor and came face to face with Withers. He half-growled at her. "Fire drill?"

"No, sir. I think something has just clicked."

With an indulgent smile, the sort one would give to a child, he let her past.

Mandy burst into the room.

"I think I know who CR is." She held the book aloft, a stupid grin over her face. "This is the book Grace was studying and where she had tucked in the bus ticket. Nia Jones told us Daphne Du Maurier was Grace's favourite author. She was doing some sort of special project on her work. This book is called My Cousin Rachel." A pause. "I think CR is Cousin Rachel."

"Wow. That's a bit of a leap," said Josh.

"Not really, now I've had time to think about it. We know Sîan had a child. Callum Rosser told us. I checked over the notes. Rose or Ruth he said. He couldn't quite remember. I think the child was called Rachel and she is the mystery woman in the photographs. She made contact with Grace at an event. Perhaps told her about the soured relationships in the family, begged forgiveness and depended on Grace's altruistic nature to come out quits."

"But to have a baby for someone is taking things to extremes, isn't it?" Josh wasn't convinced. "I mean forgiving someone for something they had no part of – sins of the mothers or grandmother in this case – is one thing. It's a bit of a step to providing them with your baby."

It was a valid point, but Mandy was prepared to counter the objections to her new theory.

"Not *her* baby exactly. If she was acting as a surrogate, she knew she'd have to hand the infant over after it was born. She was carrying someone else's child. Maybe using her eggs or maybe an embryo implanted. And, don't forget, she was being paid for it."

"Quite a bit of money too," said Helen. "All to provide her mother's treatment. The goal was set, and it was the means to an end. Unfortunate it didn't work out."

"Sort of rent-a-womb. Poor kid. Sad, innit?" said Olivia.

"Tragic. I may be off on a tangent again, but something tells me I'm right this time. Let's have another look at the woman you found with no social media, Olivia. Could she be Rachel Mathias or Jones, I wonder."

With a few clicks Olivia brought up the photographs and zoomed in to enlarge the face of the woman. There was nothing remarkable about her. Dark hair and eyes framing an ordinary face, not plain or pretty. The sort of woman who could blend into a crowd without being noticed. And yet, what was it? Mandy was certain she'd seen her somewhere. She stared at the screen for several minutes trying to remember. Then, she shook her head. If it was there, it would come to her.

CHAPTER FIFTY-NINE

Trying to find out about Sîan Jones was more difficult than anyone anticipated. Olivia rang Porthmadog station and spoke to a constable.

"Sorry, I'm new to the area. You'll need to speak to the sarge. Geraint Jones. He's not in yet. Had to take his wife to the doctor first thing. Try again later or I can leave a message. Tell him you want intel."

Mandy was far from impressed.

"How many bloody people are called Jones? For God's sake. You'd think they could do something to help." She thumped the desk and a pen rolled to the floor. "Okay. Let's see what we can dig up in the meantime. Local newspaper. Births, marriages and deaths. Go back five years to last time Sîan was showing a work record. See if anything turns up. I'm going for a walk." She grabbed her coat, leaving the others to do what they could.

As she went out of the front door, head down, she collided with someone on the steps.

"Sorry. What the–?"

Tod held his hands up. "Sorry, Mandy. I may have some information for you, about a certain baby?"

She narrowed her eyes at him as he gestured at the station. Her hesitation must have shown as he said,

"Coffee, perhaps? It'll be quiet in the museum today. All the school trips are over, thank God. Children scare me."

The remark made Mandy laugh. To think of him afraid of anything was not something she'd ever contemplated. They could go back into the station although whatever information Tod wanted to impart was undoubtedly on the dodgy side so best follow his suggestion. They walked along side by side not saying anything. When they'd rounded the corner and were in front of City Hall he grinned.

"Our first date, DI Wilde. Maybe we can go to Winter Wonderland after?"

"Fuck off, Tod. If you're going to play silly buggers, I'm going back to the station now."

"Hey. It's a joke. You'll want to hear what I've got to say if you can stop sulking. Coffee is on me."

"Naturally, except I drink green tea."

Tod opened his mouth to say something and then shut it again. They continued the short walk up the steps to the museum and then down again to the café in the basement. Tod pointed to a table in a quiet corner and Mandy sat watching an elderly couple with a small boy while he ordered. Grandparents on childcare duties she suspected. Something she'd never have to worry about.

She thanked Tod for the drink, cupped her hands around the mug and then said, "Well, what morsels of gossip have you got to feed me with today? This had better be good."

"Let's just say I have a few friends in useful places. I've been seeing a lady who works at the hospital for a while. Nothing serious you understand."

"Do I give a shit? What you do in your free time, or any time for that matter, is no concern of mine. As long as it's legal, of course."

He sniggered. "That would be telling. Lady A, my friend, remembers a young woman coming to the ante-natal unit with an older woman. Late summer. She thinks the younger woman was Grace Mathias. The older woman she recognised as one of the agency staff they used a while ago. She hasn't seen either of them for months."

Mandy closed her eyes and sighed. "What use is that? No names. A possible sighting of Grace Mathias. No confirmation. I think she's taking you for an idiot. Maybe Lady A has more sense than you give her credit for."

With a shrug, Tod said, "Wherever Grace gave birth it wasn't at the hospital."

"And how would you know?"

His grin was wider, showing teeth which were surprisingly even. "I persuaded my friend to have a look at the records. Just to check names, you know. She confirmed no-one called Grace Mathias was registered for ante-natal or post-natal care."

"Hmmm." Mandy's eyes were fixed on the wall behind Tod as she digested the morsel of information. "Confirms what we knew."

"So, am I to have an exclusive on this one?"

"There's nothing to report, is there? I'm in charge and unless you can help with some real information this conversation is over."

"I'm trying to help."

"I've no doubt about it. Who are you trying to help? Yourself, if you ask me. I've no time for this crap." She stood up, ready to leave. "If you want to make yourself useful find Eleri Mathias's older sister. We'd like to speak to her. Maybe a little trip to north Wales would open your eyes a bit. Last known to be working in Criccieth about five years ago. Oh, and thanks again for the tea."

With a vague smile towards the elderly couple, she swept out. With luck he'd take the bait and a little road trip north. It would keep him out of her hair for a while and he did have an annoying way of finding things the police couldn't get. She wondered who Lady A was, poor woman. She shuddered as she contemplated Tod as a partner. He had some redeeming features but most of the time he was a solid pain in the arse.

CHAPTER SIXTY

Josh was on his way out through the door, flushed, almost running as she arrived back at the station.

"What's the rush? Something happened?"

"Too right. Kids have found something floating in the stream by Waterloo Gardens. Probably dislodged by the heavy rain last night. Forensics are down there now."

"Who reported it?"

"Some guy. He said it looked like a dog's body had been wrapped up and dumped. Stinking by all accounts."

"Bit dramatic ringing up about a dog, don't you think?"

"That's what I thought but it had ripped open, and he could see a baby blanket. Pale blue with little sheep. It had been weighted as well. Somebody didn't want it found."

Mandy swallowed. Was it? Could this be the end of the search? Her stomach lurched. All this time she'd been convinced the baby was alive, but Grace had lived close by. It sounded as though whoever disposed of the package didn't expect it to be found.

"Bloody hell. Are you thinking what I'm thinking? Let's move it."

They tumbled into the Juke and headed towards Waterloo Gardens. It was a quiet part of the city, off Newport road with green areas for walkers. A stream ran through the middle, leading from the lake, fringed by mature trees. A few people were hanging about watching the SOCOs as they hauled the bundle out of the water and put it on a sheet of tarpaulin. Rishi was in attendance already and screens set up to avoid prying eyes.

"Can you open it now? I need to know if it's what I think it could be?" asked Mandy, her look intense.

He gave a nod of acknowledgement and prepared to open the package. He was careful as, even though it had been in the water, traces of DNA or fingerprints could remain.

As Josh had said a corner of the package had been exposed and a mud and water-stained dirty cloth could be seen. Patterned with sheep or it could just be blobs. They stood and waited while photographs were taken and measurements. Whatever was inside the packaging was small. With infinite care Rishi cut the string tying it together and peeled off the plastic cover. More photographs, more measurements. At last, it was time to uncover the contents. Lifting one corner of the blanket or cloth he exposed what lay underneath. Mandy saw a flash of white bone and felt herself tense. Not a baby then. A skeleton.

With a rueful smile Rishi called over to them. "It is a skeleton – but not human. A cat."

There was a moment of relief followed by irritation. A bloody cat for God's sake. They'd been called out to uncover the body of a moggy. Who put it in the river and why was another question but one she wasn't going to even try to answer. At least it wasn't Grace's baby.

Although they had been called out on what amounted to false pretences, the SOCO team seemed quite cheery. They had some grim things to face so this would be a bit of light relief for them. The feeling of dread in her stomach had disappeared as well.

CHAPTER SIXTY-ONE

Olivia had news for them. She'd been trawling the Criccieth newspaper archives and come up with something interesting.

"I'm wondering if this is our Sîan, now?" She pointed at the screen. "It's a newspaper report in July, five years ago. Listen here. Headline is Tragic accident kills local resident." She cleared her throat. "The body of local resident Sîan Jones, 52, was discovered on Criccieth beach early this morning. Sîan Jones, who lived on the Porthmadog Road was a strong swimmer according to neighbours. 'We'd often see Sîan swimming in the sea,' said Meredith Pugh, 'even in the winter. She was always there first thing in the morning. Tragedy it is.' An inquest will be held." Olivia looked up. "Think it's Eleri's sister?"

"Almost certainly. Well done, Olivia. I suppose a chat with the local police will confirm. When they bother to ring back."

She was still in a foul mood but intrigued by the snippet of information Tod had offered. It didn't help much except to confirm the presence of a woman. Cousin Rachel? An agency nurse? It fitted with the theory. A nurse would be able to help with the birth and stitch up afterwards. Which agency did the hospital use when they were short-staffed, and would they provide a list to the police?

The phone rang. "Yes, she's just walked in. I'll just transfer the call," Helen pointed to the phone, mouthing North Wales. "Putting you through now."

Mandy picked up the phone. A voice boomed down the line. "Geraint Jones here, Porthmadog station. I had a message you wanted to talk to me. Not often we hear from the big city now. Sorry I wasn't here earlier. The wife's had an awful cough. Keeping me awake, it was, so I had to wheel her in to see the doc this morning."

"Nasty bugs about this time of the year," said Mandy. "We're hoping you can help with tracing a couple of people."

"Of course, Inspector. What are their names?"

"It's Sîan Jones and her daughter. Sîan 's last employment was registered about five years ago with a hotel in Criccieth. We wondered if you knew where she had gone after that. Your constable seemed to think you were more familiar with the local people."

A sound, somewhere between a grunt and a sigh passed before he spoke again. "Bit of a common name around here, that is. Jones, you know. I'm a Jones myself and my sister is called Sîan, but I don't suppose you want to know about her." His laugh made Mandy tense again. The last thing she needed was a bloody policeman with a sense of humour. She managed to stop herself from swearing at him and said nothing, hoping he'd get the message. It seemed to work.

"We've got at least five ladies of the same name. What age are we looking at?"

"Late forties, early fifties we think. My constable has uncovered a newspaper report about a Sîan Jones who was found on Criccieth Beach, July five years ago. May fit our profile. Can you fill us in on that?"

"I remember it well. Rum do, it was. Woman had moved here a few years before. Friendly enough but kept herself to herself, you know. Bit of a fuss at the time as they suspected foul play at first. Lot of outsiders that time of the year you know, from over the border. Strangers. The coroner called for an inquest. Very upsetting for everyone. Kept people off the beach for a few days too as there were rumours of a shark."

"Really?" Mandy tried to keep the sarcasm out of her voice.

"Nonsense, it was. Poor woman had a heart attack and drowned was the verdict. No evidence of anything else."

"Any family?"

"She had a daughter living away as I recall. Came back to sort everything out and then left."

"Do you remember the daughter's name? What age would she have been at the time?"

There was a long sigh followed by silence. For a minute Mandy thought the line had gone dead before Geraint spoke again.

"Now you're asking. She wasn't about much. I can't remember. I could ask about and see if anyone knows. Is that who you're looking for? Missing, is she?"

Weariness came over Mandy in waves. It sounded like Sîan Mathias or Jones was the dead woman but best to check, just in case.

"You said you had five ladies called Sîan Jones? Any of the others around that age?"

"Only one person I know, and she's lived in Criccieth since she was born. Never moved away like some of them. Young people these days want the bright lights. They don't appreciate what they've got here. I'll see if I can find out anything else and get back to you if I do, Inspector Wilde."

She wasn't sure if anything Geraint Jones found out would help but it was best to keep the option open.

"Thank you," she said, then, "could the daughter's name be Rachel?"

She could hear the smile in Geraint's voice. "Well now, I do believe you're right. Biblical name for sure and it rings a bell. Could be. I'll look into it."

With some relief, Mandy ended the call. It seemed almost certain the Sîan Jones found dead on Criccieth Beach was Eleri's sister. Tragic indeed. Not much luck for that family. First the parents, then the offspring and their offspring. Perhaps Rachel Jones would be the one to break what seemed to be the circle of bad luck.

"Another dead end?" asked Josh. "We seem to be getting no-where fast, especially as we don't even know if the baby survived."

"We have *something* to go on. Rachel lived away from home."

"Where?"

CHAPTER SIXTY-TWO

Brooding was one of Mandy's things. Sometimes if she thought long and hard enough, inspiration would come to her. Today, it eluded her. With some reluctance she acknowledged they might never find what had happened to the baby. She decided to swing by and check on Jeff Davis on her way home. It was a selfish move. She hoped seeing someone in a worse frame of mind than herself might make her feel better. As predicted, Jeff was delighted to see her. Only, it wasn't her he expected.

"Joy. Lovely surprise. Come in. It's a miserable night."

Mandy opened her mouth to correct his mistake and then thought better of it. Might confuse him too much and besides it could be fun to play the old games where she used to swap roles with her sister. It hadn't always worked out but what the hell. If Jeff cottoned on or became upset, she could beat a hasty retreat.

"Sit down, cariad. I'll make us some tea and a slice of the lovely lemon drizzle cake you brought last time. There's a bit left."

With some relief Mandy sank into the fireside chair and closed her eyes. It had been a long day, or so it seemed, without much progress. With the heat from the gas fire and the exhaustion she must have drifted off. She woke when Jeff shook her arm to rouse her.

"Now then, you've had a bad day again. I can see that. It's hard this time of year. So dark and all that. My Lily hated the winter. She lived for the summer days. I didn't understand when she was with me but now," he sighed, "now I know."

He handed Mandy a cup and saucer with milk added to the tea, the way Joy liked it. She thanked him before he indicated a plate with cake. "Help yourself, my dear."

With a thin smile, Mandy took a slice. The flavour was divine. Sweet but with a bitterness. She'd always thought of lemon drizzle as being too saccharine, but this hit the spot, and it seemed to melt on her tongue. Even the milky tea tasted less cloying than usual. Perhaps her tastes didn't differ too much from those of her twin.

"How have you been, Mr Davis?"

He chuckled. "Oh, come now, Joy. I thought we'd got over all the formalities. It's Jeff, remember."

"Sorry. Force of habit."

He didn't comment on it, seeming to concentrate on his slice of cake and staring into the flames of the gas fire. They sat for several minutes in companiable silence, each lost in their own thoughts.

"Grace never came here."

It was an unexpected statement and Mandy wasn't quite sure of the significance until he put a hand on her knee and kept it there with an expectant look on his face.

"Lily knew I liked young people, but she turned a blind eye you see. But Grace, she was canny. She knew. And I knew that she knew so we were both safe with each other's secrets."

The drowsiness had worn off. Mandy was on high alert, aware of every breath and of the need to keep him talking. Although Jeff Davis looked like a harmless old man, she was in his home and God knows what was in the cake or the tea. She reached into her pocket for her phone.

"Grace told me all about the baby. She said she was going to call it Lily, after my wife. She liked flower names she told me. Names like Daisy, Fleur, Rose and the like."

Despite the almost overwhelming desire to get out, Mandy needed to hear what he had to say.

"Pity about it all. Went wrong, didn't it?"

Mandy swallowed, her throat feeling tighter by the second. She forced herself to speak. "What went wrong, Mr Davis?"

"If I'd got there earlier, she'd still be alive, wouldn't she? Grace died because I was too late." He started to sob then, heaving shoulders and red-eyed with tears coursing down his lined cheeks.

"Had you arranged to meet Grace that morning? The day you found her? Were you supposed to be there for some reason?"

He stopped sobbing, the shrewd look back in his eyes.

"Why are you asking me these questions? What is it to you? You didn't know Gracie. Sweet girl. Lily liked her too. She'd take flowers and sit by the grave and talk to her. Lily told me she was a good 'un, not long for this life. 'The good die young,' my Lily used to say. Is it time for tea yet? Shall I make some tea?"

The look in his eyes had changed again, almost glazed over and looking past Mandy instead of at her. It was disconcerting and she wondered about his mental state. Who was Jeff Davis? The kind and gentle old man, the predatory old lecher or the confused person in front of her?

"I've got to go now. Tabitha will be expecting me home."

"Tabitha, your cat." He blinked then said, "I remember now. You must bring her to see me. I like young people."

No bloody way would Tabitha ever cross his threshold.

Jeff made no attempt to stop her as she left, just sat staring at the gas fire.

Once outside Mandy gulped a breath freezing air. Her scarf, wrapped around her mouth would be wet with her breath before she'd even got to the car. What the hell had just happened in there? All her instincts were on alert. Tomorrow she'd find out a bit more about Mr Davis.

* * *

The sound of laughter greeted her as soon as she entered the hallway of Brithdir Street. Kelly was there. She recognised the giggling. It was a relief to hear Joy's raucous laugh as well. She entered the room to find Kelly with her back to the door and both Tabitha and Joy creased with laughter.

"Hey, what's so funny?"

When Kelly turned, she could see the root of the laughter. She had thick face make-up on. The result was far from flattering.

"I went and had a free make-over from my Mam's friend," she said. "She hasn't got a clue. I look like a clown." Far from being upset the girl seemed to find it funny. "I'm going to do a TikTok video but wanted to try it out on Tabs first."

"She's a natural comic," said Joy. Then, noticing the pallor of Mandy's face and the tension in her body she asked, "Are you okay? You looked wiped out, sis."

"Long day and complicated."

When Kelly's mother arrived to collect her, Mandy noticed someone lurking on the street corner. Was it the lad again? No, it couldn't be. After a quiet word with his solicitor, she had the assurance that it had all been bravado and nothing to worry about. As Mandy watched, a girl came out of the house opposite and, when she reached the lad, gave him a hug. Nothing to do with Mandy or her family. She rubbed her tired eyes. This case was taking its toll. She was becoming paranoid.

It wasn't until later, after dinner, when Tabitha was upstairs doing her homework that Mandy asked, "What are your thoughts about Jeff Davis?"

"He's lonely. Likes women. Bit odd at times but could be his age, losing it a bit perhaps. Why?"

"Bit too free with his hands?"

Joy's eyes widened and then she started to chuckle. "Oh my God. He made a pass at you. Dirty old bugger. Did you knee him in the balls?"

"No, but I don't think he's the sweet old guy I first assumed. There's more behind the façade."

CHAPTER SIXTY-THREE

DAY THIRTEEN

The ice and sub-zero temperatures were back with a vengeance. The road sparkled and crunched underfoot. The car was dusted with frost making intricate patterns as if a spider had been making webs all night. The morning air had a crispness about it and her breath made little puffs as she cleared the ice from her car. The incident with Jeff Davis had annoyed her more than she liked. She was used to dealing with the dregs of society; people who would kill their Granny for the next fix or sell their sister for a sports car. She thought she was a good judge of character, so Jeff's strange remarks made her more than a little uneasy. Maybe she was losing her touch. She'd have a word with his social worker and find out a bit more and there would be no more visits – not until it was sorted.

As soon as she got to the office Helen approached looking worried. "Is it okay if I skip off at lunchtime, please? We ordered this new game all the kids are raving about, and it was supposed to be delivered. Then we had an email this morning saying delivery was not possible until after the New Year." She hesitated, "Or, I can pick up at their warehouse off Penarth Road before four today. I don't want to disappoint the boys. Tom has some lunch thing with his doctorate students so he can't do it."

It was unusual for Helen to ask for a favour and the first one to go the extra mile when it was needed. "No problem, Helen. Nothing's moving fast with this investigation anyway. Go and play Santa. We'll cover."

The anxious look vanished. "Thanks, boss."

The phone rang and Mandy recognised the booming voice of Geraint Jones.

"Inspector Wilde. I've got a little titbit of information for you. Mrs Pugh, lives two doors down from where Sîan Jones was renting, says she thinks Rachel had gone away to do nurse training. Somewhere across the border." The way he said it made England sound like a foreign land. "Maybe Liverpool. She wasn't too sure on that. She was sure about the name though. You were right. Rachel." She could hear the smile in his voice and imagine his satisfaction at being about to impart the information.

"Very helpful. Thanks. Do you know if Rachel had the Jones surname as well. Sîan used to be Mathias."

"No. I'm pretty sure it was Jones. Mrs Pugh would have said if there'd been anything like that." He chuckled.

"Anything else?" asked Mandy. "Any idea where Rachel is now? Do you think she stayed in Liverpool or went somewhere else after training?"

"Well, now. I was coming to that. It's difficult to say. Mrs Pugh is, how can I put it politely?"

"A bit of a gossip?"

Geraint chortled again. "Now I couldn't possibly say that, could I? But she's a little prone to sticking her nose in and folk around here, well, they know it see, and spin her a yarn. You need to take anything she says with a pinch of salt."

"Or a barrelful by the sound of it. Are you going to tell me what Mrs Pugh implied?"

"Oh, of course, Inspector Wilde. She thought Rachel was going to go back to Scotland. Mrs Pugh had the impression there were relatives there, or friends or some connection. Could be true or could be a fantasy. If I hear anything else, I'll let you know."

"Thank you. It's something to follow up."

"News?" asked Josh when she put the phone down again.

"Could be. Sîan Jones was Sîan Mathias, Eleri's sister. Her daughter was called Rachel. She would be Grace's full cousin. I think she's the woman in the photos and CR. She's the one we've been looking for. I bet she knows about the missing baby. And, she trained as a nurse."

"She would be able to stitch Grace up after the birth," said Josh. "But if she was a trained nurse how come she missed part of the placenta?"

"It was a small fragment. Enough to cause extreme pain but not enough to be noticed it seems. The sarge in Criccieth seems to think Rachel trained in Liverpool. Best place to start. He's not sure if she went to Scotland after the funeral. Possibly relatives there."

"Three big hospitals in Liverpool and the dental hospital and all," said Olivia, who had picked up on the conversation and had started to search for information.

"Right. We start there. Find out if they've had a Rachel Jones qualify as a nurse in the last ten or twelve years."

Why ten years?" asked Josh.

"I'm making an educated guess. Looking at the age difference between Sîan and Eleri and taking that as a guide. I could be wrong. But we've got to start somewhere. Sort out tasks, will you Josh? I need to speak to Social Services."

Mandy was annoyed with herself. Was Jeff Davis just a randy old bugger who was stringing them along for attention or was there something else going on. She rang Social Services, expecting to be fobbed off but was put through to Jeff's social worker.

"How can I help, Inspector? I believe you alerted us to Jeff's condition a couple of weeks ago. Finding the dead girl traumatised him. We have been aware of his increasing needs over the last six months. Was there something that worried you?"

Where to start? Mandy explained about her sister visiting with a food parcel and about her own visit the previous evening.

"I found his attitude bordering on the suggestive. In my job we need to be able to assess individuals and situations with speed so when he put a hand on my knee and started talking about liking young people, I found it unnerving. Out of character from my earlier acquaintance with him. He'd seemed a genuine and charming old man, but the sexual innuendoes were clear. Now, I'm not sure whether to believe anything he says."

A sort of low breathing noise over the line indicated he was thinking about his response. At last, he said, "Jeff has early-stage vascular dementia. Some days he can be lucid, and no-one would suspect anything wrong. Other days he's all over the place. As I said, Grace's death upset him, and we've been particularly worried."

"This talk of liking young people. I've checked him out and he hasn't got a blemish on his record."

"It's his fuddled brain. Often dementia changes people. The mild become aggressive and the quiet become more sexual in their comments and actions. We've had patients strip off and wander the streets. Those people would never have done that if they were mentally competent."

"I see. At least I think I do."

"It's a dreadful disease. Some people become so ill they are frightened by their own reflections. It's quite bizarre. I can assure you the kind, gentle old man you first met is the real Jeff Davis. He started to slip after his wife died. It often happens."

It was a relief in some ways although it threw into shadow all the information Jeff had fed them about Grace.

"This niece of his, is she aware of the deterioration?"

"Indeed. We keep her apprised of the situation. She works with young children and says the situation is very similar. Safety and security are essential. She's very knowledgeable. It's still in the early stages."

CHAPTER SIXTY-FOUR

The aroma of mince pies permeated the air in the station. One of the local bakeries had sent over a fresh batch and they were disappearing quicker than a thief at a police conference. A few Christmas decorations hung limp and tired, a reminder of the festive season.

By the end of the morning, they had a list of seventeen nurses called Rachel Jones who had qualified in Liverpool during the last few years and photographic evidence taken from the records. Some of the photographs were a little blurry but they were accompanied by addresses and destination after gaining their training qualifications. As they worked their way down the list Olivia was distracted by one of the photographs.

"There's something about this one. I've seen her before. Hang on, let me check now." She clicked the keys and a different data base appeared on her screen. Helen had left and Mandy and Josh were occupied with double-checking details to ensure the accuracy of the paperwork. If they couldn't trace the baby, then they needed to make sure every avenue had been explored and their records illustrated the huge effort they'd put into finding it.

"Oh my God, it's her, it is. Look." Olivia pointed to the screen where the social media photos had been labelled and ticked off as each person was contacted. Painstaking work. "It's the mystery woman who was beside Christopher Robin at the race. I'm pretty sure it's her. She's got her hair down and it looks a bit darker. What you think, boss?"

Both Mandy and Josh looked from one photo to the other.

"Hey, Liv. I think you're right. Bit plumper around the jaw but it could be the same. Do you think?" asked Josh.

Mandy hadn't responded, staring at the screen as if she'd never seen the photograph before. "I've seen her somewhere. Recently too. I'm damned if I can remember where."

"At the hospital when you were with Joy? Maybe she's working at the Heath. Should we check?"

Frowning in concentration, Mandy said, "It wasn't there. I must be losing it. I can't recall the situation but I'm certain it was her. How could I have walked past cousin Rachel and not noticed?"

"Because we were looking for something or someone else at the time."

"It's bugging me. We passed her somewhere." Mandy yawned. "I just can't remember when or where."

"Let's hope it comes back," said Josh. "Well spotted, Liv. Now we've got a name see what else you can find about her."

"I don't think having a name will make a difference. She don't do social stuff. That's why it was so hard to find out anything. I'll keep looking."

* * *

The air in Bute Park was almost too fresh, with a sharp wind that made Mandy feel as though she'd had her cheeks slapped. No germs could survive in air so cold, and the sky was heavy with snow, at least for the hills. Caerphilly mountain would have a sugar coating by morning. Mandy needed to walk, clear her mind and try to remember where she'd seen Rachel Jones.

She stomped around Bute Park for half an hour, admiring the fairy lights and witnessing the excitement of young children, hyped up ready for Santa, or Siôn Corn as he was known in Wales, to visit. Tabitha had been three when the excitement of Christmas first became obvious. She'd played Angel Gabriel in the school nativity, her voice clear and chubby face alight with excitement. Mandy remembered the tears, mirrored by Joy's over-bright smile and glittering eyes.

As soon as she got back into the office Josh alerted her to trouble. "Withers was looking for you. He wants you in his office as soon as possible – yesterday preferably he said. What have you done now?" Josh tried hard to cover a smile.

"He probably wants to congratulate me for a year's wonderful work and suggest I take a week in Barbados on expenses." They both laughed. A loud cough from Olivia alerted them to the presence of the Super.

"I asked for you to come to my office as soon as you got in and I find you giggling like a schoolgirl. What's so damned funny?"

"A week in Barbados, sir."

The Super was not well-known for his sense of humour and Mandy thought it best not to explain any further.

"You wanted to see me, sir."

"My office, now. Tidy yourself up a bit." He waved his hand in a circular motion at the side of his head.

"Your hair," mouthed Josh.

A glance in the glass door gave Mandy some idea of her reflection and she ran her fingers through her hair, flattening it down again. The static in her beanie hat had caused it to stick up and she looked like the proverbial mad professor.

She could see someone was already in the Super's office, sitting upright with his back to the door. The back of his head showed well-trimmed hair, a few grey hairs sprinkled among the dark brown and thinning a little on the crown. Had the Super been expecting anyone? Was there-someone she'd pissed off enough in the last couple of weeks who had come in to complain?

Withers went and sat down, indicated for Mandy to close the door and sit in the empty chair. Only when she came face to face with the mysterious man did she realise who it was.

With a little cough, Withers made the introductions, or at least an attempt at doing so.

"I believe you are already acquainted with DCI Lucas Manning. As you know, DCI Manning is shadowing your team for a month from the beginning of January. He was visiting family in the area and thought it could be helpful

to come and meet the team. Break the ice a little before
he starts."

CHAPTER SIXTY-FIVE

"Miranda. It's been a long time."

No-one, other than the Super, called her Miranda. Lucas had always insisted it was a pretty name, magical even, and refused to use the shortened version.

He'd aged was her first thought. Then so had she in the last sixteen years. His eyes had laughter lines etched more deeply than she remembered, and his chin more flab, but she'd have known him anywhere. It was a miracle she'd managed to avoid him all this time. Her mouth opened and closed but her brain wouldn't engage so no words emerged.

"I hope you don't mind the intrusion." He almost seemed to purr, in the deep, melodic voice she remembered so well.

As if she'd any choice in the matter. Given half the chance she'd have been out of the door and halfway home, without a backward glance. Instead, she was sitting too close to the man who had walked out on their engagement and made a fool of her. When she didn't respond Lucas continued.

"Superintendent Withers has been getting me up to speed with your latest case. Intriguing. I'd be interested to look at what you've got and see if I can be of any assistance. I've dinner with my aunt this evening, you remember Muriel, but I can spare an hour to go over the headlines and meet the team."

Mandy opened her mouth to say something sarcastic, thought again and pinned on a false smile. Her professional face.

"Of course, sir." She put particular emphasis on the last word so he would realise this was strictly business. She was over him. Referring to his aunt was a dirty trick. She'd got on so well with Muriel. In fact, she'd lost more than a fiancée when they'd split up as she'd been too embarrassed to continue the relationship with his aunt.

Withers wittered on about the work of the department, how delighted he was with this liaison between different areas of the force and so on while Mandy took low steady breaths. What a bloody hypocrite the Super was. No doubt Lucas turning up unannounced had pissed him off too. Just what they didn't need at the mouth of Christmas. Silence in the room alerted her to the fact she'd switched off and had lost the thread of the conversation.

"Isn't it correct?" asked Withers, addressing her. Lucas watched as she wrestled with her thoughts. What the hell had the Super said?

"Yes, sir." Best to agree.

"I suggest you take DCI Manning to meet the team he'll be working with in the New Year."

"Of course, sir." Easy to do. Action was better than the brain fog she was experiencing. She stood and Lucas stood too. Even though Mandy was almost six foot tall, Lucas had a couple of inches on her. He moved to one side, and she brushed past, not pausing to see if he was following. Her whole body felt tense. She knew she'd have to see him again, but this was being taken by ambush and Mandy was not happy about any of it.

Josh and Olivia looked up from their screens as Mandy entered, Lucas in tow. Josh raised an eyebrow. Neither of them moved.

"I'd like you to meet DCI Lucas Manning from North Wales Constabulary. He will be shadowing our team in January, but he thought he'd give us a little surprise by popping in to say hello and wish us a Happy Christmas." There was no disguising the sarcastic tone of Mandy's voice.

Both eyebrows were raised now as Josh said, "Good afternoon, sir," rising from his chair and offering his hand, "DS Josh Jones."

Lucas shook his hand and turned to Olivia who looked like a doll beside the DCI. "You must be DC Wyglendacz."

The Super had already given him the set-up. He knew their names and no doubt would be checking their records before starting in January. Methodical was the Manning way to work. He was less intuitive than Mandy, less inclined to blur the lines. He'd get on well with Josh. Two of a kind.

"I believe there's another member of the team?" Lucas looked around and spotted Helen's empty desk.

"DC Probert is our liaison officer in the case we are working on at present, sir." No need for him to know Helen was off collecting her children's Christmas gift. Let him think she was doing her duty elsewhere.

"Yes. The dead girl and the mystery of the missing baby. Intriguing. Do you want to talk me through where you are with it?"

Again, no choice. Lucas was the superior officer, so they spent the next hour outlining the facts, their leads and what they had discovered. He asked searching questions, frowning now and again as he listened.

"We're trying to find the whereabouts of Rachel Jones, Grace's cousin," said Mandy. "We believe she has some connection to the case."

"Bit of a wild card, I'd say." Lucas gave her a look which seemed to indicate she was making a mistake. It annoyed Mandy, but she bit her lip and remained silent, trying not to clench her fists.

"I expect you've done the cross-checking of all her associates and those Grace Mathias has had any contact with during the last year and more. One can't be too meticulous with these things. It's the paper chase that often brings results rather than hunches."

It was a direct challenge. Mandy could feel her face flushing as she tried to maintain her professional persona.

"Of course, sir. We've checked and double checked. I have an excellent team."

A slight twitch of his lips told her it had been a deliberate effort to annoy her. January was going to be a long month if that was the game he intended to play.

After what seemed an eternity, Lucas glanced at his watch before smiling warmly. "Lovely to meet you all. I'll look forward to working with the team in January. Right now, I've got a dinner date with my aunt."

"Seems a nice enough bloke," said Josh when he'd left. "I expect we'll all learn a bit from him."

"Maybe he'll wave a magic wand and make it all happen, now." Olivia seemed less impressed and was watching Mandy's face. It seemed she had sensed the tension and was curious. Well, she'd just have to ignore her curiosity. She wasn't about to divulge her past when it wasn't relevant. Joy was a different matter. No doubt her sister would have something biting to say about men in general and Lucas in particular.

CHAPTER SIXTY-SIX

DAY FOURTEEN

It was typical funeral weather. Heavy leaden sky and an East wind that seemed to cut through clothing like a hot spoon in ice-cream. At least it was dry, and the sun was making a valiant attempt to break through the cloud.

The atmosphere was sombre. Superintendent Withers was suited and booted ready to make a statement to reporters, although Stefan had requested no press or photographers at the interment. A short statement had already been released to the media.

"Everything go alright with DCI Manning yesterday?" He was addressing the team, but his eyes were fixed on Mandy. His concern, while touching, made her squirm. She said nothing, a slight nod of the head.

"He seemed a decent bloke, sir," said Josh. "He was really interested in the case and asked lots of questions. It will be a bit different having someone else working with us in the New Year."

"He's supposed to be observing not interfering. Shadowing the team not taking control. I don't suppose I need to remind you of that, do I Wilde? Your team, your rules."

Had he winked? Mandy wasn't sure but his eyes had crinkled at the corners and there was a definite twinkle in them.

"Right, let's get to this funeral." He was all business.

Stefan had decided in the end to have a Humanist service and woodland burial for both Eleri and Grace. A broken man, he was going to go back to Poland as soon as the business of the house and contents had been decided. The money Grace had raised was given to a charity specialising in brain disorders and her name attached to the donation.

Olivia had opted to stay in the station in case any further information came through. Sometimes, with the press coverage, someone would remember something or someone they thought was significant.

Stefan, with Helen's help, had organised for the two willow coffins, to be driven to the burial spot in a horse-drawn carriage. Two white horses with plumes trotted along adding an almost surreal feeling to the occasion. Mandy, Josh, Helen and Ross Withers followed behind the other attendees.

A surprising number of people turned up at the meadow where the service was to take place. It was a beautiful spot, an open field with mature trees, a few copper leaves still sprinkled under bare branches and stunning views towards the city. Sunil and Ashley clung to each other and other schoolfriends huddled together, faces strained and almost disbelieving. Mandy recognised a few of the neighbours and Callum, Christopher and the councillor were there. A couple of Grace's teachers had also made an appearance, exchanging words as they arrived at the scene. They spotted Nia Jones talking to her successor, Gemma Cooper. One woman stood a little apart from them. She was a slight build and wore a large, brimmed hat and scarf which covered half her face to protect her from the wind, no doubt. Mandy edged a little closer to her.

The service was moving. Grace's teachers read poems, one of her former classmates recalled some funny incidences where Grace, Sunil and Ashley had got into trouble for playing tricks. Callum Rosser talked about Eleri, her strength, resilience and kindness in nursing her grandmother during her dying days. He also made tribute to Stefan and his devotion to Eleri. It wasn't depressing. On the contrary it seemed uplifting.

It was a short ceremony and when people began to drift away Mandy kept an eye on the woman in the hat. A sudden gust of wind blew the hat off and as she bent to retrieve it the scarf slipped, exposing her face. Mandy recognised her immediately. She hurried over to the woman's side.

"Rachel," she said, "You are Rachel Jones, aren't you?"

CHAPTER SIXTY-SEVEN

For a second it looked as if the woman was going to bolt. She glanced all around as if looking for an escape route. Realising she was caught she replied, "My name's Rachel. It's Rachel McGregor."

Mandy was sure of herself now. She challenged the woman. "You're Grace's cousin. Sîan Mathias was your mother. We've been looking for you."

"Who's been looking for me? Who are you?" Her voice had risen a little. It was difficult to tell if she was indignant or afraid.

Mandy pulled out her ID. "Detective Inspector Wilde. We're investigating circumstances leading up to Grace's death. We'd like to speak to you concerning the matter."

Rachel indicated the funeral party now dispersing as they descended the slope. "I don't think this is the time or the place for a discussion, do you? Now, if you'll excuse me, I need to get home."

"Not before I have your contact details, please." To hell with it. This woman was not going to escape her grasp after the merry dance they'd had up until this point.

Rachel rattled off a telephone number. "We live at Bluebell Cottage near–"

"– Whistletop Farm. I know it. We'll call tomorrow morning – unless, of course, you'd rather come into the station."

Rachel closed her eyes and took a deep breath. "I'm not an early riser in the winter. About noon, perhaps?"

The aplomb of the woman was amazing. Anyone would think she was talking about a manicure appointment or arranging a lunch date instead of an informal interview with the police. Perhaps she had nothing to do with Grace's death after all. Maybe she knew nothing about the baby. And maybe the sky was green with purple dots.

"Tomorrow, Mrs McGregor. We'll see you at Bluebell Cottage in the morning."

"Someone you know?" asked Josh when she caught up with the others.

"Cousin Rachel. And guess where she lives? Bloody Bluebell Cottage. Right under our noses the whole time. Can you believe it? We're speaking to her in the morning. There's something I want to check first."

* * *

When they got back to the station Mandy asked Olivia for the list of registered births again. She skimmed down the page before grunting in satisfaction.

"I thought not."

Olivia raised her eyebrows.

"No baby McGregor listed yet. We've found Sîan's daughter, Grace's cousin. If CR is Cousin Rachel, it could be that Grace was acting as surrogate for her cousin. It strikes me if Grace was regularly getting the Newport bus and getting off at The Dog and Bone, she was less than half a mile from Bluebell Cottage. It's where Rachel and Ian have been living for the past couple of years."

"You're allowed forty-seven days to register a birth, though. And if Rachel is a nurse, it could be Grace was just going to be checked out, like. If she wanted to keep things under the radar that is."

"My gut tells me otherwise. I need some more information from Nia Jones. I don't suppose she'll be back from the funeral do yet."

For the next hour Mandy paced up and down, checking and rechecking all the notes she'd made. Rachel McGregor was the person who could help them solve this case. She hadn't denied being Grace's cousin, there would have been no point, but she wasn't exactly thrilled to be questioned either. When she rang the farm, Nia's husband answered, his voice gruff and wary. They could hear the baby screaming in the background.

"Now's not a good time," he said, "colic. I'll get her to ring you back in an hour or so."

Frustrating, but nothing they could do about it except wait. Nia was under no suspicion or obligation, except her moral duty, to answer their queries. When the phone rang Mandy pounced on it.

"I wanted to ask you about your neighbours, Rachel and Ian. I noticed Rachel was at the funeral today. How well did she know Grace?"

"She didn't say much except that Ian had run a couple of the sponsored races and she had spoken to

Grace. She seemed quite upset. More than I would have expected for a brief acquaintance."

"Do Rachel and Ian have any family?"

"Yes. I hadn't realised she was pregnant again. She lost a baby just before I became pregnant and said it was her second miscarriage. But now they've got their little one. Maybe that's why she was so teary. Giving birth plays havoc with your hormones and the exhaustion. No sleep and constant feeding are a killer."

An unfortunate choice of word Mandy thought. Grace Mathias didn't have the opportunity to experience true motherhood. She blinked away the thought and asked, "How old is the baby?"

"Very young, I think. In the past month from what she said. She was a bit reticent to be honest but then we're neighbours and usually only exchange pleasantries. And a funeral isn't exactly the place to be talking babies. Lovely service I thought. So sad."

Mandy agreed, asked a couple more questions about Rachel and Ian to confirm what they already knew. Rachel had trained as a nurse. She was Welsh by birth, but her mother had married in Scotland and Rachel had relatives there. Ian was from outside Glasgow and worked remotely so they could move around the country. She'd lost her mother about five years previously. Nia didn't have details.

CHAPTER SIXTY-EIGHT

DAY FIFTEEN

At eight the next morning Mandy rang Josh.

"Ready for a visit to Bluebell Cottage?"

"What? I've only just got out of the shower. What's the rush? Thought Rachel said about noon?"

"She did. I think she was trying to pull a fast one. Get your arse in gear and get down to the station. See you in ten."

"Right, boss."

Joy appeared in the kitchen as Mandy was buttering her wholemeal toast. She looked tired despite having ten hours in bed. She yawned and sniffed the air.

"Early start, Mand?"

"Yeah. Gut feeling. How are you? You look like shit."

Joy made a snorting sound. "Thanks, sis. You really know how to make me feel good. I'm not sleeping. Keep thinking about the baby, you know."

It was hard for everyone. Mandy's first instinct was to wrap her arms around her sister and allow her to wallow in despair. She'd experienced the physical pain her sister had endured but the mental anguish was Joy's. She tried to imagine how depressed Joy must be feeling. Mandy also knew that it was essential to keep Joy occupied. What did they call it? Tough love.

"I understand you feel crap, but your daughter is upstairs asleep, and she needs you more than you realise. Do try, Joy. She's a real superstar that kid. I love her to bits and although I understand you need to grieve over a lost baby you also need to give that girl some idea of how important she is. To you and to me both. Don't fuck up with this one. It's too important." She grabbed a slice of toast in her hand and handed the plate with a second slice to Joy. "Now, I've got to go. And don't forget to keep an eye out for that lad I told you about."

"I saw him yesterday, hanging about. Tabs was with me. Turns out he used to go to her school. Got in with the wrong gang and wasted his schooling. She didn't seem bothered by him. His mate is the bad 'un according to Tabs. She says what's his name," she scratched her head as she tried to remember, "wants to go back to college and learn plumbing. Maybe he could fix that dripping shower head."

"God forbid. He threatened me. I've had words with his brief to make sure it was empty threats. Just be careful."

"He seemed okay. Shouted sorry to me across the street. Do you think–"

"Mistaken identity? Sure. His brief has put the fear of hell in him then. Good. One problem solved."

She left Joy standing open-mouthed while she donned coat and boots and made a getaway. Having her sister back was wonderful and awful in almost equal proportions. And Tabitha was important – to both their lives.

The journey to the station was uneventful and Josh was standing waiting, his breath making little puffs in the winter air. He got into the Juke, popped a nicotine mint into his mouth and groaned.

"Why so early?"

"Hunch. I think we're going to solve this mystery today but not if we delay. If my guess is right the owners of Bluebell Cottage will be vacating before noon." She stepped on the accelerator, and they made it out of the centre of Cardiff just as the Christmas shopping queues were building up.

"Why do people leave things to the last minute? Are they bloody stupid?" she said, viewing the long tail of traffic cruising towards the centre of the city.

"God knows. Procrastination. Laziness?"

"Done all your Christmas shopping, Josh?"

"I only buy for Lisa. She does the rest of the family."

"Bloody hell. Men. You live on a different planet, don't you? Leave it all to the little woman." Mandy gave him a sideways glance before changing gear as the traffic began to thin.

"You sorted then, boss?"

"Of course. Done and dusted. New jacket for Joy, vouchers for Tabitha and a pair of designer jeans she lusted over, and a hamper of Welsh produce sent to my folks in Spain. Tick."

Josh shook his head in disbelief. Mandy grinned at him. In reality she hadn't done anything.

CHAPTER SIXTY-NINE

As they approached the cottage the sky was apricot pink and deep blue with pencil lines of gold where the sun was trying to escape. Despite the cold and damp, it wasn't as grim as some December days and Mandy felt her spirits lift. They were close. She was certain of it. The lights were on in the cottage, but the front door was open and so was the boot of the car. Rachel was leaving through the door with a suitcase in one hand and a vanity case in the other. She stopped in her tracks when she saw the car and seemed almost to deflate.

"Going somewhere Mrs McGregor?"

It seemed Rachel didn't know how to react, staring at them with a mixture of apprehension and bravado.

"Later. We're hoping to get up to see Ian's family for Christmas. It's a couple of days to drive. We stop above Carlisle at a Premier Inn to break the journey." She glanced up at the clouds. I hope we don't get snow as it can get quite scary."

A gust of wind blew Rachel's hair across her face. She put the luggage in the boot of the car and slammed it shut. "You don't need to speak to me for long, do you?" No attempt to invite them inside the house and no sign of the husband either.

"Is your husband not at home? If you're going to Scotland later, is he not helping with the packing or leaving it all to you? Typical." Mandy smiled.

"He just went to the supermarket to get some things for the journey. I expect he'll be back soon."

"That's convenient as we'd like to speak to him too. May we come in or are you trying to heat the countryside as well as your home?"

With noticeable reluctance, Rachel led them into the cottage. Outside the building looked a typical old stone-walled cottage with a slate roof and small windows. Inside was a revelation. The place had been gutted and reshaped. Rachel took them along a corridor to an L-shaped room at the back. Kitchen, dining and lounge area. It was bright and airy with bifold doors out on to a garden. A white painted dining table and six chairs made up the dining area and two large blue leather sofas were in the other section. Rachel made no offer of refreshment. In fact, the kitchen was immaculate, as if she'd just stepped into it or she had cleaned before leaving.

"Nice place," said Josh. "You've been renting?"

"Yes. Ian's job is remote so he can work anywhere. We've been here a couple of years. I expect we'll end up in Scotland or maybe even Canada. Ian has a longing to see the Rockies."

She pointed to one sofa, and they sank into it while she perched on the edge of the other, hands clasped together.

"Would you like to tell us about your relationship with Grace Mathias," said Mandy.

"Grace was my cousin. We didn't grow up near each other, so we got to meet after we moved here. She was a gem. I became very fond of her."

"You didn't meet Eleri?"

Rachel bit her lip. "No. She was too ill. I wanted to," she looked from Mandy to Josh, with anxiety filled eyes, "but Grace said it might upset her too much. I'm not quite sure why there was all the disagreement between my mother and Eleri. Mam was a force to be reckoned with. You were either with her or against her. No half-way mark. No compromise." She rubbed a hand over her eyes. "I found a letter from Eleri in my mother's things after the accident. Eleri wanted to meet. I know it never happened. Mam was far too stubborn."

While Rachel was talking Mandy was looking around for evidence of a baby. Nothing. Not even a soft toy. It looked very much as though Rachel was leaving, not just for Christmas but for good.

"How many times did Grace visit you here and what was the purpose of her visits?"

The direct question appeared to unnerve Rachel. She started picking at her nails. "We, we were getting to know one another. She did come here, several times, I suppose."

Vague. Too vague. "Like once a month? When she was ovulating?"

"What?" Rachel stood up. "I think you'd better go now. I've packing to do."

The front door opened, and a male voice shouted, "Who's car is blocking the drive? I've got the things you needed, and she's gone to sleep as well. Motion of the car."

Ian McGregor entered the room and stopped when he saw the two detectives. The look of alarm told them they were on the right track. And the baby in Ian's arms was tiny, obviously very young.

"You didn't tell us you had a baby," Mandy said as Rachel swallowed and coloured.

"You didn't ask."

"Most new mums are only too happy to tell everyone when they've given birth."

Rachel moved to stand by Ian's side and as if sensing the tension in the room the baby mewled and turned its head towards Rachel.

"She'll be hungry now," said Rachel. "I need to heat a bottle."

Making no attempt to move, Mandy and Josh watched the interaction between the couple. Ian looked shell-shocked as Rachel introduced them to her husband. His eyes widened and she pursed her lips and flicked her eyes from side to side. Silent messages between partners.

Josh asked Ian questions about his work and his enjoyment of running; the races he'd entered and causes he supported. The man answered like an automaton, cradling the tiny infant who had now opened both eyes and was in the process of stretching, the mewling becoming louder by the minute. He'd sat down on the sofa Rachel had vacated and she soon joined him. He passed the baby to her, and Rachel pressed the bottle to the eager little mouth. Rachel gave Mandy a look of almost defiance. They could all guess how this scenario was going to pan out but for the moment they were playing games with each other.

"How old is the little one?"

"Just over two weeks." Rachel had a mutinous look on her face.

"Boy or girl? I'm guessing from the clothing it's pink for a girl although I don't suppose it matters much. It's an exciting time, isn't it?"

Neither Rachel nor Ian spoke sitting stiff-backed while the sucking of the baby provided a backdrop to the room. One tiny little baby who had caused them so much trouble. She was so small and perfect thought Mandy as a little hand stretched upwards, escaping from the folds of the pink blanket.

"We were talking about Grace Mathias before you came in Mr McGregor. How well did you know Grace?"

"We met after one of the charity races. Then we found out Grace was Rachel's cousin."

It would be so easy to feel sorry for these people. With a swift turn in Josh's direction, she let him take over the questioning while she thought about the issues involved. They'd need a DNA sample from Ian McGregor and the baby which she was certain would be a match for the placenta. There were so many other ways they could have had a child so why ask Grace to be a surrogate? Were they going to tell the whole story, or have it dragged out of them?

"You're a nurse," said Josh. "Do you specialise?"

"I'm a midwife." The words were whispered, and Rachel looked as if she was going to be sick.

"That must have been difficult for you when you had fertility problems of your own. Nia Jones told us you'd lost a baby," said Mandy.

"How? What's that to you? Why don't you stop messing and get on with whatever you want to ask." There was a spark of anger in Rachel's voice now and Ian was becoming unsettled, fidgeting.

"What has my wife's fertility got to do with you? This is intrusive. You haven't given us any indication of why you are asking these questions and frankly I'm finding this quite offensive." Ian was red in the face and his voice was raised. The baby responded by wailing.

No way around it. "We are here because I believe the baby you are holding is the baby Grace Mathias gave birth to a few days before she died. In fact, the small particle of placenta which remained in her womb and caused so much pain could have contributed to her death." She took a breath. "In addition, I believe you were paying Grace Mathias to carry this child for you, to act as a surrogate. It was all kept quiet because Grace was under the required age for surrogacy agencies. Plus, women who act as surrogates receive reasonable allowances only. The ten thousand pounds we found in Grace's room will, I am certain, coincide with a withdrawal of a large sum of money from your bank account. In addition to substantial regular payments over the last year."

Mandy turned towards Josh as she said, "DS Jones will take a sample of your DNA and of the baby's which should prove, beyond a shadow of doubt that what I'm speculating is the truth. You can talk to us here or down at the station. The choice is yours."

CHAPTER SEVENTY

Ian put his head in his hands and groaned. "It's over, Rach. We might as well tell them the whole story."

Rachel's eyes filled with tears as she removed the empty bottle from the baby's mouth and put her over one shoulder, soft pats to bring the wind up. The infant burped and then nestled into Rachel's neck making snuffling noises.

"You're going to take her away, aren't you?"

"It's not my decision to make. My job is to find out what happened to Grace Mathias. Why she died. This is her baby, isn't it?"

"It's Ian's too," said Rachel.

"What have you called her? I'm guessing Maisie. Grace had a number in her phone with the name Maisie linked to it."

With a finger stroke to the baby's face, Rachel replied, "Margherita. Ian registered her yesterday. Margherita Grace Mathias McGregor. Grace won't be forgotten."

"That's quite a moniker." Mandy's face softened. "I hope she learns how to spell. Do you want to tell me how it all happened? How did Grace become your surrogate."

"I don't know where to start."

"At the beginning is a good place."

"I suppose it all started after Mam died," said Rachel. "Ian was the one who found her on the beach. We knew each other before then but he was a rock, a real support in those awful black days following her death."

"I was just trying to help. I lost my Dad when I was a teenager, car accident, so I had some experience of the shock of a sudden death and the tidal wave of emotion." Ian squeezed Rachel's shoulder, encouraging her to continue.

"I found stuff in Mam's paperwork. Letters, a faded photograph and her birth and marriage certificates. I didn't know about that side of the family. Mam refused to talk about her early life. She said her parents had been killed but I could never get any information from her. It made her angry when I asked so, in the end, I gave up."

She was rocking now, slow movements forwards and backwards, one hand on the baby's head, the other supporting the tiny body. Ian took up the story.

"I could see how Rachel needed something to fill that gap. How important finding out about her mother's background was to her, so I started searching. With the information she already had to hand it wasn't difficult. And her aunt, Eleri, was still living at the same address. It was my suggestion we move to South Wales for a while, and she could acquaint herself with the rest of her family. We got married first."

"We were about to go when I had my first miscarriage. It was early days. I was less than six weeks, so I didn't worry too much. When I had the second one the doctors discovered I had something wrong with my ovaries and one had to be removed." She blinked several times, but the tears still rolled down her cheeks.

"We moved down here to Bluebell Cottage, and I got some agency work in the area. Ian works from home most of the time with occasional trips to London and abroad, so it was fine. We tried IVF but didn't work, my eggs were deformed or something. We searched for a surrogate."

"That was a disaster," interrupted Ian, "the woman they linked us with had a row with her partner over carrying someone else's baby. It was the same with the second match. She didn't have a healthy lifestyle. We were pretty desperate."

"Where does Grace fit into this story? When did you first meet her? How did she come to be carrying your child?" Mandy was intrigued by the whole tale but so far, they hadn't given her the information she needed. Josh sat making notes and, now and again, looked at Mandy.

"We didn't know how Eleri would greet a long-lost relative so decided to take things slowly. We hung about the neighbourhood a couple of times and then we found out about her illness and all the events Grace was staging to raise money for the treatment abroad."

"We were saving to put a deposit on a house so had a tidy nest egg set aside. I donated a couple of times by running in the races and telling her the lump sum was money I'd raised from sponsorship."

"When did you tell her you were related?"

"The first time we met."

"After the fancy dress race," said Ian. "She made a point of talking to everyone and when she saw Rachel there was an instant connection."

A faint smile from Rachel as she said, "She looked at me and said, 'Do I know you? You seem familiar.' I just blurted out that I was her cousin and, despite the age difference, when we met for coffee a few times afterwards we discovered we liked a lot of the same things. She was interested in working with children and art. She would have been wonderful too. Grace really was a star."

"You took advantage," Josh said. Rachel started, looked at Ian then back to Josh.

"She offered to carry a baby for me." Rachel said. "Believe me, it wasn't us pushing. When I told her about my problems, she suggested it. Of course, for me, it was the ideal solution as I knew the baby would have some of my family connections."

"Except it was all a bit underhand. Secret. You paid Grace to have your baby. Her death was a consequence of the birth."

CHAPTER SEVENTY-ONE

Outside it had started to rain – swathes of light drizzle while somewhere larger drops hit something plastic with a plopping sound. Inside, the baby slept on, oblivious to the fact her fate was in the balance. Rachel's face was blotchy, and Ian pulled her into the circle of his arm.

"It was Grace who wanted to keep it all secret," said Ian. "She suggested us having a burner phone. God knows why. I didn't understand. I don't suppose we'll ever know now. When we heard about her death we switched it off." He rubbed a hand across his forehead. "She came here, and Rachel checked her out every month during the pregnancy. Rachel persuaded one of her colleagues at the hospital to have a quick look, an ultrasound, to ensure all was well. She was young, fit and healthy. Nobody expected her to die."

"What happened to her?" asked Rachel. "We only know what was in the papers. I've been afraid to talk to anyone."

"She had a tiny fragment of the placenta left in the womb. The theory is that it caused extreme pain. She took two of her mother's opiates to try and ease it, but she became sleepy, and hypothermia did the rest."

Rachel gasped. "Oh my God. It was my fault. I checked the placenta. It all seemed intact." She broke down, huge gulping cries that woke the baby who joined in, aware of her mother's distress. Ian took the infant from her, and Rachel wrapped her arms around herself while he comforted the baby.

"Where did she have the baby?" asked Josh.

"Here. She had her here in Bluebell Cottage. We were both with her at the time. She was brave and very excited to see Maisie. I checked everything. I was sure it was alright." Rachel shook her head in disbelief.

If Grace had seen a doctor her death could have been avoided. The desire for secrecy, the need to keep the payment for the surrogacy hidden from everyone involved had been a major factor in the disaster.

"It was a very small piece. Easily overlooked I'm told," said Mandy. "Grace should have had proper medical attention throughout the pregnancy."

"She did. I can assure you I looked after her better than I looked after myself. It was done by artificial insemination. She had dreadful nausea in the beginning, and I was very concerned. After the first twelve weeks she blossomed. I wanted her to stay with us a bit longer after the birth. She insisted she wanted to get back to see her mam."

"Was she complaining about pain?"

"She had what she said felt like bad period pains. She also found it painful when her milk came in. I told her to go and see her doctor. There is no way on this earth I would have advised her to take anything not prescribed for her. I'm a midwife, for God's sake. I knew what I was doing."

Another silence followed.

"Are you… are you going to arrest us? What happens now?"

"We'll have to present all the facts to the CPS. We need confirmation, DNA evidence, to prove what you told us is true, plus signed statements from both of you."

"And Maisie?" Rachel's voice was a whisper.

What could she say? Although Mandy doubted if the baby would be removed it was a grey area. She couldn't give them false hope when she had no idea what the courts would decide. She shrugged. "I don't know. Those decisions are left to others. I gather the facts." She turned to Ian. "You were going to visit your mother in Scotland, I believe."

"Yes. She's eager to see Maisie. She doesn't know the whole story. As far as the world is concerned, Maisie is our miracle baby. We'll be back here about the third of January."

"The DNA results should be through by then. Give me a ring as soon as you're back and we'll make arrangements for you to come in and give your statements."

The couple exchanged surprised glances before staring, open-mouthed at Mandy.

"You aren't going to arrest us? We can have Christmas together?" asked Ian, as he kissed the top of the downy head of the baby. "To be honest, inspector, it's been a relief to talk about it all. Since we heard about Grace, I don't think either of us has slept much. We never, in a million years, expected what happened."

Josh coughed. "Boss?"

"We'll let you get on with your packing for the trip. Safe journey. DS Jones." She nodded towards the door.

Rachel looked like a sleepwalker when she saw them out, waving goodbye as if they were expected and welcome guests instead of people who had just turned her life upside down.

As soon as they pulled away from the house into the narrow access road, Josh said, "What the hell? Have you gone soft or something? They are guilty as hell, and you've more or less given them carte blanche to clear off."

"We've got the story now, Josh. When we have the DNA evidence and their statements, we can pass the information to the CPS. It's up to them at that point."

"But–"

"–Let them have Christmas together. I'm a good judge of people. I'm pretty sure I'll have a telephone call as soon as they return. Nobody expected Grace to die. We know what happened to her. Now we know her baby is safe and well cared for too. CPS will decide if it's in the public interest to prosecute. I hope neither of them is given a custodial sentence."

"Ian is the father. Paying Grace for carrying the baby was illegal. Plus, lack of care was a factor leading to her death. What do you think the Super will say about us letting them just sail off into the sunset?"

Mandy slammed the brakes on, jolting them both. She turned to face Josh.

"I'll deal with the bloody Super. We have a confession, given in an informal manner without warning them of their rights. No solicitor present.

Circumstantial evidence in the main until we have those results from the lab and that won't happen until after Christmas."

Josh turned away, wiped the condensation from the inside of the window and grunted. "Suppose you're right. The baby is the centre of their lives."

"And yours will be too if you ever have a family. Just wait and see." She crunched the car into gear, and they headed back to the station.

Josh went to put the kettle on while Mandy headed to the Super's office. In truth she wasn't sure if she'd done the right thing in letting them leave. It had been a gut reaction to seeing how tender they were with the baby and thinking about how devastated they would be if social services intervened and removed the child. She'd given them a warning. An opportunity to get legal advice in place. She squared her shoulders and knocked on the Super's door. Best get this over with as soon as possible.

Withers was staring into space, a mug with 'I'm the boss' held between his hands. Behind him a laughing Santa, his one concession to the holiday season, sat on a filing cabinet. The aroma of fresh coffee hit Mandy's nostrils and her stomach rumbled, reminding her she'd only had a thin slice of toast several hours ago.

"We've found the Mathias baby," she said. "She's alive."

Ross Withers smiled. "Wonderful news. Well done. I was afraid we were going to end up with another body. A girl. Where is she?"

"With her father, sir. I'm not sure if I made the right decision."

Withers put his mug down, taking care while doing so, and indicated for her to close the door and sit down. The smile was gone, and he remained impassive while Mandy recounted the story they'd heard from Rachel and Ian and her response.

"I'm not sure if I should have let them go. It's so close to Christmas and it seemed cruel to spoil things prematurely. It was a gut reaction but–"

He tapped the side of his mug for what seemed like hours. Mandy felt her neck tense. Had she misjudged? Would this be the thing that would have her demoted, or kicked out of the force?

"Sometimes, as detectives, we need to make quick decisions. Someone's life may depend on us. That's what gut reactions tell us. Those instincts, gut feelings, are important. From everything you've told me, I'd have done the same. A bit of humanity. Whether our DCI Manning agrees or not we'll find out in the New Year, won't we?"

With a profound sense of relief, Mandy went back to her team. The mention of DCI Manning had given her a chill. Lucas back in her life and Joy leaving it. And Tabitha? Would she go to Spain too? It didn't bear thinking about.

THE END

Printed in Great Britain
by Amazon